Rana Joon
and the
One & Only
Now

RANA JOON

and the

ONE &
ONLY
NOW

Shideh Etaat

Atheneum

New York   London   Toronto   Sydney   New Delhi

𝒜
atheneum

An imprint of Simon & Schuster Children's Publishing Division

1230 Avenue of the Americas, New York, New York 10020

Text © 2023 by Shideh Etaat

Jacket illustration © 2023 by Salini Perera

Jacket design and hand-lettering by Karyn Lee © 2023 by Simon & Schuster, Inc.

For information about special discounts for bulk purchases, please contact Simon & Schuster Special Sales at 1-866-506-1949 or business@simonandschuster.com.

The Simon & Schuster Speakers Bureau can bring authors to your live event. For more information or to book an event, contact the Simon & Schuster Speakers Bureau at 1-866-248-3049 or visit our website at www.simonspeakers.com.

Interior design by Karyn Lee

The text for this book was set in Evoque.

Manufactured in the United States of America

First Edition

10 9 8 7 6 5 4 3 2 1

Library of Congress Cataloging-in-Publication Data

Names: Etaat, Shideh, author.

Title: Rana joon and the one and only now / Shideh Etaat.

Description: New York : Atheneum Books for Young Readers, 2023. | Audience: Ages 14 and up. | Audience: Grades 10-12. | Summary: Set in 1996 southern California, high school senior Rana Joon wants to honor her deceased best friend by entering a rap contest and living authentically as a lesbian, but feels conflicted by her Iranian family's expectations.

LCCN 2022029144 (print) | LCCN 2022029145 (ebook) | ISBN 9781665917629

N 9781665917643 (ebook)

ranian Americans—Fiction. | Lesbians—Fiction. | Grief—Fiction. | Family life—

Novels.

PZ7.1.E855 Ran 2023 (print) | LCC PZ7.1.E855 (ebook) | DDC [Fic]—dc23

LC record available at https://lccn.loc.gov/2022029144

LC ebook record available at https://lccn.loc.gov/2022029145

For Elia.
Thank you for seeing the possibilities;
thank you for loving me.

Your children are not your children.

They are the sons and daughters of Life's longing for itself.

—Kahlil Gibran

The first person you have to resurrect is yourself.

—RZA

1.

There's a jungle down there, and almost a year ago, it swallowed my friend up. I'm standing at the very spot my best friend, Louie, died. Topanga Canyon is just off Ventura Boulevard, the bridge between the San Fernando Valley and the Pacific Coast Highway—dry hills and majestic beaches. It's the type of road to get nervous on. It's the type of road that Louie, with his grandma-driving skills, would've been extra careful on. He was one of the safest drivers I've ever known, always managed to stay right below the speed limit, passed his driver's test sophomore year on the first try with a perfect score, and yet he somehow lost control of his car and it flipped over and over again down the side of the canyon, into the dense brush where coyotes and mountain lions roam. It was the last day of junior year. Nobody knows why it happened.

I lost my virginity the day of his funeral. I know that sounds all types of wrong. He had one of those open-casket funerals, so I was dreading going, but I obviously had to. I was more angry than sad, though, because they put him in a stupid blue suit, like he was an old man or something. I knew he wanted to be cremated and have his ashes spread over the ocean.

So he could stay in the flow, he told me.

And if they just had to bury him, he would've wanted baggy jeans, his gold chain around his neck, a simple white T-shirt that would expose the artistry of tattoos on his arm—ocean waves, the Buddha sitting in a meditative pose, the Wu-Tang symbol, a few Alan Watts quotes, and *Janelle*, the name of the only girl he'd ever loved, who broke his heart freshman year and made him swear off love for good. He had a hookup at a tattoo spot in Hollywood— his good friend Lucky was apprenticing and needed someone to practice on and Louie was down because it was free. To be honest, some of the tattoos were shit—I always teased him, saying Buddha looked more like an Asian grandma taking a nap—but they were *him*.

I wanted to cry, trust me, especially because his face looked different; he'd had so many bruises and broken bones, but they put on a ton of makeup, as if trying to hide the fact that death can hurt. I was pissed off and almost tried to reach down into the casket to undo one of the buttons that was closed so high up on his neck. He looked like he was choking, but it didn't matter because he was already gone.

Traffic whirls by me. I parked up at the overlook and walked down to the very spot where it happened. I'm not sure why I came here today. Maybe it's because almost a year without Louie means this circle of grief is coming to an end, and I'm just not ready for it. I used to come a lot and leave flowers for him or read him some of my poems I'd been obsessively writing the year before he died. The poems, however mediocre they might've been, brought me a lot of joy—just knowing they came from me, they were *my* creations, *my* voice, and no one could take that away from me. I didn't think I had much skill, but Louie believed otherwise. He always told me they were just masterpieces in the making. That's the thing about Louie: he always made you feel like you were capable of anything. Grief has sucked all my creative juices dry, though. Here I am almost at the end of senior year, and I haven't done shit. Fuck, I miss him.

I wasn't planning on losing my virginity that day. Death isn't particularly sexy, but when we went back to Louie's house so we could eat Subway sandwiches and Jell-O with his mom and aunts, his manager from Ralphs, and some kids from school, I snuck into his room. Most would call that a disrespectful move, but Louie and I were tight, best friends since the beginning of freshman year when he took me to see Tupac in concert. Back then, I used to wear Tupac shirts religiously—I realized a little too late that I was acting like a poser, and if you really love someone's music, you don't need to wear their face on your body at all times—but luckily, because of that shirt, Louie stopped me in the halls one day, said he respected my commitment, and asked me if I wanted to go to a Tupac concert with him. I'd seen Louie around, had noticed how blue his eyes were against skin that lingered on the darker side, his hair a blond mess of curls, like a lion's mane. But this was the first time we'd ever talked.

I have an extra ticket, he said. *My girlfriend hates him, and you seem legit into him.*

That was the best night of my life.

Louie's room was decked out in Wu-Tang posters—the infamous yellow *W,* a black-and-white picture of all nine rappers, a cartoon drawing of a dragon with nine ninjas posing from its head to its tail—and quotes that Louie had copied in his perfect handwriting on poster board from his Alan Watts books on Zen Buddhism. Alan Watts was this British, hippie philosopher who Louie idolized and I'm still trying to understand. He said things like, *Man suffers only because he takes seriously what the gods made for fun,* and, *I have realized that the past and future are real illusions, that they exist in the present, which is what there is and all there is.*

I hadn't come to Louie's room to sniff his pillows and climb into his bed or kiss his old shirts, because our relationship was never like that—but it went deep. I was always down to hear about his latest life philosophies, and he was always down to eat In-N-Out with me after a crappy day.

I was in his room because I wanted a little peace and quiet and I was looking for some part of him, something to hold on to, something that would only be mine. Police said he was driving a hundred miles an hour when he died, which felt impossible to me, knowing how often he got honked at on the freeway for going below the speed limit, but the facts were the facts, I guess. I was about to pull out his desk drawer when the door opened. I turned around and saw Tony, Louie's twin brother, standing there with a black eye I hadn't noticed until then.

Did I mention Louie has a twin brother? Not an identical twin brother who would make you do a double take, but a brother who lived in the womb with him, came out first, weighing something like five or six pounds while Louie weighed a measly three pounds two ounces; a brother who grew up with him, loved him, but didn't particularly like him, and who was completely different from him. They weren't the type of twins who had a lot in common. Louie was some sort of genius, an honor roll student, tough-looking on the outside but soft and spiritual on the inside, kind to nerds, and a hardworking bag boy at Ralphs. Tony was tough through and through—got into way too many fights, smoked an excessive amount of weed, got fired from every job he started. They both had tatted arms, but Tony's were devoted to big-breasted pinup women, our 818 area code, his friend Joe's face after Joe got shot in a drive-by the year before Louie died. I'd probably had one conversation with Tony the whole time I knew Louie—he was out getting into trouble and Louie was a homebody with his nose always in some book.

I thought Tony would yell at me to get the fuck out, that I had no right to be in Louie's room, but instead he said, "Wassup, Rana?"

"Hey," I said, leaning my butt on Louie's desk, in sudden shock that I'd been discovered, but also that Tony knew my name.

"What's up with your eye?" I asked him.

"Just stupid shit," he said.

I was wearing a black dress, one of the few dresses I owned, and because my mom bought it for me, it was lacy and very feminine—not really my style. Tony had even lighter-toned skin than Louie, but Tony shaved his head, and I wondered if he would have the same blond curls if he didn't. They both had those blue eyes that looked unreal.

"You snoopin' around?" Tony asked. He sat on Louie's bed, wearing a T-shirt and jeans like Louie should've been wearing that day, and he lit up a joint, not even waiting for an answer from me. He offered the joint to me, and I knew it would've grossed Louie out and he would've gotten all judgmental on his brother, but I'd always wanted to try it, and maybe it was Louie dying so suddenly and so young, but I was starting to feel like Alan Watts was right—we only ever really have this moment. I grabbed the joint from Tony and sucked on it and immediately coughed and blew the smoke out.

"Naw, you ain't doing it right. You gotta really let it rest in your mouth," he said, and demonstrated for me. I stared at his lips, realizing that he and Louie shared more than I'd wanted to admit. I tried again, and he nodded in encouragement this time. I could feel my brain sizzling, my body letting go. I'd drank a few beers at parties before, but always stopped myself after the initial buzz. This was something else completely. Tony smiled at me. Behind the bruise, his eye was red, either from the weed or too many tears. I hadn't cried yet and I hated myself for it, but right then, despite all of Louie's and Tony's differences, it was like I was staring at Louie. And maybe it was the weed or the thought of Louie's body being eaten by worms when he'd wanted his flesh burned and thrown out into the ocean flow and there was nothing we could do about it now, but I started sobbing.

Snot-nosed and high, I covered my face with my hands, and my whole body convulsed with each sob. Tony got up and wrapped his arms around me, rocked me like a baby. Even though I didn't particularly like Tony in that way, it felt good to be touched and to feel his strength take over me. When I looked up, I saw Louie's eyes, alive and ready.

Tony kissed me. It wasn't my first—I'd kissed a boy named Ramptin in eighth grade, but it was sloppy and the whole experience was vomit-inducing, so let's not even go there. This time, the weed or the kiss or the reality of death had me really living inside my body. I could taste the kiss like candy on my tongue; I could feel Tony's breath expanding my lungs.

He undressed me. It was difficult to get the dress off because the material was so expensive and delicate. I bet my mom wasn't thinking of me having sex when she bought it, or maybe she was and that's why it felt like hours before we could get it off. Once I was naked, though, I was surprisingly not overthinking shit; I wasn't worried that my boobs were too big or my stretch marks too jagged. His touch felt easy, so I let him do it. I let him lick my neck, my nipples, my belly, in between my legs. I let him put a condom on and find his way inside me, and I tried to stay in the moment and convince myself we were doing this out of our mutual love for Louie, to honor his death, and that Louie wouldn't be upset with me, even though he would've known I was lying to myself the whole time. Louie was the only one who knew my secret.

I like girls.

2.

This morning, my mom's preparing all the ingredients for the cooking class she teaches at our house Monday, Wednesday, and Friday afternoons. She usually sleeps in, but on these days, she's too excited and is awake by six and does all the prep work before her students get here. Cooking a Persian dish of any kind usually requires six hours of hard, focused labor, but by doing all the prep, my mom cuts that in half.

"What's on the menu today?" I ask her. I love watching her in her element and can almost ignore the fact that even this early in the morning, she already has her red lipstick on, her fancy blouse and heels. Her idea of womanhood is something I could never live up to, and I wish she could just relax sometimes and stay in her pj's all day, but that hasn't happened since I was a little girl.

"Ghormeh sabzi," she says, chopping the variety of herbs it takes to make the stew, including fenugreek, which results in horrible BO.

"You better tell them to wear extra deodorant," I say. She smiles at this.

"Sometimes you have to pay a price for a delicious meal," she says, and then notices that I'm about to put two slices of bread into the toaster.

"Two?" she asks, without even looking up at me. "Do you really need two, Rana Joon? Especially since you're not playing basketball anymore these days, you know? You need to watch it." I can tell she's trying really hard to make her tone even, but it doesn't matter, because anytime my mom brings up food, my blood pressure skyrockets and I just want to do the exact opposite of whatever it is she's telling me to do. But sometimes I become extremely insecure and end up listening to her instead, which makes me feel even shittier about myself.

My grandfather moved in with us a few years ago and was my main ally because my mom also tried to control the way he ate, insisting he cut salt and sugar because of the cancer. We'd run into each other in the middle of the night at the kitchen table.

You're hungry too? he'd ask. *She's worse than your grand-mother was.*

It was during these midnight ice-cream/bread-and-cheese/cookies-dipped-in-whipped-cream fiascos that my grandfather would read me poems. Some were his own, some from famous Persian poets like Rumi or Hafiz or my favorite, Forugh Farrokhzad.

I plant my hands in the garden soil—
I will sprout, I know, I know, I know.

It's in your blood, he would tell me, *to be a poet.* He knew that I loved poetry, but back then, I was hesitant to put pen to paper.

He died the year before Louie did, and sometimes I don't know who I miss more. Louie gave me this beautiful notebook after my grandfather passed, and told me it was time, and, just like that, the ideas, the words, the memories flowed—as if I were just waiting for two people to believe in me instead of one. But, like I said, all that stopped after Louie died.

I toast one piece, slab too much butter and jam on it, and try to leave before she notices, but she stops me.

"Your orientation packet came in the mail yesterday. I left it on the table for you. I'm so proud. UCLA is a wonderful school. This is the most important thing you're doing, Rana Joon." My mom got married young, and I know one of her biggest regrets is never having gone to college. She loves her students, but I know she really wanted to help people and become a psychologist.

I don't respond because I used to think the same thing. I used to think studying hard, getting a good GPA and high SAT scores, and getting into a good college were the most important things I could do. Even after Louie died, I worked my ass off, grief making it impossible to write a poem, but somehow motivating me even more to get into what I thought was my dream school. It was always me and Louie's plan to go to UCLA together, and I was going to work hard enough for the both of us. I even quit the basketball team to focus more on schoolwork, which pissed Coach Lock off, but I didn't care. And then a month ago, the letter came—I got in. But the sadness in the pit of my stomach was still there. All that work and Louie was still dead and I was still living a lie, so what was the point?

"Oh, by the way, I talked to your dad today."

"That's cool," I say, mouth full.

"He's coming to visit earlier than usual this year."

"What? Why? How early?"

"He wants to see you graduate. He gets in this Saturday," she says, the sound of her chopping suddenly louder. I can hear the unease in her voice even though she tries to hide it. My dad has been living in Iran since I was in the sixth grade and comes to visit once a year for about a month. How can two people share a sacred bond when one lives in California and the other in Iran? It's actually really easy when there's a certain level of denial involved. If they were a normal fucked-up American couple, they'd just get a divorce and not insist that having children was a legitimate excuse to stay together, but it's not that easy.

My dad works his ass off in Iran. He owns an auto parts manufacturing company and manages four different factories and sends us a decent amount of money every month—and my mom only has a tiny bit of money from her cooking classes, so how could she survive without his money? And how could my dad survive without something to work for? He's always prioritized Babak's, my white-washed younger brother, and my college educations. Of course, he could come here and make some money—maybe not as much as he makes in Iran, but at least he'd be with us. Instead, this is their arrangement; this is what they've decided to pretend works.

And what would people say about them if they *did* get a divorce? How uncivil, how American to do something that might make you happier in the long run but would ruin your reputation and show that you're just a fucking human who has flaws like everyone else. God forbid. My mom is a free woman when my dad isn't around, and when he does come, she transforms into this manic version of herself. Let me tell you, it's not pretty.

"He doesn't need to come to my graduation," I say. It may seem like I'm being selfless—trying to spare her from him—but I'm really trying to spare myself. I haven't seen my dad since Louie died, and I'm a different person now. I mean, I'm still on track to go to UCLA, which is probably the only thing that really matters to my dad at this point. He calls us a lot, but never asks me how I'm really doing. He's usually telling me about his cousin or his friend who knows a professor at UCLA and that maybe they can give me a private tour or make sure I get all the classes I want, especially those science ones because they're important for being on the pre-med track. (Little does he know I actually applied as an English major.)

I guess my dad, like everyone else, thinks I'm over it by now— and I thought I would be too. I thought grief was something you could just stuff down, something you eat your way through or study your way through or smoke your way through. Turns out this isn't a straight line; this isn't steps in organized numerical order. This is loud chaos, the kind you can't quiet, the spiral that keeps pulling at your heart, reminding you over and over again that there's a big hole where this person used to be that no other person can ever possibly fill, that life will never be the same—*you* will never be the same. How can I express any of this to my dad? How can I be real with him when I can't even be real with myself?

"He's your father, Rana Joon. It's important for him to feel like he's a part of your life."

He's really not, though, I want to say, but I know I have to keep my mouth shut out of respect. Everything beautiful that lived between me and my dad feels so distant. Gone are the days where I'd help him in the garden, or accompany him on long walks with my grandfather, or when I was in the fourth grade and he'd pick me up after school and we'd share an extra-large pizza between the two of us.

If he were around, maybe things would be different, but he's not, and how is that my fault?

"He's paying for school. You should be grateful; without him, you wouldn't be able to do any of this. You would have no future," she says. Guilt is for sure the glue that keeps any immigrant family together, and I'm a real sucker for it.

"Fine. I'll try to be more grateful."

I take my last bite and wash it down with a cup of tea and tell my mom I'm going to be late coming home after school because I'm going to study with my friend Naz.

"Tell her I say hi, okay? I love you," she says, and gives me a kiss without questioning me because she knows Naz is more Muslim than we are and is under the impression that she's not the trouble-making type. My mom's controlling side is usually only unleashed when it comes to dictating what I put into my mouth.

I wish I could tell her the truth, starting with where I'm really going after school, but she would never understand.

"I love you too" is all I can manage.

Naz is waiting in front of school with Starbucks—a black coffee for me and a Frappuccino with extra whipped cream for herself.

"So I have a plan," she says, barely letting me thank her for the coffee first.

Everything she's wearing today is some shade of green, and her lips are bright orange, and she's lined her eyes thick like a cat's. The hijab is meant to cover women up, not draw attention *to* them—but at school everything about Naz screams *look at me*. Which is what I love about her.

"A plan?" I ask as we walk through the jam-packed hallways—people riding skateboards, making out, checking their pimples in their locker mirrors.

"Ya, I'm going to make out with Paul Stewart today," she says, like it's a fact.

Naz gets the whole living-a-double-life thing—her parents are from Afghanistan and are way more conservative than mine, and in front of them she wears zero makeup and tones down her outfits. But she wants to be a fashion designer and is always quoting Coco Chanel. Even though Naz mostly buys her fabric from thrift stores, she has an elegance about her that's undeniable. And guys flock to her—she has these really dark, majestic eyes and has given blow jobs to a few guys at different parties. But she told them her dad would come murder them if he ever found out, so no one ever spreads rumors about her or anything like that.

"Why Paul Stewart?" I ask, and then burn my tongue as I take a sip. "Fuck."

"That's what you get for questioning me," she says playfully, smacking my arm. "Dude, Rana, he's so hot, and I've never hooked up with a surfer dude. Like, he's so white, it's blinding," she says, and we both crack up.

Naz and I met on the bus in middle school, because some dickhead told her to go back to Arabia and tried to throw a glass bottle at her head, and the one and only triumphant moment of my middle-school life was throwing that bottle right back at him—missing, but breaking it near his head at least—and telling him to go fuck himself. Naz and I have been friends ever since, but we never hung out outside of school until Louie died. Naz showed up to Louie's funeral, even though she didn't really know him that well, and brought flowers—I thought they were for his mom, but they were actually for me. She was one of the only people in my life who could acknowledge Louie's death as a big loss for me and didn't expect me to grieve on a particular timeline, so we've been pretty inseparable all year.

"Well, you keep me posted on that, please. I gotta go to

English," I say, and give her another hug right as the bell rings. I head to English class.

My English teacher, Mrs. Mogly, is old. The skirt-below-her-knees, I-need-to-sit-down-every-fifteen-minutes-to-catch-my-breath-and-call-in-other-teachers-to-take-over-so-I-can-take-pee-breaks kind of old. She's been teaching for thirty-five years, and I don't think she actually cares anymore, especially now that we're done with the AP exam.

Right now we're doing a poetry unit, probably because Mrs. Mogly thinks it'll be fast and easy since we're all burnt out from studying for the exam. To be honest, I'm actually pretty excited. All year I've been hoping for that spark again, for a moment of inspiration to break my dry spell; maybe reading some poetry, even with Mrs. Mogly, is what I need to write more poetry.

"You have thirty minutes to read the poem and answer the questions. We don't have that much time left together. Just stay focused and do the work," she says. Her tone always makes it feel like we're freshmen, not seniors about to enter the real world. While everyone else drags their feet, I turn to the assignment page right away.

My grandfather used to tell me that a poem is a gift, that you have to take your time with it, unwrap it slowly, savor each word, each line, each stanza, as its own little world. I skip the poet bio and get right to the poem itself: "A Litany for Survival" by Audre Lorde. It's about people born into fear, facing moments they were never meant to survive, and how every beautiful thing also has a flip side.

I read the whole poem over and over, listening to the tiny heartbeats within every line. The only other time I've ever felt like this was when I read Forugh Farrokhzad's poems with my grandfather. But it reminds me of Louie and Alan Watts too because what Audre Lorde is really saying is that all you have is this moment and no one is ever guaranteed anything, so you need to demand to be heard even if the whole world is trying to silence you.

I turn back to the bio and read about Audre Lorde. She died not too long ago. She was born in New York City to Caribbean parents. In the fifties she established her identity as both a poet and a lesbian.

I read the last line—the last word, really—several more times, and then I get up and go to the front and put the open textbook in front of Mrs. Mogly, because I'm not about to ask a question in front of the whole class.

"Yes?" she asks, not looking up from the quizzes she's grading.

"This poem," I say.

"Yes?" she asks again, still grading.

"What do you think she means by 'who love in doorways coming and going / in the hours between dawns'?" I ask, and I suddenly have her attention. She reads over the poem and then looks up at me, her pink lipstick covering a space larger than her lips.

"What do *you* think it means?"

"It sounds like it's about having to love in secret. Not being free to love," I say.

"Well, she was a lesbian, so yes, I'd say that's about right," she says with a smile.

I've never heard any of my teachers openly talk about anyone we study being gay, and I certainly don't expect conservative-looking Mrs. Mogly to be the first, but here she is opening a door for me.

"It's good to hear your voice, Rana," she says.

"What do you mean?"

"You never share in class and barely have any questions for me. You do so well on all the tests and essays, but I was starting to think you didn't need me," she says. I give her a smile before going back to my desk to finish answering the textbook questions, and once I'm done I pull the notebook Louie gave me out of my bag, pen hovering over paper just in case.

Before the bell rings, Mrs. Mogly collects our papers and hands out another one with details about our last assignment of the year.

"You will have your final exams, of course, but I am also asking you to write a poem about *you*. It's about where you're from, but also what and whom you're from—all the smells and tastes and memories that make you who you are. And since it's the last assignment of the year I'm going to let you just do as you please. No rules, other than it has to be at least twenty lines and, well . . . good." She says this last part with a little smile, revealing her lipstick-covered teeth to us all.

Everyone groans a little bit, but I can feel the start of something beautiful rising in my chest.

3.

Instead of studying with Naz, what I really do after school is go over to Tony's, get high, watch TV, and, when I'm feeling completely low and desperate, have sex with him. This has become our ritual since Louie died.

When I walk into his room, it's so messy I have to step over pants and shoes and dirty plates to get to his bed. He has the weed ready for me and everything.

"How's school?" he asks. Tony got kicked out for selling weed at school around Christmas break, so he hasn't gone back since, but oddly enough asks me about it often. He's packing the bowl for me with love and precision. Tony seems all tough and confident, but he always sits on the edge of things when I'm around. He looks nervous sometimes, like he actually likes me.

"The same," I say.

"Why do you sound so depressed about it? You're gonna be out and at UCLA soon. I thought that was the dream."

"It is . . . it was. I don't know anymore."

I know Louie would tell me I was doubting myself for no

reason—that all we have is the one and only now, that I should be celebrating my accomplishments—but this one and only now kind of sucks without him in it.

"I mean, don't get it twisted. You're still going to be stuck at home. That drive on the 405's a bitch. You could've at least stayed in the dorms or some shit."

"You know my parents won't allow it. Dorms are for white kids. Plus, my dad's stingy ass would never pay for it," I say, and immediately feel bad for saying it.

Louie and I kind of bonded over the whole dad thing, even though my dad hadn't completely abandoned us. When Louie and Tony were five years old, their white dad ran off with an equally white woman, started a new family up north, and didn't speak to his kids again. Louie always talked about how he wanted to find his dad, how he was a musical genius for a white dude, jazz and shit like that, and how his mom had probably demonized him to make herself feel better. He always said that when he turned eighteen, he'd just say fuck it and drive up there himself and even try to convince his dad to take him in.

Tony's version of their dad is completely different though—a cheater with a cocaine addiction. A musical genius, yes, but only when he was on something. A dude who couldn't handle having kids whose skin color made it look like they didn't belong to him.

Louie just couldn't accept it, he told me once. *He wanted to see what he wanted to see and couldn't get over the fact that our dad decided one day that he didn't want anything to do with his half-Black children.*

"You think you'll go back?" I ask Tony.

He shrugs. "You know school was never my thing."

We both smoke way too much weed. Puff, puff, pass. Puff,

puff, pass. Back and forth, back and forth, until it feels like nothing does exist but this one and only now. Louie didn't smoke weed because he was on meds—antidepressants, to be exact. He said his breakup with his girlfriend, Janelle, triggered something; he felt like he was drowning, like his thoughts weren't his own, and his mom who works in a drug rehab center hooked him up with the psychiatrist there. He told me he hated taking meds, that he felt like a zombie, but he knew he needed them, at least for now.

Although they had their differences, the one thing Tony and Louie did have in common was their taste in music. They both loved artists I'd never heard of, like Hieroglyphics and Company Flow, and were obsessed with Wu-Tang. Tony plays "Bring Da Ruckus" and raps along and nods his head just like Louie would, except when the song is done, he doesn't insist on playing it again and again or pull out his bruised and tattered copy of Alan Watts's *The Way of Zen* or insist we sit in silence and meditate. Instead, he turns on the TV and we watch *Beverly Hills, 90210* because it's only the greatest show in TV history. If it's not that, then we're watching *Fresh Prince* or *Martin*, close runner-ups. I've never met anyone who loves watching TV as much as I do.

On this episode of *90210*, it's Steve's twenty-first birthday party, and the Goo Goo Dolls are playing.

"I can't believe people think this shit is music," Tony says. We both start cracking up for no specific reason at all. Tony looks at me and I think he might kiss me, but then he says, "Louie could never hang like this. He was always so high and mighty with all his Buddhist bullshit." He grabs an Oreo, splits it in half, and starts licking the cream in the middle.

"It wasn't bullshit," I say.

"You still defending his ass, huh? Come on, tell me it didn't annoy the shit out of you when he made you sit in silence and do absolutely nothing."

"It didn't," I say, even though it did always make me more anxious than relaxed. I grab the side of his cookie without the cream and eat it.

"Shit, you're a horrible liar, Rana."

"What? There has to be a deeper meaning to life. He was just curious," I say, but Tony just shakes his head no, like I'm backing up the wrong brother, and eats a few more Oreos and then turns off the TV. I should probably go because I have World Religions homework, but Tony hands me a fresh bowl, so I stay a little longer. The smoke fills me up and then claws at my throat. It climbs toward my brain—the sizzle and crackle entering my ventricles, forcing my mind to quiet down. I ask Tony to put Tupac on even though I know he doesn't like him.

"He's too mainstream, Rana. Wu-Tang is a way of life. Not too many people get it." I smile because that's the kind of shit Louie would always say. Tony never talks about missing him, but I know he feels it.

Tony inches his body toward mine and stares at my lips. He puts his hand on my thigh, and the first thing I think is that it doesn't feel right, and that it probably never did.

The heat of the first time we did it had vanished quickly, and now it feels like I'm having sex with a ghost. He barely uses his tongue when we kiss, and so his chapped lips hurt sometimes. He touches me with one soft finger while he's on top. He puts on a condom, and little by little enters me, like he's afraid he'll do some real damage if he does it all at once. But it doesn't hurt, and I open wider and wider because I like how it feels to have another body pressed up on mine. I like how our sweat mixes and how he tries to find a rhythm to match mine, and I like that we can be quiet and close our eyes and I can imagine Brianna Asher, my former best friend and longtime crush, instead of Tony. I can feel myself opening up for her even though she'd freaked out on me when I tried to kiss her in sixth grade, pulling away before our lips even touched, and I should be over it by now. I had told her I liked her, and she said she liked me too. I thought we were in some sort of safety zone, but I guess it all felt like too much for her. Still—she's the one who makes me wet, not Tony.

"You good?" he asks, too carefully.

"Ya. I'm fine. Keep going," I say, because I want him to shut up so I can keep pretending. And I don't dare open my eyes until after I come. I'm not even sure if he comes or not, but he rolls away and immediately pulls the condom off, tosses it, and then goes to put on some music.

"This was Louie's favorite," he says, lying down next to me.

It's "Protect Ya Neck," and I know Tony's right. Louie always said Wu-Tang wasn't just music; it was a whole movement that was transferring ideas into your mind through sound. *It's like their tongues are swords,* he'd say. *Our words are the most powerful weapons we have.*

The only person I've ever come out to is Louie. It was the day after my grandfather's funeral, the same day Louie gave me my notebook. He took me to the beach. Everyone was in their bikinis and board shorts, eating Popsicles, and we wore hoodies and drank our coffee hot and black. Then we took the same windy roads of Topanga Canyon where Louie would crash a year later, and parked at the overlook.

Sitting up there, I just blurted it out to him.

I'm gay.

Alright, alright, he said, sounding impressed, and then he pulled out his notebook.

I was listening to Alan Watts on the radio, and he said something I had to write down. You're gonna love this shit, he said, flipping through the notebook. *Here it is. You ready for this shit?* he asked me, and I nodded yes. He read:

> *If you see yourself in the correct way, you are all*
> *as much extraordinary phenomena of nature as*
> *trees, clouds, the patterns in running water, the*
> *flickering of fire, the arrangement of the stars,*
> *and the form of a galaxy.*

Fuck, that's good, I said.

It's like, there's nothing wrong with just being you because you're the most natural thing that exists, he said.

After a long silence and a parade of seagulls scurrying by us, Louie said, *I want to be a fucking rapper.*

I kind of laughed, but it actually made sense. I was horrified by public speaking, but Louie was a star. Just that year we'd been partnered up in English to do an oral presentation on a poet of our choice, and I refused to get up and talk in front of the class. Louie said he'd do the whole thing, but our teacher wouldn't allow it, and we ended up compromising and did a pre-recorded video presentation instead. My fear of voicing my thoughts in the actual moment, in front of real, live people, has always been my weak spot, the reason I always get As, but never an A+. And as much of a homebody as he was, Louie was magnetic in front of people.

I've been writing all my thoughts down, he said. *I know your grandfather was all into poetry and shit, so you get it. I've been spitting in front of the mirror at night, and I think I'm pretty damn good. It helps me actually feel something even though my meds just try and numb me up. There's this battle every year, the Way of the Wu. It's not that amateur type of shit, like win a gift certificate to The Cheesecake Factory or whatever. If you win you get to perform at one of Wu-Tang's shows. I can't even imagine sharing a stage with them. I mean, I'm nowhere near ready right now, but just the thought of it gets me all hyped.*

You should rap for me.

Right now?

If not now, then when? I said, using his own advice on him. Right then and there, with the sun setting over the water, the sky bleeding pink and red and purple, he closed his eyes, opened his mouth, and told me about learning to flow with life, his mind like a whirlpool turning in a circle:

*I got this Buddha brain
Letting me be one with the pain.
My word is bond like covalent.
Strong, motorized genetics,
My cytoskeleton is tapped with cybernetics.*

Let's promise each other something, he said when he was done. *By the end of senior year, I'll enter the battle and win, and you'll come out.*

Fuck no, I said.

Aren't you tired of staying quiet? Of not feeling anything? Sometimes you have to speak up so you can feel alive, he said.

Then he handed me the notebook.

Write your thoughts down, process your shit, and fucking liberate yourself, Rana. You down or what? he said, and put his hand out for me to shake on it.

It was an offering, an invitation, a doorway into a world where he wanted me to be a truer version of myself. I shook his hand, because with Louie around, anything felt possible.

After that day, the poems just came to me without much effort. I'd be flat ironing my hair, watching TV, doing the dishes, and an idea would pop in my head, and I'd sprint to write down the poem in the notebook Louie gave me before these golden nuggets of truth disappeared. But that ended after he died.

All those memories feel so vivid right now, and the pain is an added weight on my heart I'm not prepared for. My dad will be here in a few days, and it seems like the perfect opportunity to keep my promise to Louie, to finally liberate myself, but even the thought of it sends my whole body sweating and the anxiety churning in my gut. I need to get out of Tony's bed and leave this room as soon as possible. Why did Louie have to die? And why did he leave me to do what feels like the impossible?

"Wait, where you going?" Tony asks me as I get up and start throwing on my clothes.

"I don't feel good," I say.

"Just take some deep breaths or something," he says, because he probably notices how panicked I sound. I take his advice and breathe in deeply. "What's wrong?"

He says it with such earnestness that I think maybe he'll understand. I take another deep breath and let out what I was thinking about the other day when I visited the spot where Louie died. "I guess I've just been feeling weird because it's almost been a year. It's like I should be over it by now, but I'm just stuck. I can't find a way to move forward. I think about him all the fucking time." The relief of saying the words out loud is immediate, but then I see the confused expression on Tony's face.

"You're gonna drive your ass crazy with this shit. You gotta let it go, Rana," he says.

I can't believe how easy this is for him—and it pisses me off. "So you don't think about him? You don't miss him at all? You don't feel like something was up with him? None of it makes sense, Tony."

I don't finish my thought out loud, but it echoes in my mind: That I could have done something to stop all this from happening. That *we* could have done something.

Tony shakes his head. "You trippin', Rana. Of course I do, but torturing myself over it isn't going to fucking help."

"But I knew Louie. He would never drive that fast."

"You didn't really know him, Rana. Sometimes he even surprised me."

"What the fuck does that mean?" I say, a little too aggressively.

"It means you need to chill out," Tony says.

"How can you be so calm about this? Why am I the only one who's still angry? You know what, never mind. Why do I even try? Everything with you is about weed and video games. I should go."

"Wait. Don't be like that. I'm sorry," he says, immediately switching from tough boy to desperate-for-love boy. He runs his hands over his face—his beautiful, chiseled face that any girl but me would swoon over.

"You know my mom. She'll get worried if I'm not home soon," I say. I take another puff from his pipe and leave.

⟨℮⟩

Except I don't leave the house, and instead sneak over to Louie's room. Tony's really high and has Wu-Tang blasting, so he won't hear me. I haven't stepped foot in here since the funeral, but right now I miss him. I want to feel that pang, to sit in my grief and just fucking cry.

I expect it to be locked for some reason or empty or a home gym by now, but when I open the door as quietly as possible, it's exactly as I remember it. Shit isn't even dusty—it's obvious his mom's been keeping it clean.

I want to hear his voice, his laugh, the rhymes he'd spit. I want to see him as vividly as possible. I'm desperate for any part of him I can find—I open his desk drawers and shuffle through, looking for pieces of him so I can put him back together and make him whole. I find old receipts, light bulbs, incense, nasal spray, rocks he collected on days spent at the beach, old essays he'd written all marked up in red with the most positive feedback any high school student has ever received—*Brilliant! College material! Are you sure you wrote this?*

I hold them all to my chest and try to find a heartbeat.

I go through his dresser drawers—socks, underwear. I smell his shirts and am immediately hit by a wave of sadness so deep, I'm suddenly dizzy and have to sit down on his bed. I cry quietly at first, and then sob loudly into my arm as I wipe my tears away. Fuck, the tears feel good.

I get down on all fours and rummage through everything that's underneath his bed—basketball shorts, jerseys, hats, scratch paper, a box of markers—and when I think my hands can't reach any deeper, I touch something solid. I grab ahold of it and pull it out from the clutter. It's his overly used, fat-as-fuck spiral notebook, black cover with graffiti letters scrawled in Wite-Out pen saying *KEEP OUT*, and it feels like all of him—everything I've missed and have been searching for this past year—sits within these pages.

Louie poured his whole soul into this notebook. He was never without it. After that day at the overlook where we'd made our promises to each other, he started performing at open mics, school pep rallies, but he'd never made it to the Way of the Wu. I quickly flip through the pages, seeing hundreds of Louie's rhymes, some that he'd shared with me and others that he hadn't. Some crossed out and rewritten, others highlighted with notes scribbled in the margins. There are pages filled with affirmations he'd written for his own eyes: *I will win this battle. My voice matters. I want to be free. I will win this battle. My voice matters. I want to be free. I'm not crazy. There is nothing wrong with me. I am human. I am me. There is nothing wrong with me. There is nothing wrong with me.*

If there's any part of Louie left in this world, it's in this notebook.

Tony turns the music down in his room, and I quickly put Louie's notebook in my backpack and leave for real.

When I get home, I'm still pretty high and hoping my mom has saved me some ghormeh sabzi after her cooking class, but, like usual, she hasn't. She's also adding salt to the wound because she's made a whole pan of French fries and says they're for my brother's water polo team potluck. I stare at them and ignore her.

I think she senses how desperate I am, because she says, "Okay, just have one or two." They're thickly sliced and brown all over, like how she used to make them when I was a chubby little girl and she didn't seem to give a shit. "How was Naz?" she asks.

"Great. She says hi. We got a lot done," I say, poking at the fries, trying to find the biggest ones.

"Did she hear back from schools yet?" she asks me as she sits down with a glass of tea and I continue to hover over the fries.

"She got into UCLA too, but who knows with her dad. They might send her back to Afghanistan to marry her cousin or something."

"Eh? Cheh hayf, what a shame," she says.

She turns on the radio too loud, and I have to stop myself from rolling my eyes. I know what you're thinking—the radio is fun, the radio plays music and is a lively and entertaining machine—but it's not like that at all when my mom's in control. She's obsessed with this program where the saddest Iranians from all over the world call in and ask this semicompetent psychologist questions.

I hover over the stove and keep eating the fries slowly because she hasn't told me to stop. I pour ketchup carefully onto each one, letting the grease soak my fingers, as some mom weeps to the psychologist about how her son has just come out to her and how she thinks it's just unnatural and dirty; how could such a thing be happening to *her* son?

The psychologist isn't the smartest, but he isn't such a bad guy either. He's actually pretty real with the people who call in, and he tells this woman, "Lady, he is your son, and nothing will ever change that."

My mom's putting on crimson nail polish now and she barely looks at me, so I think maybe she doesn't notice my French fry crime, and maybe she'll also just ignore this highly sensitive personal topic she has no idea is related to her own daughter. But then she says, "Bichareh, poor woman," and I stop eating and stand there for what feels like fucking eons, my brain crackling inside me, my stomach begging for more fries as the woman on the radio sobs.

I know she's not head over heels about the concept. I've heard her talking sometimes about her cousin Ladan's gay neighbor in West Hollywood who throws ragers in the middle of the week and how inconsiderate and selfish he is, and how she thinks it's absurd that Ross's wife on *Friends* left him for another woman, but like most controversial things in life, we've never had a real conversation about it.

The words come out of my mouth before I can stop them.

"Why is she such a poor woman?"

It's only after I speak that I start to panic. My mind races at all the possibilities of how she could answer. I try to calm myself down. I take a deep breath and allow myself to think just for a moment that she is capable of giving me the answer I need—not that this woman on the radio is unlucky because her son is gay, but maybe that the woman is unlucky because she's stuck in a limited way of viewing the situation and that this is preventing her from loving her son completely.

She finally looks up at me, and in her face I think I see something like malice, dragon-like, but maybe it's just Tony's weed getting to me.

"The neighbor's child being gay I can handle, but not my own. Not ever you or Babak."

I look away from her, afraid she'll see my teary eyes. It's the opposite of what I wanted to hear, and after that I pretty much eat the whole pan of French fries—and let me tell you, it's a big pan, more like a cauldron used for feeding a tribe of people. My mom finally notices what's going on and says I'm overdoing it, and what will Babak take to the potluck now? Babak with his quick metabolism. Babak who can eat whatever the hell he wants and can go wherever he pleases and can do no wrong.

"You don't know your limits, Rana. You have to know when to stop," she says, and then adds, like always, "I only want the best for you. You know I love you." As if those words will lessen the sting.

There's a favorite memory I have of her cooking up a storm in the kitchen when I was a little girl, probably seven or eight. She's not beautiful in the perfect, put-together way that's her trademark now. She doesn't have lipstick on, is barefoot, and still glows like the goddess that she is because she's immersed in this act, this thing she loves most in the world—grilling onions, slicing the fat off meat, pouring in just enough salt, just enough cumin, just enough turmeric, covering the bottom of her pot with oil, ripping the leaves off the parsley stem. She's put out a beautiful golden place setting just for me and sits me down to eat a piping bowl of saffron rice covered with pomegranate-and-walnut chicken stew, saving me extra pieces of crispy rice; or lamb shank cooked in tomato sauce with lima-bean-and-herb rice; or meatballs the size of my fists, filled with rice and prunes. Offering me passion, love, comfort, life—the grease, the mess, the flavor—all of it without hesitation.

Do you know what's in this, Rana Joon? she'd always ask me, and I'd guess all the ingredients and was usually right because I'd obsessively watch her as she cooked.

You forgot love. Love is the most important ingredient of all, she'd always say, and then she'd kiss me while I ate. I was eating the food, but I was also absorbing a piece of her soul, and I felt safe. As long as she was cooking with such passion and these smells enveloped our home and I got to be on the other end of this ritual, I felt like all was right in the world.

Back then she hadn't started teaching her cooking classes yet, but it was hard for her to sit still and do nothing, so she was constantly cooking when my dad was at work, which was usually until nine or ten p.m. When I started sixth grade, my dad moved to Iran because his uncle was getting old and couldn't handle running the factories anymore. Around the same time, I got my period and breasts. It felt like overnight, I lost my dad and my mom started telling me I was getting a little too chunky and needed to watch my weight. My body changed, and she started treating me differently, like she had to protect me from myself. When Babak's body changed, she started treating him like a fucking king.

Soon after my dad left, she decided to help other people cook the foods we loved, but began to save her salads and grilled chicken for me. Only when my dad shows up once a year, or when Babak has one of his potlucks, does she fill our dinner table with her most beloved recipes.

Sometimes I can see my mom's control as love, but right now, with my dad suddenly arriving this weekend, and her comment about not being able to handle her own child being gay, and how she's looking at me like I'm a disgusting ball of grease, I feel some sort of hatred toward her. And the thing is, I know it's not right, but I can't fucking help it.

"If you don't want me eating them, then you probably shouldn't be making them," I say.

"I told you they're for Babak's potluck."

"I know, but I'm fucking hungry too!" I say, a little too loud and a little too stoned.

"Eh, Rana Joon, ladies don't talk like this," she says.

"I don't give a shit about being a lady," I say, and then go to my room and slam the door hard. For a really long time, I stare at my walls, covered with posters of Tupac, and then blast "Ambitionz Az A Ridah," which is my go-to song when I feel small and insignificant and want to fucking scream.

I lie down on my bed and try to focus on something good. Maybe UCLA *is* the ticket out that I need—sitting in lecture halls, surrounded by people from all over the country and beyond, people who know nothing about me, walking from class to class, meeting girls, kissing girls without being bombarded with memories of Louie. Maybe I'm just standing on the edge of something, and once summer is over, life will really start for me.

Louie would be disappointed that I haven't kept my end of our promise, that I'm just waiting for life to start instead of making it happen for myself. That I have no plans to come out and no prospects for a potential girlfriend or even a kiss.

I take his notebook from my backpack and open it up. I start from the beginning, take it page by page. I read his rhymes more carefully. They're mostly about his life philosophies, finding his purpose, life without a dad, his mom struggling to make ends meet, being a twin so disconnected from the person he shared a womb with. He pours his heart out on the page while I'm still trying to protect mine.

He would have killed at the Way of the Wu.

This is the one and only now—
Life, a ship wrecked,
The freedom of a mic checked.
I'm reckless and young,
This blood-soaked blade sharp on my tongue.
I don't know what this all means, let's just say I do.
I'm just a shadow in the shade who dissipates on cue.

His words shoot off the page and come alive in my mind and make me think of my life and all the things left unsaid.

Suddenly I'm inspired, that electric buzz in my heart that's been gone as long as Louie has, alive again. I grab my own notebook from underneath my bed and open it up, attempting to write a poem about the significance of eating French fries.

> *There are too many reasons to eat the French fries—*
> *The grease another layer to hide my shame,*
> *The feeling of fullness a home I have built for myself,*
> *Like my body isn't the enemy, but the only thing*
> *protecting me.*

It's the first thing I've written in almost a year and it's not amazing, but it's not shitty either. At least it's something. I reach for Louie's notebook again, and a small paper slides out from between the pages. When I pull it out, I see it's a flyer from last year's Way of the Wu. The date underlined a few times with red marker.

Maybe this is a sign. There's a way I can liberate Louie, at least—release his words into the world and make sure he fulfills his end of our promise. And maybe it's also a way to let go of this heaviness that still sits at the bottom of my heart. I'm over waiting for my life to start.

I take the flyer and pin it to the corkboard on my wall, because as nervous as I feel in my body, it's up to me now—I'm going to enter for him and give him a chance to win this thing.

4.

School starts at seven forty a.m., and it takes me
twenty minutes to walk over. I usually get up at seven and throw
on my best T-shirt and jeans, but today is Thursday, so I wake
up at five to shower and flat iron my hair. This once-a-week flat-
ironing ritual is simple. Shampoo once, condition twice, blow dry
the fuck out of it, clip it up, and then let one piece loose at a time
and iron it section by section. The iron has to be on the highest
setting possible, and you can't use one of those shitty Target ones;
it has to be ceramic, bought from one of those specialty beauty
supply stores. Sometimes it feels like this ritual—and this ability to
flatten all my frizz out—is the one thing I can control, so it's actually all pretty meditative.

I'm down for breakfast by six forty-five and grateful that my
mom loves to sleep in at least a few days out of the week so I can
eat as much bread as I want. Babak's already finishing his coffee
and is about to head out. He always leaves super early because he
has practice before school starts. My brother is probably the only
child of Iranian immigrants who's ever played water polo, and he

spends most of his time before and after school at practice, hanging out with the team, or with his girlfriend, Samantha.

"That's a lot of bread," he says, nodding toward the three slices I've taken out.

"Jesus, you sound like Mom."

"The woman does have a point. I mean, I could eat all that bread and it wouldn't matter because I'll be in the water for the next hour, but you haven't moved your ass in months," he says, mostly referring to the fact that I quit the basketball team. Babak was surprised when I told him, but I guess so was everyone, especially Coach Lock, because I was really good and loved playing so much. "I still don't get it, Rana. It baffles me every day that you quit."

"It's just not my thing anymore. People change," I say. I take a huge bite of toast smothered in butter and jam and wash it down with the darkest version of Persian tea possible. What I should say, though, is: Why should I care about a stupid game after what happened? How could I—how *dare* I—take joy from something when my best friend is gone? I never could find a way to articulate this to anyone, even Coach Lock, but I quit because it was easier to concentrate on the things I didn't love than the things I did.

Babak should understand people changing—he's the type of guy who assimilates to the girl he's dating, so the fact that he continuously dates needy white girls with bad taste in music and perfect nuclear families just means that's more or less who he's pretending to be. He wears puka shells around his neck, spikes his hair, and waxes his eyebrows. Everyone calls him Bobby, and his girlfriend, Samantha, insists on calling him Bobby *Joon*, a term of endearment in Persian, something like "dear."

Growing up, Babak and I were really close, and we even looked similar because both of us were chubby and had unibrows. People always assumed we were twins, but he's a year younger. We were both obsessed with basketball and used to shoot hoops any chance we got. When our parents were fighting about bills or about my dad being messy, Babak and I would walk to the park down the street and play ball until the sun went down. I think he lost interest right around freshman year, when he didn't have a growth spurt and I did. It's not a requirement to be tall to be a good water polo player, so the sport suits him well.

Lately, though, he's turned into my worst nightmare—there's just a certain level of cockiness to him I find disgusting. I want to have an intervention and have him go away to rehab before he becomes the biggest douchebag in the whole world. I know it's a cultural thing to worship Babak just because he's a boy, but I had hoped for more from my parents. At least my mom. But Babak was born with a penis, and in my parents' eyes, it's like a golden penis (Iranians actually have a term for this—doodool tala), so he can basically do no wrong.

It wasn't always this way. When we were younger, he was the mischievous one—getting lost on purpose in the mall, light-ing things on fire, breaking an antique vase my mom had brought from Iran—and the time-outs and lectures always seemed fair and adequate. Somehow, once he hit puberty, he could crash cars, break curfew, and have a girlfriend, and they just let all that slide. But when I started wearing a bra and begging my mom to let me shave my legs, it was suddenly all about watching my figure, not walking around the neighborhood after dark, making sure my parents knew the history of my friends' entire families before I could hang out with them.

All this goes over Babak's head, of course. Or maybe he just chooses to ignore it and let me suffer.

"I mean, it's your body, but I can help you get back in shape if you want. We can start shooting hoops again. If you won't help yourself, at least let me help you," Babak says, which is kindness wrapped up in a whole lot of bullshit.

"I'm good. Thanks," I say.

"Whatever." He grabs his gym bag and backpack, says bye, and leaves.

Naz and I meet at our usual spot at the back of the school before the bell rings, and she greets me with our black-coffee-and-Frappuccino ritual. We take a seat on the ground behind a bench and hide from the morning chaos.

"I don't know how you drink it black," she tells me, slurping loudly and getting her hot-pink lipstick on the straw.

"Dude, my dad's coming. Like, on Saturday. I hate when he comes."

"At least he's not up your ass all year long," she says, taking a compact mirror and tweezers out of her backpack and plucking her eyebrows to perfection, "but ya, that must be weird for you."

"Ya, he's not even here most of the time, but it's like I feel like he's controlling me anyway. Like I have to live up to some bullshit image of who he thinks I should be."

"If it doesn't make you shine, don't waste your time," she says. "You got to go toward the shit that makes you happy."

"Are you, like, a motivational speaker now?"

"All I know is Oprah better watch her back," she says, and we both crack up.

"I found Louie's notebook."

"You found it? Like on the street?" she says, and by her tone, it's as if she already knows what I've done.

"Okay, okay. I took it from his room. I went snooping. I had to, dude. I needed to hear his voice, to have these pieces of him. I'm scared of forgetting."

"I get it, don't worry."

She puts her arm around me, squeezes, and we finish our drinks in a beautiful kind of silence.

My favorite class this year has to be World Religions, except for the fact that the classroom is right next to Coach Lock's office. Usually I'll avoid him by going the long way, so I can end up on the other side of the hall, but some days I forget and we cross paths. He says hi to me and I say hi back, and we stand there staring at each other and I think he might finally yell at me for disappointing him, but he always just nods and smiles and tells me to have a good day.

It was Louie's idea to apply for this elective class. He'd been tight with the teacher, Ms. Murillo, for a while, because she held these meditation sessions in her classroom at lunch that he went to pretty often, leaving me to fend for myself or find Naz. I didn't really care whether I got in, but I guess Ms. Murillo liked my essay about being Muslim but not knowing what I believe in. Ms. Murillo's pretty young, and she wears cool, flowing dresses and a lot of jewelry from all her world travels. Her family's from Mexico, but she could pass as Indian or even Persian. She's the type of woman who is stunningly beautiful, but has a lot of masculine, tough energy, which I imagine makes her seem unapproachable to most men.

She's also the only adult I've really spoken to about Louie. We start every class by writing about a journal prompt Ms. Murillo puts on the board, and the first week of school, she asked us to write about what we believe in, so I wrote about Louie. I wrote about how he believed everything happens for a reason, and that even though the pain of losing Louie was sometimes too much to bear, I also believed there had to be a bigger purpose to his life ending so abruptly. She asked me to stay after class the next day, and she told me she'd spoken to Louie many times about Buddhism and meditation.

He had such a wise soul, she told me, *way beyond his years. How are you doing with all this?*

Okay, I guess, I said, because there was no way I could articulate how I was really feeling—how getting out of bed felt like I was climbing out of mud, how I was starting to forget what his voice sounded like. That was what scared me the most—the idea that he could disappear even from my memories.

I know a lot about loss, she said. *My husband died three years ago, the day before his thirtieth birthday. He had a brain aneurism, and I found him unconscious on the bathroom floor.*

Fuck, I said.

So you don't ever have to feel like you're alone, she said, and she wasn't smiling or patting me on the back like she was trying to wrap all this shit in a bow; she was speaking her truth to me. It was the first time an adult had spoken so candidly with me about death.

All year she's been inviting me to her meditation group, but I just haven't gotten around to it.

At the start of class today, I get out my notebook and pen to start answering the journal prompt, but for some reason, when I go to write the date, I'm overwhelmed. It's May, which means June is right around the corner. How can it be so close to June already? How can it be almost a year Louie's been gone? I can feel the tears coming, the sob stabbing at my throat trying to find a way out. How am I still this fucking sad?

"You okay?" Ms. Murillo bends down low next to me so I can see her face, one hand gently pressed against my back.

"I'm fine," I say, trying to snap out of it. I know she can tell I'm not fine, but to Ms. Murillo's credit, she knows when not to push, so she just pats my hand and lets me be.

After the journal prompt, we watch a short film on how widows are treated in India. The practice of treating them like shit started with sati, where a long time ago some Hindu communities would basically make widows burn themselves during their dead husband's funerals.

"My intention isn't to shock you, but to show you that every religion has its extremes," Ms. Murillo says. "We have suicide bombers killing in the name of God, Serbian Christians killing off Muslim men and boys by the thousands, Hasidic Jews demonizing and disowning anyone who chooses to leave the community, Buddhists lighting themselves up in protest, and women in India basically losing their identities and being destroyed right alongside their husbands."

She has us journal again, and then she asks us to share our thoughts on the film. Normally my palms would be sweating in a situation like this when I know there is pressure to share, but Ms. Murillo and I have a silent agreement where she gives me space to just be, and I never feel awkward about keeping my ideas to myself or sharing them with her in my work.

The class is mostly girls—Jews, Hindus, Christians, a girl named Joyce who I think is Buddhist, a Persian Zoroastrian girl named Marjan, and me, the one Muslim. The only two boys are CJ, the Thai kid who immigrated last year, and Marcos, whose grand-father was some type of shaman in Mexico and seems to have some herb or elixir that can cure anything.

Krishna, as always, starts the discussion off. "Obviously at this point, you all know my family's from India. I think there's a fine line between spirituality and sexism. Like, if two people's souls are connected when they're married, then why don't the dudes stop living when their wives die? As spiritual as my dad is, I know that if my mom died, he'd find another woman to cook and clean for him as soon as possible."

Rain, the white girl who's known for doing really bad spoken word poetry, snaps for Krishna like she just finished reading a poem.

"Preach, sister," Rain says. "Religion shouldn't be about oppression. I mean, look at these women in the Middle East wear-ing burqas, covering their whole face, for what? So their husbands don't have to worry about them enticing other men? Like, how can they be so insecure? And those women just do it without giv-ing them a fight because they're scared. A long time ago, men saw how powerful we were, they saw us bringing life into this world—like, whole human beings come out of our vaginas—and they just freaked out and decided it was their job to make sure we never were actually given more power than them."

Marjan interrupts. "First of all, not *all* women in the Middle East wear burqas. You see it in Afghanistan and Pakistan mostly. Wearing a burqa means your face is covered; wearing a chador or hijab, like they do in Iran, means it's not. So let's just be clear what it is we're actually talking about here. And I think this is more about women's rights. Like the right to choose. The burqa or the chador or the hijab isn't inherently bad; some women might make that choice for their own reasons. It's the forcing of it, the being told to do it by a man, that's the problem."

Marjan for the win. There's a bit of silence after that, and I'm thinking Ms. Murillo's going to end it before things get too heated, but her eyes laser-focus on me and she passes me a warm smile.

"What do you think, Rana?"

Did she really just say my name? My mind goes blank, and the room starts spinning. My stomach gurgles, and I stare at her in shock that she's calling me out like this. The words are there, but they're all jumbled up and I'm just staring at the ground. I'm quiet for way too long, and everyone is staring at me, and I stare at the door, planning my escape.

"Rana?" Ms. Murillo says, but the bell rings, thank God. I try packing my stuff up quickly, but Ms. Murillo asks me to stay after.

"You know I'm calling on you because I think your opinion matters," she says. "I'm not trying to embarrass you. I know you're a little shy about speaking up in class, but you have important things to say. At some point you're going to have to make the choice to do it, especially now that you're going to college."

"I know, I'm sorry. I just freeze up. I don't know what to do," I say.

"You don't have to be sorry; just be open to the possibility. I still think you should come meditate with us at lunch. I think it'll help," she says. A few students are loud coming in, and are cussing for no reason at all. She tells them to stop, turn around, and walk back in when they're ready to be calm and respectful.

"The classroom is a sacred place. Don't screw it up for everyone else," she says. Instead of arguing with her, they apologize and do as she says.

5.

Later in the hallway, I see someone taping flyers up by the boy's locker room. "Hey, Jordan," I say.

Some people are intimidated to talk to Jordan, but we're cool. He's a Black kid with hair like Bob Marley and has a chill, teddy-bear vibe most of the time—except he can suddenly explode and get into fights, especially with rich white kids who sag their jeans and pretend to know what hip-hop is all about. Our school's pretty diverse, and we also get really high scores on all those bullshit standardized tests, but that doesn't mean kids don't get into fights.

"What up, Rana?" he says as he struggles with holding the flyers and cutting pieces of tape at the same time.

"Here, give me those," I say, and take his stack of neon pink flyers so he can get a better grip on the tape. The day after Louie died, Jordan came up to me at school and pulled me in for a hug, and even though he's got a tough reputation, I could feel him shaking in my arms. He knows I can play ball and has been inviting me to shoot hoops with him and his friends all year, which was unheard of because (a) I'm a girl, and (b) I'm not Black, but I told him I was too sad to play, and he said he understood.

Sometimes you just gotta let yourself be sad, he told me.

"Why is it that I can do the most complicated shit, like fix my grandma's broken air conditioner, in five minutes tops, but simple shit like tearing a piece of tape is fucking calculus or something?" he says, giving me a half smile.

I take a closer peek at the flyer—bright pink with black handwritten letters that immediately grab my attention.

WAY OF THE WU
COBALT THEATER
JUNE 14th, 8 P.M. ALL AGES
FIRST PRIZE: THE CHANCE TO OPEN FOR
WU-TANG. ONLY SERIOUS RAPPERS AND
ARTISTS NEED ENTER.

I stare at the words so long, Jordan has to nudge me.

"Don't leave me hangin'," he says, finally managing to secure a piece of tape for the flyer.

"You going to enter?" I ask him, snapping out of it and handing the paper over to him.

"Nah, I do all the sound and lights and emcee and shit. I don't have that actual raw talent."

"Do you, like, just show up or whatever if you want to enter? Or you gotta apply? How does it work exactly?" I ask.

"Yup, just show up. There'll be a sign-up sheet night of. First come, first serve. Spread the word to any of your homies. Too many people spittin' these days without even thinking twice about what they're saying. This battle is for those who rap with intention, like, with an actual message, you know what I mean?"

"That makes sense," I say, because that's the type of shit Louie talked about—how it's not how fast you flow, but the meaning behind what you're saying that counts. I want to tell Jordan my plan, but I know he'll just laugh. And maybe it is a big joke—me on that stage, Louie's words falling from my mouth like broken teeth. I'm scared to even peep a word in any of my classes. But Louie's gone and I'm standing here perfectly capable of speaking my truth, perfectly alive, and maybe it's easier to change than to hold on with a tight grip to the safe little bubble I've created for myself.

Coach Lock walks by and gives Jordan an elaborate handshake—not the same one he used to give me before we started a game, but something along the same lines. Jordan is tall, but looks pretty small standing next to Coach Lock.

"Hey, Rana," Coach Lock says without looking at me. Gone are the days of his wide, dimpled smile he'd always welcome me with. He points to the flyer and says to Jordan, "You know, I have a few friends who've won."

"Oh, I know—don't think I haven't heard the rumors about you, Coach. They say you were one of the illest back in the day! Man, you should do it. That would be so dope," Jordan tells him.

Coach? A rapper? I can't imagine it. Coach Lock laughs, but then catches my eye and gets serious again.

"Naw, naw, I'm too old. I'm a freaking geezer, and it's all over for me." He gives Jordan another elaborate handshake, nods at me, and leaves.

"Can I keep one?" I ask, even though I know by any "homies" Jordan definitely didn't mean any girls, and especially no girls who are flooded with anxiety when faced with speaking up in front of more than two people.

"Why? You know someone?" he asks me, eyebrows scrunched together.

"Maybe," I say.

"Cool," he says, and hands one over to me. "Just make sure he's good, Rana. We only want that crème de la crème."

My stomach won't stop turning the rest of the day. Now that I have the flyer, have a date for the competition, it all seems so real, and I'm scared as hell about getting up on that stage. My pits are sweaty, and I can't focus or think clearly about my next steps or if my plan makes sense at all. I don't even notice when Ramptin walks in.

He's an Iranian kid in my Spanish class who likes to harass me about the way I dress, how I like to keep my eyebrows thick, and anything to do with Tupac. The weird thing is that he's the one who introduced me to Tupac in middle school, which was cool, but then at the party in eighth grade where he laid my first kiss on me, he wanted a blow job afterward. Actually said the words, *Put your mouth around my dick.* Real classy. I said, *Fuck no.* Ever since then, he's been a total asshole to me. Freshman year he started worshipping Biggie and making sure I knew I was an idiot for idolizing a sellout like Tupac.

Ramptin is tall and muscular and on the basketball team and gets a lot of girls because if you squint really hard, sometimes his sleaziness can be mistaken for charm. When he sits down right behind me, it smells like I'm walking through the cologne section at Macy's.

You could say what happens next starts with him tapping his

pencil on his desk, but it doesn't really. Like I said, shit between us goes way back. This is the kid who terrorized me for years, and when I told my mom, she said he must have a crush on me—because nothing says love like being called a whore in Farsi. Now, I was already feeling on edge about entering the battle, and it felt like he knew it and was actively trying to make it worse with that tapping. I usually bite my tongue when he starts in on me because of the potential risk of having to explain myself to the teacher, but today I can't.

"Stop," I turn around and tell him. He looks satisfied and continues a few seconds later. I turn around again, and I'm harsher this time. "You're annoying the shit out of me. *Please* stop."

But he won't. I thought my emphasis on the word *please* was a nice touch, a way for it to seem like I was at least trying to be nice, but it doesn't work. While Señor Mariani's explaining the use of the future tense, Ramptin leans forward and whispers into my neck, "Tupac's a fucking poser."

I resist the urge to turn around again, because I'm better than this, because I know Ramptin is enjoying getting a rise out of me. I try to go back to just hearing Señor Mariani, but it's impossible with this asshole.

"He's not a true G. He ain't got nothing on Biggie. His rhymes are weak. He's a fucking talentless piece of shit, just like your friend Louie was."

I turn around and smack Ramptin in his face so hard, my hand actually burns from it.

I've never slapped anyone before, but also no one has ever insulted Louie in front of me. Something wild came over me, and it takes a minute to really sink in—how my body can be powerful and do some real damage if needed. Ramptin yelps like a confused dog, and everyone's looking at us now. He looks like he might slap me back.

"Señor Mariani!" he yells. "Rana just slapped me!"

"En español, por favor, Jorge," Señor Mariani insists. Everyone has a Spanish name except me because "Rana" means "frog" in Spanish.

"Rana . . . me . . . me slaparon. She fucking slapped me!"

"Jorge, no uses esas palabras, por favor."

"Lo siento, pero she slapped me."

"Es la verdad, Rana?" Señor Mariani asks me.

"Sí, es la verdad," I say like my normal, quiet self because I don't yet know how to say in Spanish, *This fucking asshole was talking shit about shit he doesn't know shit about.*

Señor Mariani tells me to go to the principal's office. As I'm leaving, I squeeze the flesh of my right hand, trying to get the sting out, but despite my best efforts, it still lingers.

6.

I get a referral for slapping Ramptin and have to come to school on Saturday to do detention for five hours, which I have never done in my life. They also call my mom, which I'm not looking forward to dealing with. Ramptin gets off with a simple lunch detention because, according to Señor Mariani, I was the aggressor.

Naz is waiting for me outside the front entrance after school.

"What the fuck? You slapped Ramptin?" Apparently word was getting around.

"The asshole had it coming. It was like a reflex or something. I didn't really think about it," I say.

"He's so sexy," Naz says. "I bet it turned you on just a little slapping him like that."

"Ew. Fuck no," I say.

We head to our after-school spot—the only shopping center nearby. It has a Ralphs, a Subway, a cheapo trendy clothing store, and Starbucks, which is obviously where we're headed.

The line's too long, but the last place I want to go is home, where my mom will surely tell me slapping a boy is not something *her* daughter does, and I can't even tell her about what I plan on doing to honor Louie because she'd never understand, and I certainly can't tell her the real, real truth. I see Brianna Asher at the front, and staring at her helps keep my mind off my problems.

"Let's just stay, it'll move fast. It's on me," I say to Naz.

"Are you my sugar mama now or something? I can get down with that," Naz says, and she kind of waves her hips around like she's humping the air, which makes me laugh. Naz's parents may want to send her to Afghanistan so they can marry her off, but she doesn't overanalyze every moment of her life like me and has a pretty damn good attitude about most things.

"Oh my God, you totally stole my thunder," she says suddenly.

"Why?"

"I made out with Paul Stewart today during sixth! He's so fucking dreamy. I think I want to take surfing lessons or something."

"Where? In class?"

"I'm not a slut, Rana Joon. I was very ladylike and had him meet me in the girl's locker room. We almost got caught by Irena the janitor, but I made Paul hide and did the whole 'innocent girl who doesn't feel comfortable getting dressed in front of other girls for PE' routine, and it totally worked."

"Wow, sounds like the plot to a rom-com," I say, but at least one of us is getting some. Then I tune Naz out for a second because Brianna's picked up her drink and is walking past us. I miss playing ball for a number of reasons, but one of the top ones is playing with Brianna. Like now, her hair's up in this messy bun because she just got done with practice, and she has her gym shorts on and is drinking an iced tea because she's always avoiding sugar.

"Hey," I say. "How was practice?"

"Pretty good," she says. "We're playing Chaminade next week."

"Cool," I say like an idiot.

"I guess I'll see you later," she says.

"See you," I say.

"Jesus, she's such a snob," Naz says when Brianna walks away, probably because Brianna didn't even say hi to her. "I mean she acts all down-to-earth and stuff, like she's not into wearing makeup or stuffing her bra like those other white girls, but I can tell she's a snob. Bad vibes all around."

"You're making a lot of assumptions about someone you barely know," I say, defending Brianna even though she doesn't really deserve it. After what went down between us in sixth grade with our almost kiss, she stopped answering my calls, was cold to me when I swung by her house to see if she was up for a swim.

I thought you said you liked me too, I told her as I stood in front of her, wearing my swimsuit and shorts.

She said, with arms crossed, *Ya, but not like* that.

I could have sworn she wanted the kiss—even leaned in a bit for it before she suddenly pushed me away—but maybe my instincts were all off. It was in that moment I realized how confusing it would be to ever know if a girl really did like me.

If it weren't for us being on the basketball team together, I don't think she would have spoken to me ever again.

"Don't you know I'm really good with vibes, Rana? It runs in my family. My mom says she can see ghosts and spirits. Maybe that's why she's so fucking sad all the time. And I'm like psychic or some shit. Except for you. Before we really got close, I thought you had this whole I-don't-give-a-fuck vibe."

"Me?" I say.

"You were just always hanging out with Louie, doing your thing with him, writing in your journal with your headphones on, wearing whatever excuse for clothing was lying on your bedroom floor that morning. You didn't seem to care too much what other people thought."

"And now? Now that you really, really know me? What's my vibe, oh wise one?"

Naz looks at me with some goofy expression on her face, really making a show of it. But then she turns serious. "You have so much love and life inside you, and it scares you to let any of it out. That's your vibe. I know you got a notebook full of poems sitting around somewhere. Just own that shit. By the way, when are you going to let me read one? I know you have mad skills, Rana. Stop hiding them from me."

I go in for a hug and catch Naz off guard.

"Whoa," she says, because I'm not much of a hugger, but that was exactly what I needed to hear. To be seen like this feels overwhelming and beautiful, especially after the past couple days. "So I figured you out, huh?"

"Ya, pretty much," I say, wiping my tears away and letting them melt into laughter. "Honestly, I haven't felt inspired at all lately, but I read some of Louie's old stuff in his notebook yesterday and then . . . this." I pull out the Way of the Wu flyer and hand it to her.

"I don't get it," Naz says.

"Louie wanted to win this thing, Naz. He really thought he could do it."

"That's cool," she says. She looks at me and cocks her head curiously to the side. "But why do *you* have this?"

I take a deep breath, because after I say it out loud, there's no turning back. "I . . . I think I need to do it for him. Or for me. Like, to honor him, or to release him finally, or, I don't know . . . ," I say. My palms are already starting to sweat thinking about it, and I can feel panic locking up my throat. But there's something else there too, an electricity I haven't felt before. "It's been almost a year, and I just still feel so fucked up about losing him. I need to do *something*. I don't want to forget him. Have him be forgotten."

"Wait a minute. Wait a minute. *You're* going to rap? In front of *other people*?" she asks, laughing, but then quickly stopping because I'm not. "You're serious? You hate public speaking so much you'd write down your questions on my paper last year in Econ and make me ask them for you. I actually don't think I've ever heard you speak to more than, like, three people at once."

"What happened to 'my life didn't please me, so I created my life'?" I ask her, citing her favorite Coco Chanel quote. She literally has it Sharpie'ed everywhere—on the inside of her locker, the side of her sneakers; sometimes I see her writing it on her arm like a tattoo. "People can change, can't they? It's not too late to use my voice for good. I fucking slapped Ramptin today! I'm tired of hiding, Naz," I say, and grab the paper from her, fold it back up, and put it in my pocket.

"Daaaaaamn," she says, putting a fist to her mouth in admiration. "You got a point. Maybe this is the type of thing you need to push you out your comfort zone. I could get down with it. I can be your stylist. Or your coach. Or your cheerleader. Whatever you need. I can read some of your pieces and see . . ."

"I mean, I'm probably just going to do one of Louie's pieces or whatever."

"Fuck no! If you go up there, it has to be from you."

I stay quiet, but Naz quickly breaks the silence.

"Look, if you really want to get up in front of a bunch of sweaty, aggressive, lyrically savvy dudes and read them a poem, I will one hundred percent be there backing you up. I'll even make a poster that says *I'm with the badass Persian bitch!*" She finally gets a smile out of me and seems pleased. "But we got some work to do, girl. Maybe just start by reading *one* person *one* poem? Or actually raising your hand in class tomorrow?"

I nod my head yes, almost in tears again. Losing Louie was huge, but it's nice to know I still have a best friend here who has my back.

I order a grande Mocha Frappuccino with extra whipped cream because I'm tired of drinking just plain old coffee. Naz splurges and gets a venti Mocha Frappuccino. She has the I-eat-whatever-I-want-and-never-gain-a-pound type of vibe.

"Venti? Really?" I ask.

"Don't be all sugar mama one second, and cheap ass the next," she says. I smile and hand over a twenty to the cashier.

Naz asks me to wait with her until her mom gets here to pick her up.

"Do I look like a sinner?" She sips her drink and adjusts her hijab so it's covering more of her hair, and then hands me her drink for a second. She takes out a wipe from her purse and removes her eyeliner and lipstick, checking everything in her small pocket mirror.

"You're fine. Just chill out," I say. Naz lives in Van Nuys and can't walk home like me. Despite her confidence earlier, she seems paranoid, like her mom will be able to smell Paul Stewart's bad breath lingering on her lips.

"Shit, that's my mom," Naz says as her mom's old burgundy

station wagon pulls up. Naz is clearly back to panicking as she shoves her wipe in her bag and grabs her drink from me.

"Just take a deep breath; she has no way of knowing."

"Shit, I'm so dead. She's going to smell the sin on me," she says. "That's actually a really good line for one of your poems. *She's going to smell the sin on me.* Oh my God, maybe I should enter? Okay, focus, Naz. Just act cool. You are a strong, confident, beautiful, smart woman who has sexual skills well beyond her years," she tells herself. She does this sometimes, boosting herself up before she's about to enter a stressful situation.

But the closer her mom's car gets, the more Naz's confidence disappears. "It's funny; I actually like covering at school because no one is on my back about it. I feel like it's my choice. But as soon as I'm around my family, they make such a big deal about even a strand of hair coming out! It's just annoying when they think they're the ones in control of my body," she says, and then waves at the car like an innocent little preschooler.

I say hello to her mom, and she's just as beautiful as Naz, except she has some stray chin hairs Naz would never allow and definitely doesn't have her daughter's style. She smiles at me, but not so much at Naz.

"I can totally help you with your homework. No worries at all, just call me later," Naz says in an overly energized voice as she gets in the car, even though we don't have any classes together. She has the I'm-so-desperate-to-look-like-a-nerd-in-front-of-my-mom-so-she-won't-send-me-back-to-Afghanistan-to-marry-my-cousin vibe going on. As they drive off, I can't hear them, but it looks like Naz's mom is already yelling at her for God only knows what.

7.

I walk home from Starbucks. We only have one car, which my mom keeps on reserve in case of an emergency. My grandfather barely used the car because he took walks every day, sometimes for hours. He said it was the only way he could clear his mind, by moving his body, and that's when the ideas for all his poems came to him.

Maybe this walk will bring me ideas. Doing one of Louie's pieces up onstage was already a big stretch, but Naz suggesting I read something of my own just took my anxiety level to complete shutdown mode. I can't even picture doing that in my mind, so I bury the idea somewhere deep inside and remind myself to look up, to admire the palm trees, the mountains that surround us.

Most people think the San Fernando Valley's boring, but I actually like it. The truth is, if you ever decide to come to LA, you'll go to the Santa Monica Pier and Hollywood Boulevard, or you'll go to Universal Studios and spend way too much money doing all that touristy shit, which means you'll never come to the Valley.

LA is fucking huge and we're technically a part of it, but it's a whole different vibe here. There's so much space and parking and less traffic here, and the people are just more down-to-earth, which is what I appreciate the most. You can also see the stars at night, and sometimes it's so quiet you feel like you're completely alone, which is a lot different from feeling lonely.

Sometimes it feels wild that, out of all places, my family ended up here. Most Iranians came this way during the Islamic Revolution because Los Angeles had the beauty, hype, and perfect weather to ensure them a problem-free life. Having to flee their country and watch it transform overnight were enough problems for one lifetime. Some Iranians decided to settle in Beverly Hills and Bel Air when they got here because either they had the money, or it was important to them to pretend they did. Other Iranians, like my family, found homes in Woodland Hills, Encino, and Tarzana because houses were bigger and cheaper, they didn't care what their zip codes were as long as they had pools, and after experiencing the chaos of a revolution, they were ready to just chill.

I pass the gas station, where the workers whistle and holler at me as I walk by, as usual.

"Ey, mami! Qué linda! Guapa! Guapa!"

How do I know what they're saying if I have my headphones on and am listening to Tupac? You can just feel when your ass hypnotizes. Too bad it hasn't hypnotized any girls yet.

I try to channel my grandfather as I walk, try to observe the world like a monk and not a horny teenager buzzing on caffeine.

If he did have to leave us, I wish he would have just died in his sleep or been hit by a car on one of his walks and died instantly. That was the one thing about Louie's death that I could make peace with—he didn't suffer in that moment. But my grandfather had stomach cancer, and so it was ugly and tragic. My mom was there, taking care of him day and night when no one else was. That's why she doesn't really talk to her sisters anymore, which is fine by me. They all live in mansions, and my mom and I can't stand them, even though she'd never say that out loud.

All my mom's sisters basically disappeared when my grandfather got sick—their excuse always their precious husbands they had to attend to. If you don't know this about Iranians, we're horrible when it comes to dealing with death. We like to believe if we don't utter the words or prepare ourselves for it, death will somehow skip us, jump over us, leave us the fuck alone.

He's going to be okay, my mom would insist when I asked her about my grandfather. Pretending isn't really easier because the thing you're hiding from just grows and grows until it's bigger than you and you no longer know what to do with it. The day he died, she fell asleep, and I was just sitting there watching my grandfather, his skin yellowed, his head bald and shiny like a bowling ball. He woke up and asked me for water, and then he said:

The truth is nothing to fear, Rana Joon. Your mother is scared, but I'm dying. And that's okay. I lived a good life. I'm okay with it. It was filled with love and poetry, and that's more than most men can say. Without love, life is shit. Write a poem about this for me. Please, Rana Joon, don't forget, he said. *Even when I'm dead, come to my grave and read me your poems, okay?*

I told him I didn't have any.

Not now, but you will, he said.

He took my hand and squeezed it, and I helped him drink water out of a straw. And then an hour later, it just happened. My mom was awake, and Babak was at water polo practice, and I was looking for something to watch on TV, and then my grandfather's breaths became sharp and violent. My mom was screaming, a shrill scream that didn't sound like it was coming from her, but from an animal being tortured. I wanted to close my eyes, cover my ears, but I also wanted to see how life ends, as proof that it does. The strange thing was, his last breath wasn't aggressive and didn't look painful; it was like a sigh of relief, like he could finally rest easy and didn't have to be in pain anymore.

My dad came from Iran after my grandfather died and was supposed to stay for a month, but ended up staying only four days, not even long enough for the funeral, because I think it was unbearable for him. He lost both his parents in a fire when he was seven. His eighty-year-old uncle raised him until he was old enough to go to boarding school in London. My mom's father was the closest thing he ever had to a real dad.

My mom kind of kept things mellow for the last few years, but six or seven months ago, *bam!* She started wearing fancy dresses and lipstick, staying out late at her friends' houses playing cards, taking trips to Santa Barbara with her cousin. It didn't make sense to me, but I didn't question her much because she seemed happier than I'd seen her in a long time.

The immensity of all that's been lost hovers over me like a heavy cloud. I can feel the tears coming, so I try to snap out of it; I change the song up and listen to "Only God Can Judge Me" on repeat on my Discman, and I'm stuck on this line that goes, *Is it a crime to fight for what is mine?*

When you listen to these lyrics long enough, they're not just words anymore. Tupac wrote in isolation, but they feel like little messages he's wrapped up in a tiny bottle and flung your way, just for you—if you're open to them. In the end, it all just feels like poetry to me.

I switch songs after a while and wipe my tears—because sometimes, no matter how much I try to distract myself, they come. In that slight pause, I can hear some pestering voice behind me, like a tiny dog barking. I turn around and see Farbod, or Bod as most like to call him, which is quite ironic considering how skinny he is.

"Rana! Wait up!" he yells. I walk even faster, crossing the street while the red hand flashes, trying to channel my grandfather, who was a master speedwalker. "Rana!"

"What do you want?"

"My mom told me she'd pick me up from your house today," he says, almost a whimper, and I don't know if I should feel sorry for him because there's not a mean bone in his body or tell him to leave me alone. "Wait, were you crying?"

"No," I snap, and he immediately shuts up about it. Farbod is the only child of my mom's best friend, Faranak. My theory is that Bod didn't turn out to be ideal, or even close to it, and so they decided one was enough. From a young age, I've been forced to hang out with him because our parents are best friends. On the bright side, his parents loved feeding me since Bod usually picked at his food, so it wasn't always so bad. He's a grade younger—same as Babak—but as irritating as a freshman to me.

He's yapping about something I probably won't care about, so I turn my music up. He lifts one of my headphones off my ear, and I give him the look of death. Louie always had more patience than I did. Sometimes Bod would run after Louie and me and try to get in on our walks after school, and Louie wouldn't mind it at all, would try to calm me down and say it was cool when I told Bod our walks were private.

"What you listening to? Tupac again?"

"Ya."

"Don't you ever get sick of him?"

"That's the dumbest question you've ever asked me."

"Did you hear Sahar got a nose job?" he asks me, because he's the type of person who thinks gossiping makes him sound cool.

"Good for her," I say, because I couldn't give a shit.

Last summer, Bod kissed this girl named Sahar, who has a thicker mustache than him. Don't get me wrong, I have plenty of hair too, but I handle that shit. You shave it, or Nair it, or wax it, or use one of those turbo machines they have late-night info-mercials for, or go old school and have your mom use some string, but you take care of that shit. The point isn't even that. The point is that Bod—skinny, studious, math league champion, smudgy glasses, can't grow a real mustache, does the running man when he dances—has kissed a girl, and I haven't.

"I saw your mom at my uncle's house yesterday," he says.

"That's weird," I say. Bod only has one uncle, and that's Faranak's brother, his uncle Reza, who is extremely attractive when it comes to older Iranian men. He has that whole George Clooney vibe going and still has all his hair because he's at least twenty years younger than my dad. He's acted in a few Iranian plays and is super artsy and always fundraising for this and that organization in Iran. I've only ever seen him at get-togethers at Bod's house. "What was she doing?"

"She was cooking."

"Like, *teaching* him how to cook?"

"I guess," Bod says, which is weird because my mom never

told me she makes house calls when it comes to her cooking lessons. "My mom told me your dad's coming."

"Ya," I say.

"Does it piss you off?" he asks me.

"That he's coming?"

"No, that he's away for so long," Bod says. I don't say anything for a while because I realize no one has ever asked me this question. So maybe that's why I tell him the truth.

"I guess I wish things were different sometimes, but I also wouldn't know how to function with him here all the time," I say.

"That makes sense," he says. For some reason, I don't put my headphones back on the rest of the way, and Bod is smart enough not to talk my head off, so we walk in silence, Bod aligning his steps to mine like I can do him no wrong.

8.

"Ladies don't hit people. Where did you learn this from?" my mom says when I get home.

I want to ask her, *Do ladies daydream about kissing other ladies? Do ladies worry that no one will ever know that they like ladies and so they'll be alone? Forever? The end?*

Her obsession with being a lady doesn't surprise me at all. In the world she comes from, the goal is to become a dutiful wife. The funny thing is that my grandfather always told me he didn't want her to marry my dad so young, that unlike my grandmother, he wasn't convinced by my dad's wealthy family and European education. My mom was the one who pushed for it, who wanted to get married at eighteen to my dad, who was already in his thirties.

"Well, my life goal isn't to just be a lady, unlike some people," I say. I can tell by her silence that she's taken this personally. I wish I could fill the silence by telling her about what I actually want out of life. Instead, she's the one who breaks the quiet.

"You need to grow up, Rana Joon. In the real world, you can't just slap people when they upset you."

"And what do you know about the real world?" I snap back. By the way she crosses her arms, I know I've hit a real nerve again. I want to take it back, hug her, tell her I'm sorry, but I've dug myself into this hole of disappointment and there's no way out.

I go to my room, sit on the floor, pull the neon flyer out of my backpack to distract myself. It's like I can't be real with my mom unless I'm snapping at her, and snapping at her just makes me drown in a swamp of guilt.

I open Louie's notebook for inspiration, for some sign. I flip through all the pages and find one with the corner folded, as if Louie had marked it as special.

Your face a prophecy
Of all that is wrong with me,
But you're the man, the myth, the legend, my one wish,
Coming in and out my life like a slippery fish.
They tell me I don't need you, but I feel like I do.
They tell me not to see you, but that shit I can't chew.

I read it over and over again. I knew he felt a certain kind of way about his dad not being around, but I never realized it bothered him this much. Louie hardly ever talked to me about it, but as I flip through more pages, his dad shows up on most of them. Why was Louie hiding this from me? And how did I not notice?

I jump when my mom knocks on my door, but I pretend I don't hear it over Tupac. She knocks too many times. The song stops.

"Rana! Rana!" she says. "I'm sorry. I was being too harsh with you."

"I just want to be alone," I say.

"I know, but I don't." I can tell she's been crying by the sound of her voice, so I open my door and see her snot-nosed with mascara running down her cheeks. Maybe it's the power of mothers, how I can feel so close to her while knowing she will never completely know or understand me, but I can't ever stay mad at her for long. I let her in my room, and she gets on the bed and lies down, and I lie down next to her.

"Are you happy Baba's coming?" I ask her, trying to find something to change her mood. Even though I could never understand their relationship, and I don't particularly like who she becomes when he does come around, she usually seems excited. But this time, she hesitates. She nods yes, but cries even harder. "What? What's wrong?"

"Nothing," she says, which is a stupid thing to say because I know she'd only ever cry like this if something were wrong. Like that day at my grandfather's funeral, when she couldn't keep it together and instead of my dad holding her up so she wouldn't collapse, I was the one making sure her two feet stayed on the ground.

Afterward she thanked me.

You shouldn't have to do the things a husband should be doing, she said.

It's okay, I said.

No, it's not, she said. *He should be here for me. You shouldn't always be the one helping me,* she said. I was surprised because she never usually complains about my dad not being around, but that day she was hurting.

I know that while she's lying here next to me, there are all these empty holes inside her heart, and I'm the only one here who could possibly understand or fill them, even though the holes in my own heart feel like they're starting to swallow me up. I wrap my arm around her.

"I'm sorry," I tell her, not really sure what I'm apologizing for.

9.

That night, after doing some homework, I head to the living room to watch *Friends* and wait for my mom to share some butterless, saltless, flavorless popcorn with me. She walks down the stairs wearing a black dress, heels, a red scarf around her neck, and lipstick to match.

"Where are you going?"

"I'm going to play cards at Ladan's. Is it too much? I've had this dress for so long, to save for something special, but I decided every day should be special," she says. I wonder if this is something she heard on the psychologist's radio show. The dress is tight, but it looks good on her because my mom is the same size she was on her wedding night.

I remember what Bod said earlier and decide to push my mom for more info before she leaves. "Bod says you were at his uncle's house teaching him how to cook. You're making house calls now?" I say. She pulls out her compact and flips it open as if I didn't say anything at all. "Mom?"

"Oh, yes. You know how his uncle is, thirty and still not married. I feel bad he has no wife or mother to cook for him, and we both know Faranak's cooking is awful. Too greasy. He asked me if I would teach him a few dishes, and I said yes," she says, without looking at me.

"Why can't he come here for a class?" I ask her.

"His kitchen is beautiful, Rana Joon. It would be a shame not to use it," she says. She examines her makeup in her compact mirror, fixing errors only she can see.

We stay in silence for a moment, and I wonder if, in these rare moments of stillness, she starts to slowly see through all my bullshit—if she can see that I dream of kissing girls in open fields and bathroom stalls, on kitchen sinks, on basketball courts. It's less shame that lives inside me and more an overpowering sensation of guilt, a feeling that's embedded in our culture like a thick cord that keeps you eternally tied to your parents—this guilt of not being the ideal child, of not attending to your parents' every need, of not fulfilling their expectations, because after all, didn't they attend to all your needs without you even having to ask for it?

How could *she* raise a girl who likes other girls? I knew that would be the first question my mother would ask herself if I told her.

"Sinehat khayli bozorg shodan," she says suddenly, out of nowhere. *Your breasts have gotten too big.*

I look down at my boobs—my thin white tank top revealing the outline of everything that lies underneath. At first I'm pissed and I'm ready to tell her to mind her own fucking business, but the woman's got a point. They've definitely grown at an exponential rate since the last time I bought a bra, and especially since I stopped working out, and little pockets of fat stick out the top of each cup.

"It doesn't look nice, Rana Joon. You don't want to look like a sloppy girl. Let me take you shopping," she says. This is the kind of move my mom typically makes—harsh criticism followed up by a shopping spree.

She extends her hand out and rubs my forearm comfortingly, her manicured nails perfection just like the rest of her. I look down at my own nails, bitten down like those of a careless child, the skin raw and chewed off.

"I'm sorry I'm not staying for our TV night. And I might come back late. Why don't you call Naz to come over and watch it with you?"

I shake my head. "It's okay," I say.

Even though she said she's doing her usual card night with friends, I can't help but wonder if Bod's uncle will be there, or if maybe she's going to have a glass of wine with him somewhere, just the two of them. But it's a ridiculous idea because that's something Iranian women just don't do. They sacrifice themselves, their pleasure, their desires for the good of the family. It's like some sacred code or something, an agreement not to make selfish choices once you have a husband and kids.

"It's good to have company. Too much time alone is bad for you."

"I'm really okay. I'll probably make some popcorn and watch TV like usual," I say.

"No butter?" she asks, when it's really an order.

"No butter," I say.

"I'm proud of you," she says, and kisses me goodbye. Her sticky red mark lingers, and for a second, I remember what it was like to be a kid and to see her beauty as something to aspire to instead of something that feels like a ghost haunting me, her version of womanhood something I could never in a million years live up to.

After my mom ditches me, I decide to go through Louie's notebook, since I'm still planning on picking one of his pieces for the battle. I flip to the longest one he's written, which feels the most complete.

> *Every night same fight, same fright, same dreams,*
> *Climbing the razor's edge trying to find the extremes,*
> *Asking myself what happened to the yesterdays I knew?*
> *Now every day's the same daze like it's déjà vu.*
> *In the light of day, I fight for the right call.*
> *I meditate my mind so I stay up and don't fall.*
> *Breathe in, breathe out,*
> *There's no figuring out—*
> *You don't need to be a genius, just know*
> *You ain't really living unless you're living in the flow.*

I read and reread and try to make it a part of my body, try to let the echo of each word vibrate through me, but my mind wanders too far ahead and paralyzes me. I pretty much suck at this. I'm going to need someone on my side who actually knows what they're doing. But who?

I turn the TV back on and worry about fictional people's problems instead of my own.

Babak gets home from water polo practice just as *Friends* is ending. It's the one where Rachel sees the old prom video and realizes Ross was going to take her because her date had ditched her, but he didn't get a chance to because her original date showed up. The episode ends with Rachel kissing Ross in the present moment, and my heart is fluttering for them. My mom's going to be so pissed she missed this.

"This show is so stupid," Babak says, sitting down next to me and ripping open his bag of greasy Jack in the Box. My bowl of popcorn is done, and I'm dying on the inside because he's biting into a spicy chicken sandwich and has a box of curly fries too. I try to resist, but end up grabbing a fry anyway.

"By the way, I need you to go with Mom Saturday to pick Baba up from the airport," I tell him.

"I can't. Practice," he says.

"Dude, I have Saturday school."

"You, Saturday school? For what?"

"None of your fucking business."

"Well, he doesn't get in until the afternoon, you'll be done by then. And I thought you were on a diet or something," he says. He finishes his sandwich and takes out a couple crispy tacos. I've never heard my mom tell Babak what he can and can't eat. I've even seen her sneak him a plate of leftovers from her cooking classes after she told me there was nothing left for me to eat.

"Mom always thinks I'm on a diet," I say.

"I mean it's cool to eat fries or whatever, but you just can't sit on your ass all day. My offer to play ball still stands," he says.

"I just don't feel like it," I say, dipping the fries in some ranch.

"You know, I actually used to look up to you, but you're so bleh lately. I know you're still upset about your friend Louie or whatever, but you can't just carbo load your pain away. You're not the victim here—you're not the dead one," he says, which is probably one of the cruelest, most observant things my brother has ever said.

"Fuck you" is the only thing I can manage to say back to him.

10.

Saturday school is exactly what it sounds like—the
last place you want to be. Even Ms. Reynolds, the art teacher,
clearly doesn't want to be here. She looks hungover, wearing a
top that could double as flannel pj's. She doesn't take her sunglasses off and eats Cheetos out of a jumbo bag and tells us that
all we have to do is either finish our homework or just sit quietly
and do nothing. I'm pretty sure the teachers who come to monitor
Saturday school have fucked up in some way themselves, and this
is their punishment too.

"Can we listen to music?" I ask her, because I have my Discman ready to go.

"No, no music," Ms. Reynolds says. "If you think you'll enjoy
doing it, don't do it."

There are only a couple of people in here I recognize, like
Ricardo, who's colored his hair an electric blue and is already
asleep and every two minutes wakes himself up with his own
snoring. He has Saturday school every week, I think, because
he showed up drunk to school and vomited all over Principal

Denado. Jordan's in here too, I'm not sure for what. He looks my way and nods.

I'm sort of relieved I don't know anyone else. I'm actually excited to work on my "I Am From" poem for Mrs. Mogly's class with no distractions. I get my notebook out to start, but pen never gets to paper.

"Hey, hey," I hear someone eagerly whispering. Jordan's standing in front of me. Ms. Reynolds hasn't looked up from her Cheetos long enough to notice. "You got any gum? I forgot to brush this morning."

"No, sorry," I say.

"It's cool. Hey, how's Tony?" he asks, which is a bizarre question to ask because no one knows we really hang out, but I guess he knew I was close with Louie and so I must know something about Tony.

"He's okay, I guess."

"You should give him one of those flyers. For the battle. Who knows, maybe he's got chops like Louie did. Did Louie ever tell you his stage name?"

"He had a stage name?" I never knew.

"Bravo Mad Mad. At first I was like, *What the fuck?* But then it just made sense. I mean, he did so much good, but there was a little chaos in him too."

"Bravo Mad Mad." I repeat it a few times, as if casting some spell to bring him back. It's so wacky and not what I expected at all, and I love it.

I don't say anything to Jordan about it, but Tony definitely doesn't have Louie's talent—he never even tries to rap along when his favorite songs come on. And Jordan bringing up the battle makes me nervous all over again. I practically wince, thinking back on how much I stumbled last night practicing. I really need some help . . . and suddenly I remember something Jordan said the other day.

"Hey, the other day when you were talking to Coach. He used to do this kind of stuff?"

"Yup, he's as real as they come."

And then, before I can stop myself, I say, "I'm actually thinking of entering for Louie. Well, you know, entering to honor him. I'm thinking maybe Coach Lock can help."

Jordan laughs, but then sees that I'm serious and quickly stops.

"For real?"

"Yes? I mean, ya," I say, even though the booming of my heart feels louder than the words coming out of my mouth.

"Alright, alright. I see you, Rana. I see you. Maybe we should call *you* Bravo Mad Mad now," he says with a smile, and then Ms. Reynolds barks at him to get back in his own seat. He does, but not before giving me a look that is surprise and respect and maybe even belief in me, all wrapped up in one.

I try to get back to my poem, but before I can, there's someone behind me who has the hiccups. Normally I wouldn't be so annoyed by it, but she's ruining my flow. The sound feels deliberate and so irritating, I have to say something.

"Do you need some water?" I ask her, looking over my shoulder. I've never seen this girl before.

"Already tried," she says. It looks like there are a thousand red coils on her head, freckles splattered around on her face, and she has light green eyes. "It's not like—*hiccup*—I have control over it. You can't—*hiccup*—control your hiccups."

"Just hold your breath then," I tell her.

"I already tried that."

"Try again."

"This might sound weird, but will you count for me? I think it's easier when someone else is counting," she says.

"You want me to count for you?" I ask her, because why the hell would I do that?

"Please," she says, "you can just count in your head." She closes her eyes and is already holding her breath, so I don't have any choice.

She holds it and holds it and I'm counting in my head and I push it further and further until her eyes almost pop out and she's shaking her head because she might burst into tiny little red pieces of confetti.

"Okay, you can breathe now."

She exhales and then quietly sits there, staring at her desk, just waiting for the jolt in her chest, but it never comes. She smiles at me, and I can see a tiny gap between her two front teeth.

"See, it just works better when someone else is counting."

I turn back to my notebook and try to start writing the most amazing poem I've ever written, but Ms. Reynolds interrupts and tells us she needs to go to the bathroom. She has a pack of cigarettes in her hands, though, so it's obvious what she's up to.

"If you leave this room, I'll give you next Saturday too. I don't think you want to test me," she says.

Once Ms. Reynolds is gone, I hear the girl ask, "Hey, what's your name?" I want to tell Medusa I'm not in the mood to talk; I'm trying to be a real poet over here.

"Rana," I say without turning around.

"What? You're not going to ask me mine?" she says.

"What is it?" I snap at her.

"Yasaman," she says, kind of like how my mother would say it. Not Jasmine or Jesamine, not that at all, but *Yasaman*—the way only an Iranian would say it.

"Wait, you're Iranian?" I ask her, turning around for this. It's probably a ridiculous question to ask someone who has such loud red hair and such pale skin, green eyes, and so many goddamn freckles.

"Half. My dad was," she says.

"How?"

"How was my dad Iranian?"

"Ya, I mean, you're so *red*."

That makes her laugh. "My mom's a redhead, and my grandmother on my dad's side was also a redhead. She was originally from Afghanistan and came to Iran when she was a teenager."

"Wow," I say.

She's been nervously chewing on the end of a pen even though she's not writing anything. I expect her to say something, but she's just quietly staring at me and it's starting to feel awkward, so I get back to my notebook.

I am from
A monarchy turned theocracy—
Ruby-studded crowns and lashings on bare skin
To commemorate the holiest of men.

I get these words out before she asks, "So what brings you here on this lovely Saturday? You just can't get enough of this place, or what?"

I turn around again. "I'm sorry, but I'm trying to get some work done. Can you focus on your own thing or something?" I say.

She smiles and raises one red eyebrow like I've suddenly become more interesting to her. For some reason, all her attention is fixed on me, and I don't get why.

"Well, I told this kid to go fuck himself," she says.

"What?"

"That's why I'm here. He was doing a presentation in front of the whole class."

"The presentation was that bad?"

"He said something about a woman's place being in the kitchen."

"What was his presentation on?"

"I have no fucking clue; I wasn't really listening."

"And the teacher didn't care?"

"Oh ya, Mr. Rodriguez cared that I told this shithead to go fuck himself. He didn't care so much about the misogynistic comment. It was totally worth it, though. That little fucker can't talk like that. The teachers at this school enable boys to be total douche bags and don't call them out on their shit, and if I don't say something, it's like I'm adding to the problem. Do you know what I mean?" She says it with real passion, and it reminds me of how Louie used to talk about the things he cared so deeply about, like he'd discovered the secret to life and wanted everyone to know about it.

I put my pen down and turn completely so I'm fully facing her. "I slapped someone."

"You *slapped* someone? How is that even possible? I thought in high school you upgrade to punching."

"I know, I know, but he had it coming."

"What did he do?"

"Insulted Tupac. And my best friend. My best friend's . . . dead, so, you know," I say. I'm not really sure why. It's not something you just blurt out.

"Wow, that must suck," she says, which is a pretty casual thing to say in response to death, but actually sums up the feeling pretty well.

"Ya, it does really suck."

"My dad died when I was four. I don't remember too many things about him except his hands. He was an artist, so they always had paint on them, and he was always using them to make something. My grandma has all these pictures of him from Iran up in her apartment—like it's a museum dedicated to him or something. It's, like, totally creepy, but also cool."

I've never heard someone other than Louie talk about death so easily and have so much to say about it, but I guess she's had a lot of time to process. She also just seems like the type of girl who's so comfortable in her own skin that she can basically strike up conversation with anyone about anything.

"You speak Farsi?" I ask her, totally forgetting about my poem.

"Mm-hmm. My grandma was determined. So, baleh, yes, I do," she says. We're both smiling at this. My eyes keep flicking to the space between her teeth—it feels like an invitation, like a dark hole I can jump into and forget myself completely. But I'm sure Yasaman is just talking to me because we're in Saturday school and she's bored out of her mind.

Ms. Reynolds is back, her fingers a faded neon orange from the Cheetos.

"No talking, ladies," she says. She sits in her chair and I'm pretty sure falls asleep sitting up, but I can't tell for sure because of the sunglasses.

"What are you working on?" Yasaman asks me, whispering softly now.

"Just some poems," I say.

"Can I read one?" she asks.

"Oh, uh, they're pretty rough," I say.

"Well, when you feel good about them, like they're ready for the world to see or whatever, I really want to read one. I would do anything to be able to write a poem, but mine always suck." She doesn't even wait for an answer, but just jumps to the next topic. "Can I draw you?"

"What?"

"I need to draw someone for my art class. Just keep writing. Act natural."

Before I can say no, that the last thing I can do is act natural when someone is trying to scrutinize my face and capture all the details, she's gotten up and taken the empty seat next to me so she can get a better angle. I look at her, confused.

"It won't take too long. And I promise I'll stop bothering you after this so you can concentrate on your poem." She smirks at that before looking down at her paper and starting to sketch.

Pretty much speechless, I turn back to my work. I can feel her eyes on me, and it's different from when Tony looks at me. I'm tiny and bigger than my body all at the same time. Is she drawn to me the way I feel drawn to her? When I steal a glance back at her, her tongue is falling out of her mouth in concentration, and I start to imagine us kissing, the dizzy spell of our bodies touching, what it would be like to be really seen by this person.

After twenty minutes, she shows me the drawing. When I look at it from far away, it doesn't really look like anything special, but when I hold it up close, I can see all the details and the random lines that perfectly align to create my eyes and my chin and my ears and my perfectly straight hair. I look vulnerable without being weak, quietly confident. I look how I want to look—like my face and my body and my whole life are here, pulsing inside the one and only now.

"You like it? I know I'm not really that good," she says.

"It's actually really good, but I don't think it looks like me," I say.

"Of course it does, you're fucking beautiful," she says, like it's nothing at all to tell someone something like that, and then Ricardo wakes up and lets out a loud yawn, jolting Ms. Reynolds out of her trance.

"What time is it?" Ms. Reynolds asks, even though she's the one facing the clock. We have thirty minutes left, but she lets us go early. Our sacred Saturday school bubble bursts as everyone packs their bags and gets ready to leave. Maybe I'll see Yasaman in the halls one day and we'll reminisce on that one time she drew my portrait and we talked about the dead people we love, but I don't expect anything more than that.

Then Yasaman asks me, "You want to go to Starbucks and get a drink?" I'm stunned and almost say yes, but remember my dad's coming today. I'm even more annoyed about him coming now.

"I can't, I have to go with my mom to pick my dad up from the airport," I say.

"You sound like you're dreading it," she says as we're packing our stuff up.

"It's kind of complicated," I say.

"I get it. Maybe I'll see you later—you going to that kid Marcus's party tonight? I don't really know him that well, but he invited me," she says. I didn't even know Marcus was having a party. I'm sure Naz will definitely be going, but with my dad here, it would be near impossible.

"I can't. My dad's pretty strict," I say, and she nods. I move toward the door, but she stops me.

"Wait," she says, and she tears out her drawing of me from her sketch pad.

"I thought it was for class," I say, hesitating to reach for it.

"It is, but you can have it. I'll do another one," she says, smiling.

"Thanks." I take the drawing and carefully put it into my backpack. "I'll see you around?" Maybe this doesn't have to just be a fleeting moment.

Yasaman smiles. "For sure."

As I walk away, I put my headphones on and press play and don't turn around to see if Yasaman's still looking at me, even though that's all I really want to do.

While I wait for my mom to pick me up, I see Coach Lock in the parking lot, probably here on a Saturday for practice, and I take it as a sign. Shit is still weird between us, but if what Jordan says is true, then Coach is probably the only one who can help me not make a fool of myself at this battle—assuming I can make it onstage in the first place. He's loading his trunk up as I approach him.

"Hey, Coach," I say, realizing suddenly how weird it is that I'm calling him this when he's not my coach anymore.

"Rana. What's up?" he says, not stopping to get his things together. If he's surprised I approached him, he doesn't show it. I don't know where to start. *I'm sorry? I need your help?* It all feels too desperate. I reach into my backpack and hand him the flyer instead.

He glances at it and says, "Ya, I saw Jordan putting those up the other day. You gonna tell me to enter too?"

"No, I am. I mean, I'm entering. I mean, like, *I'm* not entering. I'm entering *for* Louie. Or Bravo Mad Mad or whatever his name was. With one of his pieces. But I need your help. I heard you used to be dope as hell, and I need to learn how to be dope as hell too if I'm going to have a shot," I say.

Coach stares at me like I've grown a second head. "I don't understand. You know it's for serious rappers, right? And from what I remember, you passed out the one time I asked you to give a pep talk to the team," he says.

Why does everyone have to keep reminding me of these things? "I know. It's a pretty insane thing to do, but I have to do it for Louie. He wanted to enter. It was his big dream to win, and I feel like I owe this to him."

He looks at the flyer and then back at me and then back at the flyer.

"You know, I was pretty hurt when you just up and quit like that. You didn't even come talk to me, Rana. You just stopped showing up."

Unlike every member of my family, Coach has no problem with open communication. Normally I'd shut down or lash out in defense, but he's right, and I've felt guilty about it the entire year. There's a reason I've avoided Coach for so long.

"I know. I'm sorry, Coach. I was so screwed up over the Louie thing. I wanted to pour all my energy into school and getting into UCLA."

"But I don't understand. You could've gotten an athletics scholarship, you're *that* good."

I shake my head. "It just didn't seem right, Coach. Why did I get to keep doing the things I loved and he didn't?"

Coach waits for me to continue. Everything I've been thinking about this week comes pouring out.

"But now I get it. I shouldn't stop doing shit because he can't. I should start." And now I'm crying. Coach Lock's eyes widen.

"I'm sorry, Rana, I didn't mean to upset you."

"No, no, it's not you. I'm just such a mess. I screwed up, Coach, but I need your help with this. It means a lot to me. Please?"

Coach looks at me in that intense way he would in the middle of a game when we were so close to winning and he needed me to pull us through.

"One last favor and soon I'll be gone for good," I say.

Coach rubs his hand over his face with a groan. "Alright. Let's figure out a time to meet at school," he says, "but you better be serious about this. No shutting me out like last time. I see you putting yourself out there, and I can get down with that. And Louie deserves to win," he says, nodding in respect, which is pretty much all I've ever wanted from him.

11.

When my mom picks me up, she insists we go to Victoria's Secret for new bras before we pick up my dad.

"What? Now? It's going to take us forever to get to the airport with all the traffic."

"His flight is getting in later than I thought. This is important," she says.

"You're being weird, Mom," I say.

"I just want the best for you, Rana Joon. This is not a crime, is it?" she says.

At the mall, she speeds through the parking garage and immediately finds us a spot. She checks her face in the mirror, as usual, before getting out of the car, making sure she's satisfied with what she sees before opening the door. I steal a glance at myself too and try to catch a glimpse of what Yasaman saw when she drew my portrait. For a moment, I almost think I see it.

I've never stepped inside a Victoria's Secret, let alone been fitted for a bra. It smells like shimmering vanilla cupcakes in here, which

I imagine is what most strippers probably smell like. Everything I see is pink or covered in lace or fur or has magical push-up powers.

While my mom convinces a saleswoman to measure me, probably giving her a well-detailed account of my predicament and how I've put on a few extra pounds since I don't play ball anymore and refuse to cut out carbs from my diet, I spray some perfume on my wrist. When I close my eyes and sniff, all I can see is Yasaman—the roundness of her breasts, her pressing her lips gently against mine and then slowly letting our tongues touch, her biting the flesh of my neck—and I'm so wet and horny I might explode.

I try to push it down—because what if she wants to just be friends?—but it's hard. I'm impatient, desperate, and lonely. My daydream bursts into nothing but sparkling dust as my mom shouts my name from across the store, near the dressing rooms where she's standing.

"Rana Joon, biya! Come!"

The white, shaggy carpet is so clean, it's as if no one's stepped foot in this store before, and the mannequins have these perfect little bodies where lingerie hangs like expensive works of art, and I know my body will never take this shape. For a second, I suck in my stomach and wish I listened to my mom more.

As I walk over to the dressing rooms, I see women fondling hot pink panties that look like nothing more than strips of lace and pieces of string, old women trying to find ones that cover the entirety of their saggy asses, and flat-chested twentysomethings desperately asking saleswomen if they have any bras that can double their cup size. Aren't we all just looking for a miracle?

Standing next to my mom is possibly the most beautiful woman I've ever had the pleasure of witnessing in my life. She wears a black blazer like all the other Victoria's Secret employees, but everything else is uniquely her. One side of her hair is braided in neat rows against her scalp, and the other side is a huge explosion of brown curls. Her lips are thick, glossy pink with a whole galaxy of stars living on them, and her eyes are as shiny as chrome. I don't just want to kiss her; I want to find a way to live inside her.

"Rana Joon, she's going to help you find the right size," my mom assures me. I swallow hard and nod yes, not sure what the next steps are. Do I just take my shirt off right here in the middle of the store? Do I actually have to bare my breasts to this human angel? I should probably step inside the fitting room first, right? She tells me in a soothing voice her name is Charlie, as if she's a doctor preparing me for surgery. She unlocks a fitting room door with her keys, measuring tape wrapped around her delicate wrist, and leads my mom and me inside. I pretty much want to die because Charlie is about to come near my bare breasts while my mom looks on.

"Boloozetoh behkan, take your shirt off," my mom says.

"This really is such a common problem. So many girls never get fitted for bras, and they end up wearing the wrong size for years. It's like an epidemic." Charlie smiles wide at me, and I'm hypnotized by her. I don't move. My shirt is still on, and it feels like a straitjacket I don't know how I'm going to get over my head. Charlie watches me, and maybe it's the high I still feel from my exchange with Yasaman, but I convince myself there's a sparkle in Charlie's eyes that must mean she's into me too.

"Rana Joon, you need to take your shirt off so she can measure you."

"Oh," I say, and I don't think for a second longer because sometimes you just have to let your fucking mind go. I face

Charlie, take my shirt and bra off, and my top is now naked with a solid, pounding heart underneath. Charlie gets close.

She smells how I smell; she probably samples the perfumes around the store when she gets bored. She wraps the measuring tape around the base of my bust, her hands warm and lotiony smooth. She lowers herself a little so she can read the number and then sneaks a glance up at me and winks, like she's trying to catch a piece of me in her silvery eye and take me with her back to whatever land she's come from.

"Lift your arms, please," Charlie says, and then wraps the tape around the roundest part of my chest. Her hand grazes my breast now, and I can feel my nipples immediately getting hard. Maybe this isn't just her doing her job—maybe she's trying to hold on a second longer just to feel me.

"Perfect. It looks like you're a 36DD," she says, smiling at me as she wraps the tape around her wrist again. I want to know where she's from, how she got here; is this a side job or are bras what she's really passionate about?

"See, I told you," my mom says.

"How can I go from a C to a DD?" I ask, trying to ease my nervousness by making small talk.

"It's normal," Charlie says. "Not everyone knows which size is right for them."

Please take me with you, I almost say out loud, but Charlie says she's going to go pick some bras out for me and leaves my mom and me alone with her actual C cups and my newly acquired DDs.

I stand there naked, nipples hard, the AC blaring on my body, missing Charlie already. I tune out my mom, who's giving me a lecture about taking care of my body and how if I'm not careful,

I'm going to become fat, and fat people aren't healthy people, but what she really means is fat girls have a hard time finding boyfriends. Well, joke's on her, since I'm not looking for one. But I wonder if I'll just have a hard time finding anyone.

"You're too pretty to let this happen," she says, a compliment that's like a slap in the face.

It feels like Charlie's been gone for hours when someone finally knocks. Instead of Charlie, a white girl with a tight blond bun comes in. I cover my breasts.

"Oh, I'm sorry, I was just bringing you some bras."

"Where's Charlie?" I ask.

"She went on her break," she says, and hands me ten bras, all either pink or red.

"Why?" I ask, panicked.

"Why did she go on her break?"

I nod yes.

"Because she was hungry?" the blond chick says.

I feel silly now, thinking Charlie was feeling the vibe between us too.

I buy two bras. One that doesn't itch, is black, simple, probably the only one in the store made of a stretchy cotton material and that actually offers support, and the other one light pink, lacy, uncomfortable, something I'll never wear, but that also makes my mom happy because she says it's beautiful and very elegant and feminine. On our way out, I spot Charlie at the food court eating French fries. She sits alone but doesn't look lonely; she almost looks happy.

I tell my mom I want to get something to eat, but she says I should start counting calories and there's nothing in the food court that's good for me anyway. "All this grease is disgusting.

Plus, I cooked for your father, so we will eat after we pick him up," she says.

I turn around and get one last glimpse of Charlie eating her fries, gracefully dipping each one in a pile of ketchup, savoring each bite, nothing about her disgusting at all.

"It's fine, he doesn't need flowers," I tell my mom as she searches for a spot in the Ralphs parking lot. I feel like she's doing anything possible to delay actually picking my dad up, but according to her, he doesn't get in for another hour. I roll a cold water bottle on my arms and forehead, close my eyes, and imagine that gap in between Yasaman's teeth, her freckles, how her lips moved when she told me I was beautiful. I'm trying not to make a big deal out of this human I barely know, but it's hard not to. I'm sweating so badly, my ironed-out baby hairs are frizzing up, so I tuck them neatly behind my ears.

"It's good to show him some respect. Make him feel loved," my mom says. Us being respectful to him has always been super important to her.

"You know he hates flowers. He says they're a waste of money because they die so quickly. Buy him a plant or something."

My mom insisted we light some esfand and fill our house with the smoke last night. Iranian moms are superstitious as fuck—meaning burning some weird seeds will ward off the evil eye; meaning you knock on wood; meaning if someone says too many nice things about you, something bad is about to happen; meaning if you ever leave the house on a trip, they throw a glass of water behind you. I'm not sure why, because you never ask why.

I stay in the car with the air on full blast while my mom goes into Ralphs. A key detail about my dad: the only thing he's really passionate about is planting things in our garden. The last time he was here, he planted some tomatoes and cucumbers and mint and lavender and these big purple flowers and a bunch of other things he asked me to look after, but nothing ever bloomed—most likely due to the fact that I hadn't tried hard enough, or really at all. Because he hadn't stayed around long enough to teach me what to do. When I was little, I'd follow him around the garden, admiring the tall purple bushes and hanging vines of jasmine on the back wall, and I'd bring his tools or help him spread the fertilizer or cut the dead flowers. These are the only memories I have of us alone, the only moments where I actually felt connected to him.

We'd chat about the garden during our phone calls, and I'd pretend it was fine, that everything was fine, and I'd fake listen to his vague instructions:

Don't let the tomatoes hit the ground.

Make sure to fertilize.

Those are the only two instructions I remember. But now my dad's going to actually see that it's all lifeless and dead and blame it all on me, which I probably deserve.

Soon my mom is back in the car with a potted orchid, which is a good compromise, except there's an obnoxious silver-and-purple balloon attached to it that says, *Welcome Home!* He's going to hate it.

"What do you think?" she asks, and I can feel the anxiety in her voice. I tell her it isn't so bad. I hold the orchid while we enter the freeway.

"Do you know any Iranians with red hair?" I ask her.

"Like they dye it red?"

"No, naturally red. Like their whole family has red hair."

"Yes. Maybe if their families come from Turkey or Afghanistan. It's possible. Why?"

"Just curious," I say, because I can't get the image of Yasaman watching me, drawing me, bringing me to life on paper, out of my head.

"That man pretends he doesn't want attention, but it's all he wants," she says, completely changing the subject. Usually before my dad gets here, she's giving me a pep talk on how I need to behave—no cursing, no short shorts, no staying out late, no fighting with Babak—but she seems distracted by her own unease. "He comes here once a year and thinks it's enough. And we all have to pretend like this is normal," she says. Her voice is part anger, part tremble, and I'm not sure where all this honesty is suddenly coming from.

"What happened to showing him respect?" I ask, but she's tuned me out, staring blankly ahead.

All the cars in front of us are braking and it's a sea of red, but my mom's in her own universe and puts her foot on the brake way too late; our car makes a horribly loud sound, and we come so close to hitting all the stopped cars in front of us. Her arm instinctively comes out to protect me, but my heart's beating too fast and I have to take a few deep breaths to calm down.

"Mom! What the hell?"

"I'm sorry, Rana Joon," she says. Her arm is still stretched out in front of me, even though we've been stopped for a while. "Sometimes I just wish things were different."

We finally make it off the clogged freeway and park at LAX, and my mom seems like she's literally going to have a nervous break-down before we even get inside the airport.

"You're acting weird," I say to her.

She reapplies her red lipstick, rubs her lips together, checks her face in the mirror, even does a fake smile to make sure it's going to pass as real. "I'm sorry. I'm fine. Don't forget the orchid," she says, as if this stupid flower is the thing that's going to fix this whole experience.

It's bizarre to call someone your dad, for him to always be that person to you no matter how much you think everything has changed, no matter how much you believe he doesn't have it in him to accept who you really are in this moment.

Why do I have to work so hard for his love?

People who wait with us hold up signs and nervously peek around the corner to see if their person has arrived. My mom cradles the orchid and attached balloon like it's my dad's newborn child he hasn't met yet and bites her lip nervously. I'm standing here gnawing at my nails—I don't want to feel nervous, but I do. My body overpowers my thoughts, tenses up, turns hot.

It's important to understand something: my mom's hot, and my dad is, to put it lightly, nothing special. He's also way older than her, which I've never really noticed until this very moment, when he turns the corner and slowly makes his way toward us, his tired face emerging from a crowd of chatty Iranian women. His body is about ten pounds heavier than the last time we saw him, his eyes squinted and strained, his hair and mustache dyed a shoe-polish black. *My dad is so old and will probably die soon* is the first thing I think. The guilt of not being there for him consumes me. Who's going to take care of him if he has a heart attack in a year? Who's going to take him to his doctor's appointments if he has to start getting chemo for the cancer that will inevitably come?

My mom's calling out his name, waving him over, and I want to excuse myself and dart toward the bathroom so I don't have to see the awkward way my parents reunite after all this time. My dad looks around, confused, like the sound of my mom's voice is a delusion that only exists in his head. He finally gets that she's real, though, and heads our way.

My mom gets a very formal kiss on each cheek, no hug, and then it's my turn. I stand in front of him, wearing my shorts and baggy T-shirt, barely any makeup, straight hair piled on top of my head in a bun. I can't imagine this is who he expected his daughter to turn out to be, and I can't say that this is the kind of dad I would've chosen.

"Salaam, Rana Joon," he says. He also leans in and gives me a kiss on each cheek, his mustache dye so potent, I think my cheeks will turn black. He tries to hug me and I let him, but it feels forced.

"Salaam," I say, trying to be nice.

He hands me a plastic package of lavashak, sour fruit roll-ups that I used to love as a kid. I'm not twelve anymore, and I'm not going to jump in his arms and kiss him all over his face just because he remembered to bring me my favorite goody from Iran, but I'll gladly accept it and most likely consume all of it by Monday.

"Merci," I say. My mom hands him the plant and the balloon.

"What is this?" he says as we make our way to baggage claim.

"It's for you," she says.

"I don't want it," he says. "Here, Rana Joon, you hold it."

And somehow I get stuck carrying the orchid all the way back to the car.

12.

"Nothing has changed at all," my dad says as he unzips and folds his brown slacks and rests them on a chair. I still can't stand how my dad immediately takes his pants off the second he walks through the door. Maybe he does this at home in Iran and thinks it's okay to do it here too, but it feels jarring considering he's barely ever around; in my eyes, he doesn't deserve this level of comfort and ease.

He investigates and doesn't seem to notice the lingering scent of the protective seeds, or how weird it is that he's walking around in boxer shorts and everyone can now witness how his upper thighs have hair and his calves are bald. His belly is rounder and his legs are thin, and if I'd seen his body evolving and was forced to live with a half-naked dad on the daily, this wouldn't be so annoying, but it makes me uncomfortable, and even more so because he pretends like it's no big deal at all.

My mom takes a break from her cooking classes when my dad's around. She says it's because she wants to focus on cooking for him so we can enjoy meals as a family, but I also know that although my dad's aware of her classes, he's not thrilled with a bunch of strangers dicing onions, grilling meat, and laughing over a glass of wine in our kitchen.

She started cooking last night to prepare my dad's favorite foods for lunch: ghormeh sabzi and rice—oily, crispy tahdig, which, if we're talking about carbs, is the greatest kind of all. The three of us sit around the table, and even though I can't see my dad's chicken legs, just knowing they're under the table weirds me out.

"Where is Babak?" he asks.

"He has games or practice every Saturday," I say.

"He doesn't eat with you?" my dad asks, sounding disappointed.

"Sometimes," my mom says with a smile.

"We barely see him these days," I say, because I'm always trying to see if there are ways to get Babak in trouble, even though he can do no wrong in their eyes.

"Khob, well, the exercise is good," my dad says.

I reach for the bread first and grab too many pieces, and I also take a huge wad of the crispy rice and pour the stew on it. My mom's less likely to say something about my eating habits when he's here. Sometimes she squeezes in a subtle nudge or a dirty look my way. But my dad could not give a shit what I eat, which gives him a lot of bonus points as far as I'm concerned.

I watch my mom pick at her food, smiling like she's really holding in a scream. I've never been in an actual relationship, but I know a thing or two about denial and how it makes life so much harder pretending you're something you're not. Secrets aren't treasures; they're balls of fire that burn holes into your heart. It's painful to watch her attend to all his needs—

Does he need more rice?

Is his tea too dark?

Is the stew too salty?

The stew's too salty; she knew it.

Why did she put all that salt in it?

She looks like she might start crying from the panic of disappointing her once-a-year husband. If this is the only model of a relationship I have, I'm pretty much fucked—boy or girl.

I try not to smile, just to make up for her fake smile, and my dad asks me what's wrong. I'm the center of attention at this meal because Babak is still at his game, and I know the investigation is about to start.

"Khob, so, I have an old friend who works at UCLA. He is a professor of engineering, I think. I can talk to him and see if he can make sure you get all the classes you like," he says.

"That sounds good," I say.

"If you are going to be pre-med, you have to start on those classes right away," he says.

What would they do if I told them the plain and simple truth that their daughter likes girls, and she won't marry a proper Iranian man and have proper Iranian babies, and she's definitely not planning on becoming a doctor and is trying very hard to become a good poet?

They'd make me an appointment with a psychologist tomorrow, tell me I'm too young to know what I want. My mom would cry for sure, give me the silent treatment for a while, and then guilt-trip me for years or maybe forever. But even though she's vocalized her distaste for her children being gay, I know I'm kind of all she has right now. The only person who really gets her. She'd have to get over it one day. My dad, though. My dad would forbid me from leaving the house ever again. Maybe he'd even force me to move to Iran so he could keep his eye on me and I could live under a government that views homosexuality as a crime worthy of death. I'm not saying my dad would want me dead or believes people who are gay should die; he'd just want to scare the shit out of me, to teach me a lesson about how difficult a life I'm in for.

"I'll be fine. The food is really delicious," I say. Secrets aren't treasures; they have no value, no worth once they stop protecting you, and I no longer feel safe in my lie, but everything feels like it's whirling inside me with no way out, so I keep my mouth shut.

"Your mom is an artist with this food," my dad says.

"I think it was salty. Not my best."

"Khob, okay. Now tell me about the garden. How is the garden doing?" he says. Fuck, the garden.

"I tried, Baba, but I think the soil needs more fertilizer or something," I say.

"I see, I see. Let's take a look after I have some tea," he says.

"I actually have a lot of work to do. Haven't graduated yet," I say with clenched teeth and a smile. If I'm going to survive the Way of the Wu, if I'm going to hook up with a girl before high school is over, I just need to stay on his good side for now, because I can't handle a battle with him on top of everything else. My dad nods in approval and lets me go up to my room.

When I get to my room, I pull out Yasaman's drawing of me from my backpack and lie down on my bed with it. I see pieces of myself in it, or maybe who I wish I could be. Something about my eyes. The way she's captured them makes it seem like I can protect myself if I need to but can also be totally vulnerable at the same time.

I look around my room. So many things feel so childlike suddenly. A ceramic bank of a bear holding a heart that I'd painted once at Kids N' Paint, a bowl filled with beaded jewelry I used to obsessively make in elementary school, a stuffed hippo I called Hippie that my mom got me when I was eight and refused to sleep alone in my bed, Paula Abdul and En Vogue CDs. It all feels like it belongs to someone else.

I shove everything that feels outdated into an old shopping bag, tie a tight knot, and put it in a corner so I can throw it away later. The only things left are my Tupac posters and my CDs and the black-and-white photograph of my grandparents underneath the Eiffel Tower when they were in their twenties and the drawing Louie did of my name in bold-colored graffiti letters. These are the things that really belong to me.

I put Louie's drawing and the framed photograph of my grandparents right next to what's left of my stack of CDs. My grandfather's handsome in the photo but has a puny mustache and is wearing an oversized trench coat, as if he wanted to seem bigger and more powerful than he actually was. I put Yasaman's sketch of me on my desk, so I can see it every time I walk in the door and remind myself of the potential that lives inside me.

13.

After my dad goes to bed early because of his jet lag, my mom wants to watch the news, which is so unlike her. It's all plane crashes, hurricanes, and bombings, and I'm not sure why anyone would sit around and intentionally increase their anxiety level like this. For a few hours I worked on reciting Louie's piece in front of the mirror, my focus on nothing else but just getting the words out of my mouth. Knowing Coach is on my team now helped me get through it, but I couldn't get over how unnatural it all felt to me. I needed a break, so I came to watch TV with my mom.

"Can we please watch something else?" I ask her. "I think *Friends* is on."

She's pretty hypnotized by the TV, though, and doesn't budge.

"Mom?"

"What did you say?"

"This is so depressing," I say.

"It's important, Rana Joon," she says, but starts flipping the channel anyway.

"You missed Ross and Rachel's kiss the other night," I tell her.

"I know. It was on at Ladan's house," she says.

"You think it'll last?" I ask her.

"I don't know," she says, stopping on an episode of *I Love Lucy*, which is the definite go-to show when you just want to tune the whole world out.

"Can I ask you a question?"

"Chiyeh? What is it?"

"Why are you so afraid of him?"

"Of who?" she asks, staring at the TV. It's the one where Lucy's working in the chocolate factory and she can't keep up with the speed of the machine, so she keeps stuffing her mouth with the chocolates so she doesn't look incompetent.

"Come on. You become a totally different person when Baba is around. Like someone cut your tongue out or something," I say.

She looks at me when I say that and is quiet for a really long time. We're not used to having an open dialogue about her relationship with my dad, but something about her freak-out in the car makes me feel like she's inviting me to ask these questions.

"Rana Joon, relationships are very complicated. One day you'll understand. Sometimes you lose yourself, you forget what makes you happy, and you feel like it doesn't even matter anymore. But we make our choices in life."

"You say that like it's a bad thing. Why can't we make *good* choices? Choices that actually make us happy? I won't be mad if you guys get a divorce. I promise you I won't think you're a bad person," I say.

I can't tell if she wants to laugh or cry. She kind of does both, pulls me in, and holds me close.

"You know I love you, Rana Joon. I'm sorry to put you in the middle like this," she says, wiping the tears from her face. She takes a big breath like she's getting ready to tell me something else—something she can't easily spit out. I'm waiting for it, but nothing ever comes.

The phone rings, and I quickly run to the kitchen to pick it up so my dad won't wake up from the sound.

"Hello?"

"Yo," Naz says, "you ready to get fucked up or what?"

"What the hell are you talking about?"

"Marcus's party, duh. You're obviously coming."

"My dad's here," I say, even though he's not awake to tell me I can't go.

"Shit," she says, and then after a pause, "I have the best idea. Just tell your parents you're volunteering at the mosque with me. I'm going anyway and am just going to skip out a little early. They'll die of happiness if they find out you've decided to spend your Saturday night surrounded by such pious and noble young men and women, but in reality, you'll be double-fisting Jell-O shots and hopefully making out with too many dudes to keep track. Trust me."

"I don't think they'll buy it," I say.

"We're almost out of here, Rana. You got to live it up. I'll pick you up in an hour," she says, and hangs up without leaving me a chance to argue. I'm not sure if my parents would buy it, and I should probably stay at home and keep practicing for the battle, but Yasaman did mention she was going. Louie's voice pops into my head—*Rana, this is it. The one and only now. No one's going to live it for you.*

I tell my mom exactly what Naz told me to say—the part about volunteering at the mosque, not Jell-O shots and make-out sessions. My mom knows Naz wears the hijab, that her family's conservative, that they pray five times a day and fast for Ramadan and have gone to Mecca and everything, so she's way more willing to trust Naz than your average well-behaved non-Muslim teenager.

"We should ask your dad," my mom says.

"He's asleep. You want to wake him up?" I ask her. And I expect her to say no and that she doesn't feel like getting any shit from him so it's better if I don't go, but she thinks about it for a minute, probably realizing there was some truth to what I'd told her—how she loses herself when he decides to show up. She's back to the news and seems sucked into the tragedies of the day, as if she's intentionally depriving herself the joy of watching Lucy fuck up over and over and over again.

"Be back by ten. Any later than that and your dad might wake up and see you're not here. Even if you're out reciting the entire Koran with Naz, he's not going to care, Rana Joon."

Louie and I rarely went to parties together—we mostly stayed in and had writing sessions or drove down PCH listening to music or watched boring documentaries because that was all he'd watch on TV. As magnetic as he could be with people, he always felt like crowds just weren't his thing. We'd eat out sometimes, which was mostly my doing. I introduced him to Persian food, the secret menu at In-N-Out, and Thrifty's ice cream, which he was forever grateful for.

Naz lives for parties, though, so this past year I've gone with her to a few. We always leave on the earlier side so neither of us will get in trouble, but making an appearance is enough for her. It's still not really my scene—I don't like to smoke weed at parties, and drinking just makes me feel dizzy. I usually stop at one drink, but maybe the key to enjoying it is drinking more.

The thing that still amazes me about Naz is that she comes from a super strict family, especially her dad, but she can convince anyone of anything, and she usually uses her mosque friends or school as her excuse for going out—or she literally lies to her dad's face, says she's going to sleep, and just sneaks out. But she sets rules for herself too, has clear boundaries she sticks to—she never comes home past ten p.m. and she never has sex with anyone. So far I haven't seen her get into any major trouble. I think she's just too confident and smart—or maybe she's just really damn lucky.

Marcus lives in a fancy gated community but still somehow falls in the zip code for our school. Naz is on the list, and the security guard buzzes us in once she gives her name.

"Holy shit. These houses are ridiculous. My house is totally going to look like this one day. Pool, tennis courts, a bathroom I don't have to share with a disgusting human being and his wife who doesn't even know what a tampon is," Naz says, referring to her older brother, Ahmad, and the girl he was arranged to marry in Afghanistan and brought back to the US. Naz's parents had an arranged marriage too, because that's what everyone in their small Afghan community did, but her mom was the one raised here and her dad was the one who came from Afghanistan, so he's way more conservative.

"All these houses look the same to me. I'd get bored," I say.

We park pretty far and have to walk over. Naz is wearing tight white jeans and Doc Martens even though it's almost summer. She's taken off her loose tunic and has left it in the car; now she's in a long-sleeved white shirt that makes her boobs look massive. She's also wearing her white hijab and red lipstick. I have jeans and a boring black tank top on, gold hoops for some flair.

"Here. Put some of this on," Naz says before we walk in. She holds her lipstick out to me. She probably has every shade of lipstick MAC makes and is always trying to give me makeovers.

"I told you, lipstick doesn't look good on me," I say, because it always makes me feel like I look like a clown, and my mom insists I wear it when we go to fancy parties. But I *do* want to look a little more dressed up than when Yasaman saw me this morning.

"Just trust me," Naz says, and so I take the lipstick. I glance at the color before applying, and it looks just like the shade of red my mom wears. Once it's on, Naz smiles. "Much better. Have some faith, Rana."

We go inside, and the party is high school on steroids. It's so loud, I have to focus really hard every time Naz tries to talk to me. The cool thing about Marcus, though, is that he's one of those kids who doesn't fall under one label, so his party is a mix of jocks, theater nerds, kids from the debate team and Model UN club, skateboarders, stoners. Jordan's even here and comes up to me while Naz gets me a beer.

"Red looks good on you," he says with a smile while he stares at my lips. He's flirting with me, but I think he sees me too much as a friend to try to make any moves. He has his dreadlocks tied in a huge bun on top of his head, and the tattoos covering his arms are exposed. (He and Louie had the same hookup.)

"Thanks," I say.

There's a DJ and not just a stereo playing CD mixes, which

I appreciate, and the DJ is playing "This Is How We Do It" by Montell Jordan, which I love.

"What the fuck is wrong with this guy? I'm about to lose my shit if he plays one more whack-ass song."

Suddenly embarrassed that I like a "whack-ass" song, I steer conversation to safer territory.

"So I asked Coach to help me with the battle. He said yes."

"Word? Hope you're ready to work. The Way of the Wu is no joke—and neither is Coach."

"What does 'Way of the Wu' mean, exactly?" I ask him.

"Well, if you're asking, then you haven't really done your homework," Jordan says. He sits down at a little side table in the kitchen and starts rolling a blunt.

I feel so embarrassed. "I know. Louie was always trying to explain it to me—like, they're more than a rap group; it's about a way of life, like a whole philosophy or something?"

Jordan nods. "Think of it like this, Rana. Do you know what a lotus flower is?"

"Ya, I think so," I say.

"The lotus flower is a ridiculously beautiful flower. I mean, there's no flower more beautiful than a lotus flower. But when it first begins to grow, it's underwater with all the mud and shit and nasty bugs, all the rough conditions that occur in that deep kind of darkness. Despite all that chaos, though, the lotus stays strong and moves beyond the obstacles to make its way to the clear surface and blossom. So these nine dudes are like fucking lotus flowers, born into the madness of poverty and violence, and they figured out a way to use their words, their intelligence, to rise up and fucking be free, Rana. And rich as fuck." With this last thought, he licks the paper and seals the blunt and then lights it up, and the crowded kitchen is soon covered in smoke. "That right there is the Way of the Wu."

"Definitely sounds like the type of shit Louie would be into."

"Hell ya. Bravo Mad Mad was legit. He was smarter than all these dorks combined."

"Ya, I've been reading his pieces. It's hard to choose just one to perform," I say.

"You're not performing any of your own stuff?" he asks. "Why not a Rana original?"

"All my stuff is pretty rough," I say, which is the easy way out and I know it. But now that both Naz and Jordan brought this up, it feels like another nudge, pushing me even more out of my comfort zone, pushing the lotus flower even closer to the surface. "I'll think about it."

Jordan's buddy walks by, and they do an elaborate handshake. I stand by awkwardly as they say hello.

"I thought you were gonna be out performing tonight, man," Jordan says.

His friend shakes his head. "Nah, that shit got canceled."

"Sucks for them," Jordan says, and then it's like a light bulb goes off above Jordan's head and he gestures toward me. "Yo, Buddha Boy, this is my homegirl Rana. She was homies with Bravo Mad Mad. Rana, you should spit something for him! He's legit and has no problem telling you when your shit is bogus," Jordan says.

Buddha Boy is incredibly tall and skinny and unlike a Buddha statue in that sense, but has a Zen-like look in his eyes, like he's half-asleep or something, which feels more fitting. My heart starts jumping around the way it likes to when I'm put on the spot. "Oh, shit. No. I don't think that's such a good idea. I'm not ready," I say, frantically looking around for a way out.

Buddha Boy inches closer to me, puts his hands on my shoulders, and gazes down at me. "You're ready when you can let all the bullshit go," Buddha Boy says, "when you know how much power your voice holds."

And then he starts spitting in this electric way that makes it seem like there's no other sound at the party but his voice:

Son, check this.
I wear the fang of the beast on my necklace!
This beat's a labyrinth and Imma run it till I'm breathless.
Put my wisdom in a tetanus, then inject the reckless!
Semiautomatic vernacular, crack your back and scapula.
Pick it up with a spatula. Hand it back to ya.

Even in a loud and crowded party where I'm sure no one can hear him, Buddha Boy commands the room. Jordan and I are floored. We're hooting and hollering for him, for the flow, for the release that feels so effortless. Is it even possible for me to come anywhere close to that?

"That was insane," I say.

"You just gotta find your flow, and the rest will come," Buddha Boy says, like it's the easiest thing in the world. There are only crashing waves and what feel like hurricanes inside me.

Jordan and him start smoking, and I tell them I'm going to look for Naz.

"Don't forget about the lotus flower. Don't get stuck in the mud, Rana. You can do this. You ain't no mud type of girl. Let me know if you want any help," Jordan says. Buddha Boy puts his hands in prayer position and bows to me as I walk away.

I can't find Naz, so I just eat the Cheez-Its I *did* find and check out the crowd getting down on the living room turned dance floor. The DJ's playing Outkast, and everyone throws their hands up in the air when the song tells them to. It's a cool beat, but no one's actually dancing to it—all I see are guys and girls grinding up on one another as if dancing is some type of foreplay.

"I'm still waiting for my poem," I hear, and turn around to see Yasaman, red curls piled like a messy beehive on her head. She's wearing green, glittering eyeliner that makes her eyes pop and pink gloss that makes my mouth feel wet, a white T-shirt with a V-neck so her collarbone's visible, and a simple, thin gold necklace.

I smile but feel immediately embarrassed and wish I had that beer Naz was supposed to get me.

"I'm just messing with you," Yasaman says, sipping on her own red cup. The DJ switches to that song that goes on and on about riding a train, and everyone dancing goes wild.

"I'm working on it. I need to find the right one," I tell her. I'm almost yelling in her ear; the music is so loud. Naz walks up to us double-fisting beers—she apparently had no problem finding me. She hands me one of the cups, and I introduce her to Yasaman.

"I've never seen you around before," Naz says. "You go to school with us?"

"Ya, I transferred a couple months ago."

"You get kicked out of your old one or something?" Naz asks, intrigued. I'm almost annoyed by Naz's line of questions, but if it bothers Yasaman, she doesn't show it.

"Honestly? We had to sell our house in LA and move to an apartment in the Valley we could actually afford."

"Oh, shit. You got that whole I'm-honest-as-fuck vibe, huh?"

Naz asks, and Yasaman laughs, and I'm overjoyed that Yasaman gets her.

Naz examines the crowd like she's looking for someone, probably trying to see if there's anyone cute she can hook up with, or someone she's already hooked up with who wouldn't mind making out again or feeling her up in the bathroom.

"Can we dance or something?" Naz asks us. I usually sit out on the whole dancing portion of the evening because Naz finds some dude to grind with in under two minutes, but Yasaman seems into it and looks my way like she's expecting me to be a part of this—the slight space between her teeth inviting me to lose myself and let go. I chug my beer and follow the two of them to the dance floor.

I wish I were just a little bit more buzzed because I can feel myself being stiff and overthinking how my body's moving to this shitty techno song, but then the DJ abruptly transitions to Tupac's "California Love" and everyone starts cheering and Naz hands me her cup and I finish it off for her.

I yell in Yasaman's ear, "I love Tupac!" She nods and closes her eyes and sways her hips like it's some sort of slow jam.

Naz is less dancing and more scoping the scene. I hand her the empty cup and take the new one that's magically appeared in her hands.

"What the fuck?" Naz says, and I just shrug. I'm expecting beer, so I almost gag when I taste vodka mixed with Coke. I give her a look of disgust, and this time she smiles and shrugs. I drink most of what's left, which is a good amount, and hand her the rest.

Tonight will be different from any other night. My feet feel loose, and my mind chatter is gone—maybe this is the flow Buddha Boy was talking about. Most of the time it's like I'm watching life from above, like I don't see myself as a part of this ocean of bouncing bodies so excited about the opportunity to be in high school and have our whole lives ahead of us, so willing to trust the moment. But now I'm pretty buzzed and feeling good in my body and suddenly live on a planet with no problems, no promises or secrets to keep, and no ten p.m. curfew. This song is my jam, so I start singing along to the lyrics and let myself move freely, sticking my ass out, thrusting my hips, throwing one hand up in the air to these lines:

We in that sunshine state where the bomb-ass hemp be
The state where you never find a dance floor empty!

I see Naz out of the corner of my eye all up on Marcus, and for once I don't feel so alone because Yasaman is dancing in front of me, cracking up because I probably look like a dork, but I can't help it. I start laughing too for no reason at all. I'm not sure how, but Yasaman ends up turning herself so her ass is facing me. She's lightly pressing it against my pelvis and I can feel how it bounces as she shakes it side to side. I've seen girls doing this before—like a whole train of straight girls dancing together in this overly sexualized way to make up for the fact that no guy wanted to dance with them. I always found it annoying, but Yasaman doing it to me is a completely different story. I'm so nervous suddenly, but also the familiar urge is there—I want nothing more than to turn her around and kiss her.

She gets down low and I follow her, and when we come back up, she turns around and smiles at me, and then we're both laughing again. Despite my buzz, my heart's beating fast and I can feel the heat rising to my cheeks. I might actually pass out.

"Damn. You've got moves," she says, and I just nod because I'm not feeling very articulate at the moment. I snap out of our booty dance trance and look around for Naz, but I don't see her. "Wanna take a break? I'm burning up," Yasaman says. She takes my hand and leads me to the kitchen to get some water, and I hesitate to let her go, but somehow our skin comes apart. We're both quietly sipping water, observing the crowd. She smiles at me, and I'm thinking it's very possible I'm not the only one feeling this spark. "I like dancing with you," she says, which is definite flirting in my book. "Some people can be so awkward. Like they have a stick up their ass or whatever. But you were really getting down." Looking straight into her green eyes is so intense, and my teeth are chattering even though I'm burning up. I try to divert.

"I gotta pee," I say.

"Cool. I think I need some air anyways. Meet me outside?"

"Ya, I'll be quick," I say. I wait in the three-person line for the bathroom, which is in the back of Marcus's house by the washer-dryer. I try to take deep breaths and not get too in my head and question my ability to actually go for this—to actually connect with a girl on a mind, body, and soul level. The alcohol definitely helps; instead of questioning if I'm making all this up in my head, I feel excited. This is the very stuff of my dreams, and I can't panic now.

It's not clear how I missed this, but suddenly there are two people hard-core making out against the washer-dryer, and it's so heated, it's hard to take my eyes off it. When the girl comes up for air for a second, I see it's Brianna Asher. I can't tell who she's kissing, but he looks tall and clean-cut from the back, wearing a collared shirt and khakis. She looks drunk, but not drunk enough to not be aware of what she's doing. Her straight blond hair, usually up in a bun and sweaty after basketball practice, is spread across her shoulders, and she's wearing a tight little black dress that shows off her legs.

I watch her lips as she kisses this dude and can't help but think of how she pulled away when I tried to kiss her so long ago. She'd told me she liked me too when I asked her, but that had obviously meant something different to her. I can't imagine she still thinks about it, but sometimes it's like the little girl in me is being held hostage by those events, how quickly I pushed someone I loved away just by being myself with them. I'm older now, though, wiser for sure, and things with Yasaman just feel different.

When I get out of the bathroom, the party's still going strong, but I head outside, where it's a little quieter. People are smoking weed, a few are in the pool with only their underwear and bras on, and couples are spread out, feeling each other up and hiding their desires in the darkness. I find Yasaman sitting on a bench right on the edge of Marcus's backyard. She's looking up at the full moon like she's asking it to guide her, and I almost don't want to ruin this moment for her.

"That was a long pee," she says as I sit down next to her.

"Sorry."

"It's cool. The moon is insane tonight. Do you know the phases of the moon control the waves in the ocean? Like, when it's a full moon, the high tides are super high, and when it's a new moon, the low tides are super low. Everything's connected," she says.

"How do you know that?" I ask.

"I read a lot of random shit. My mom has, like, a thousand books on our bookcase. She's kind of a nerd. Ever since my dad died, all she does is read. And travel," she says.

There's a fat silence between us. No one's ever looked at me like this before. Tony's eyes always seem desperate for my touch, but Yasaman looks excited and happy as she watches me. Maybe the alcohol has me reading too much into things, but I'm pretty sure she might kiss me, and this moment I've waited so long for, to be kissed by a girl, the way I want to be kissed, is finally upon me—but she just gently touches my hair instead and says, "Dude, you should totally leave your hair curly. I know you have those strong Persian queen genes."

I deflate a little but try not to let my disappointment show. "Nah, it's too frizzy. Your curls at least behave. My hair is just one big pouf if I don't straighten it."

"I'm sure with the right product it would look amazing," she says. Her fingers are still in my hair, and she seems shy all of a sudden. She removes her hand and looks back at the moon. "Do you know where you're going next year?"

"UCLA," I tell her. And maybe it's because I'm drunk—but really, I think it's just because of how comfortable I am with Yasaman—I confess, "It used to be everything I wanted, the answer to all my problems, but I'm not so sure anymore." It's wild that I'm admitting this to a girl who I had no idea existed before this morning, but maybe that's how life works? Sometimes we feel less judgment from strangers than our own families, who carry impossible expectations of us. "What about you?"

"Still figuring it out. Probably Pierce," she says, referring to the local community college. "How'd you get into writing poetry?"

"My grandfather. He was reading me Persian poetry when I was, like, eight. He had this Hafiz poetry book, and he'd always tell me to ask a question, like some deep, burning question I wanted an answer to, and to open the book to some random page. He said whatever poem I turned to would have the answer to my question, but he said it would never tell me anything I didn't already know. The poems just help you find the answer already inside you."

"That's dope."

"Ya. He's dead now," I say.

"That sucks, but it's cool he inspired you to write. I wish I'd gotten my dad's artistic genes. I swear to God I wouldn't know what to do with myself without art, but I've never been good at it."

"That's not true. That picture you drew of me was great. You seemed like you knew what you were doing."

"Thanks," she says.

There's an awkward silence between us, probably more on my end because I'm feeling shy and don't know what else to say.

"Have you ever been to LACMA?" Yasaman asks. "They have this Frida Kahlo self-portrait where she has a thorn necklace with a hummingbird on it, and a monkey on one shoulder and a black cat on another, and all these butterflies in her hair. It's so badass. She's hands down my favorite artist."

"I don't know her," I say, feeling like I've been living in some sort of cave.

"Dude, Rana. You don't know Frida Kahlo? Oh my God, I'm *so* taking you to see that portrait. It's, like, a spiritual experience. A whole other level," she says. Yasaman sounds way too enthusiastic about everything, but with her it feels genuine, like she has this zest for life and wants everyone in on it.

"Rana!" I look around and find Naz and her harsh whisper in the distance. Somehow she's located us at the edge of the party, where I thought no one would be able to find us. "We gotta go. Like, *now*."

"What happened? Are you okay?"

"Yes, we need to leave as soon as humanly possible. I'm so fucking embarrassed. You have to be home in, like, five minutes anyways," she says. I look at my watch and realize she's right.

"Oh, shit," I say. I wasn't trying to push it on my dad's first night here. I ask Yasaman if she has a ride, and she says she drove and will probably be leaving soon anyway. There's a moment when we're both just standing there, and I don't know what to do because really all I want is to kiss her, but I can't, so I do the only thing I can do with Naz right there: I hug her goodbye.

"LACMA," she says. "Frida Kahlo. You and me. Don't forget."

I follow Naz as she scurries through the party as fast as she possibly can. I think maybe she got her period or something and it leaked all over her white pants—she's freaking out that bad—but I don't see anything.

"Naz, what happened?" I ask again. She's walking so fast I can't keep up with her.

"I don't want to talk about it," she says, and then adds after a short pause, "Marcus is a fucking asshole."

"Why? Dude, I'm cramping up. Slow down a little."

"I'm sorry. I'm just so pissed. Marcus and I were all feeling each other. I mean, I could feel his hard-on against my thigh when we were dancing. I thought he was going to fucking ejaculate right there, so I told him to meet me in his room upstairs in, like, five minutes so I could freshen up and then give him a blow job, or he could go down on me, and he seemed so into it. We even kissed before we split up. Like one of those kisses that makes you so wet, your nipples immediately get hard. I went to reapply my lipstick and whatever, and when I walk into his room, I see some white girl riding him like a cowgirl. I watched long enough to see that she'd completely shaved her pubes like she was in a porno. Totally gross. Like, what happened in those five minutes that made him think it was okay to pull some shit like that?" she says, talking so fast, yet not losing her breath.

"Wait, you stood there long enough to see the girl's vagina?"

"That's not the point," she snaps at me.

"Sorry. What did he say?"

"He asked me if I wanted to join," she says, unlocking her car door. "Guys are such dicks. I'm never touching one again."

"It's probably a good thing that you didn't hook up with him if he's such a dick, right? You deserve better than that and you know it, Naz. You're a fucking queen," I say.

"I know, but still. I really like him," she says.

She's driving way too fast, speeding down the hill toward the security gate, but I've tuned her out at this point and am warped into a fantasy of my missed kiss with Yasaman and the thousand different ways it might actually happen sometime soon.

14.

In the morning I hear a knock on the front door. Everyone is upstairs getting ready for our family day out, so I answer it.

It's Tony. Tony, who never comes over, who my parents have
no clue I hang out with sometimes. Tony, who looks like he's
twenty-five and whose arms are covered in tattoos and who is
definitely not on the Persian parents' list of who their teenage
daughter can hang out with.

"Yo. Where have you been?" he asks. He's wearing a white
T-shirt and jeans—the same thing he always wears when he leaves
the house, which is pretty rare.

I step outside and close the door behind me. "What are you
doing? We have rules, Tony. You can't just come over here."

"You're embarrassed of me, huh?"

"What? No. My parents are just really, really strict. And my
dad's here."

"Shit, Rana, how do you expect me to know that? You ran out
on me, and I haven't heard from you for three days. I don't know
anything that's going on because you don't tell me shit."

"And you tell me everything? What's up with your dad? You never say shit about him, but I know Louie was fucked up over it." I don't want to tell Tony about the notebook because I don't want him to know I was snooping around. Plus, he'd probably demand I give it back, which I have no intention of doing.

Tony stares blankly at me. "So what?" he asks.

"Did Louie talk to you about him?"

"A little, I guess, toward the end," he says.

I just look at him, waiting for more.

"Listen, alright," he says, sounding tired, "he went to see our dad and he was a total dick just like I'd warned Louie he would be."

It's like I've been slapped in the face by another one of Louie's secrets. "He went and saw your dad? What do you mean? When?"

Tony runs his hands through his nonexistent hair, exasperated. "Why do you care so much? Is this about what you were saying the other day? You've got to let this fucking go, Rana. Louie is *dead*," he says, his voice rising. "You act like he was this god or some shit who could do no wrong. Louie was fucking messed up, Rana!"

"You know he had zero respect for you. You didn't really even matter to him," I say, because I don't know what else to do but to make Tony feel as shitty as he's making me feel right now. But he doesn't yell or hit me or try to hurt me back. He just looks at me, wide-eyed.

"Fuck you, Rana," he says quietly, and leaves, going the fastest I've ever seen him walk.

After what happened with Tony, I'm not in the mood for family day, but I have to go. Sundays were always family day when my grandfather was around. We'd play miniature golf or go to the movies or eat sushi. We stopped the tradition after he died, but now that my dad's here, we're expected to spend Sundays together, so the four of us end up at the promenade in Santa Monica. The street is so crowded that we don't actually have to interact with one another, which I'm okay with, but kind of defeats the point of quality time if you think about it.

The street is lined with shops and booths selling shit you don't need, like personalized key chains and hats that light up and make your head look like a disco ball. Every few minutes we stop and see a crowd gathered for different street performers. My dad seems into it and insists we stop and watch the break dancers, the man spray painted in silver doing the robot, the little Asian girl playing the violin, and this insanely skinny man who has one hand on a stick and his whole body somehow levitating above it. My dad doesn't leave money for any of them, but as we walk away from the levitating man, I sneak a dollar into his bucket because holy shit, how is he just sitting on top of air?

My dad also gets to pick where we eat; obviously, he chooses the one place that serves Persian food in the indoor mall that connects to the promenade. When it comes to food, he likes to splurge, so we end up with a whole spread: kabobs, rice with melted butter on top, eggplant dip, yogurt and cucumber, pickled vegetables, and the best part—the greasy lavash bread they serve underneath the kabob, which he insists I eat.

I'm more than happy to dig in, but I don't like him telling me what to do, so I make a little comment: "Mom's food is better."

"Your mom could never make kabob like this."

"Ya, she can. She made it with her students a few weeks ago," Babak says.

My dad looks to my mom in surprise. "You're still doing this? I thought we talked about you stopping," my dad says.

My mom looks at her plate as she responds, "I'm taking a break for now, and of course I can't make kabob like this. Everyone knows you go to a restaurant for kabob, and if it's stew or polo you're looking for, only your mom or wife can do it right."

"I'm just not comfortable with these strangers in our house. What about the kids? Where do they do their homework?"

"We just do it in our rooms," I say. My dad takes a bite out of a raw onion and chews on it sloppily. I have heartburn just watching him. Babak shrugs like it's no big deal, and my mom picks at her food while I eat too much. We've got this whole open family communication thing down really well. But I don't want to think about my fucked-up family or what happened with Tony this morning. I distract myself by replaying last night with Yasaman in my mind—our dance, our almost kiss, Yasaman's fingers running through my hair.

"Rana?" my dad says.

"Ya?" I say, shoving greasy bread into my mouth.

"Your mom says you went to volunteer at the mosque with your friend Naz last night."

"That's hard to believe," my brother says as he chomps on his kabob. Babak doesn't know when to shut the fuck up. I give him the look of death.

"It's not a big deal. I just wanted to check it out," I say.

"It is good to spend time with good Muslims," my dad says.

"Babak, did you tell Baba that Samantha is dying to meet him?" I ask. Even though my parents still idolize him and his golden penis, I know my dad wouldn't be thrilled with him dating a white girl.

"Who is Esamantha?" my dad asks, adding a shit-ton of sumac to the previous shit-ton of sumac on his rice.

"Babak's girlfriend," I say. Now it's my brother's turn to give *me* the look of death.

"Have you met her?" my dad asks my mom, who's taking small bites and chewing for a while before swallowing—one of her weight-loss methods she always tries to push on me.

"Once or twice. She seems nice. Very skinny, like a tooth-pick," my mom says.

"Babak Joon, it's important to find a girl similar to yourself—similar background, family, values, goals in life. These American girls are very different from us. Sometimes it feels like they are aliens," my dad says.

"But *I'm* American," Babak says. My dad drops his fork, and my mom chokes on her small little bite and has to wash it down with a swig of water. I just wait for the shit to hit the fan.

Even though Iranian tradition and culture give Babak the upper hand in our family, I'd still never label myself as American the way Babak just did. Iranian American, maybe, because my grandfather's poetry and my mom's cooking are just as much a part of me as Tupac and In-N-Out burgers.

Babak has waxed his eyebrows so thin, it's hard to determine what emotion he's actually experiencing, but he seems like he's just thinking out loud and not actually trying to challenge our dad. Still, my dad looks pissed.

"Put this nonsense aside. You're smarter than this. Yes, you were born in this country, but we have a very strong culture. You can't turn your back on it," he says, "right, Mitra Joon?"

"Of course," my mom says, and I can hear her silently counting how many times she's chewing in her head, all the way to thirty.

15.

When we get home from the promenade, I tell my
parents I have to go to the mall to return something, but instead
I drive down Ventura Boulevard, hang a left on Topanga Canyon
Boulevard, and drive far enough toward the beach that the road
gets windy and my palms start to sweat. Mental pictures flash
through my mind—Louie speeding, Louie angry about God
knows what, Louie's out-of-control car rolling down the side of
the mountain.

I park the car and get out just as the sun is setting. I walk
along the side of the road until I get to the spot where I can see the
entire Valley below me. There, I put down a bundle of lavender,
the only flowers that have actually grown in our garden, for Louie.

The weeks and months leading up to that day feel like a blur.
I try to look back on the end of junior year, how excited I was to
become a senior, so close to my dreams of life beyond high school.
The last month of school, I remember wanting to celebrate, go to
the beach, hang with other people, and Louie told me he couldn't
because he was doing these "meditation retreats" at home and he

needed quiet and solitude. I gave him his space because I trusted him—or at least that's what I tell myself. Maybe he was depressed and having a hard time, and I just hadn't wanted to see it.

The sky is a burning pink color, and I'm grateful and devastated all at once. There are people in the distance, couples watching the sunset too, but most of them are just making out, and in this moment, I don't care if they hear me. I close my eyes and imagine Louie's face, everything he wanted, and everything that disappeared in a second. I feel him, his joy and his pain, inside my own body. I open my mouth and release his words:

> *Every night same fight, same fright, same dreams,*
> *Climbing the razor's edge trying to find the extremes . . .*

My voice is louder than when I practice in the mirror at home, loud enough that if he's watching over me, he would hear it too. I'm astonished I remember all the words, but I do—they're a part of me now.

When I get home, my brother has gone to the gym and my mom's taking a nap, which is something she does when she's feeling a little depressed. Outside in the garden, my dad's standing in an undershirt and white boxer shorts, slippers on, smoking a cigarette with one hand, holding a shovel with the other. He looks puzzled, frustrated at the mess I've made by neglecting this sacred space. His face looks even older than when he stepped off the plane. His wrinkles are etched into his face permanently. All I keep thinking is my dad's going to die soon, and do I even really know this man?

"What are you doing?" I ask him.

"This is a disaster," he says, sounding less angry and more just deeply saddened by the whole thing. "Did you even follow my instructions?"

"I tried, but it was too hard," I say, lying to his face because I hadn't tried at all. The garden isn't big; it's a small square patch of land just beyond our concrete patio, with large orange and lemon trees surrounding it. I take it all in—the dried-out soil, the shriveled-up flowers, the tomatoes that never became anything more than tiny, pale green buds. There are too many weeds covering everything, and although some of them have surprisingly beautiful flowers blossoming, they're too wild for my dad's taste.

I remember being a little girl, digging my hands in the dirt with my dad and observing him like an apprentice. I could see the love he held for these tiny seeds even before they became beautiful. Back then I felt like he loved me the same way, and it seemed anything was possible in our garden. But then he started leaving, coming and going. For a while I still tried to garden the way he wanted me to, but it started to feel like a chore—a burden more than anything else.

When he did show up, he wouldn't stop talking about the garden, and even early on, I could sense that his obsession with it was mostly about wanting control. Even if the garden was in shambles, he could pick up right where he'd left off—but with us, it was completely different.

"You've become like these American children," he says to me now. "You have to learn about responsibility. In this world, you can't just think about yourself. Don't worry, I will buy some new plants, some fertilizer. I will show you this time, and this time you will do it right," he says.

"Okay, Baba," I answer, playing the role of the dutiful, guilt-filled daughter he so desperately needs me to be.

That night, I open my notebook, and within seconds, the words just flow. I don't know if it's being immersed in Louie's words or all the Audre Lorde poems I've been reading, but something is starting to click again.

It's a poem about a garden, but it's also a poem about a father wanting to teach his daughter about life when he doesn't even really know her at all.

I'm the rootless one,
The bud stuck in smallness
Afraid to bloom,
I'm the weed, wild, beautiful, unacceptable.
You can't even see me anymore.
Father, I am tired of pretending
These flowers will do just fine—
What would it take to finally tell you that
I am the one in need of your love?

Ms. Murillo's big black eyes get even bigger when she sees me walk into her classroom at lunch on Monday. She gives me a huge hug and welcomes me like a friend and not a student. She's arranged the desks in a smaller circle for the meditation group than she does for class—seven or eight instead of fifteen.

"I'm so glad you're here," Ms. Murillo says.

"Me too," I say.

It felt so good releasing Louie's words the other day, and I'm hoping this will help me connect with him even more. All the times Louie tried to get me to meditate, the silence and stillness only made me more anxious, but it meant a lot to him and was even something he believed could help his depression more than medication. I figure I might as well see if meditating can help calm the recent chaos of my mind. Plus, I'll try anything to help me chill out before my first practice with Coach tomorrow.

I'm the first one here, so I take a seat and look around at the walls. Instead of decorating her classroom with cheesy teacher posters about doing your best and how success is about getting up instead of giving up, Ms. Murillo has put up photographs from her travels—ruins in Mexico, temples in India, waterfalls in Argentina, mosques in Morocco. There's a colorful shaggy rug in the corner and a small velvet couch, with a sign on the wall that says *A Moment of Zen*, which I'd never noticed before.

Soon the rest of the group walk in: Krishna, Rain, that surfer boy Paul Stewart who Naz made out with, Buddha Boy, this kid Jesus who's one of the star soccer players at our school, and a few others I don't recognize. Buddha Boy nods in my direction when he sees me, and I nod back.

Ms. Murillo closes the door, turns off the lights, and tells us to get as comfortable as we can before we get started.

"I know all we have are these crappy desks, but just do your best," she says, "and please feel free to go sit on the rug." A few people get up and do just that. Ms. Murillo tells us to close our eyes, sit up straight, and put our feet flat on the floor if we're at our desks, so we can ground ourselves.

"Let your awareness move through your body. Pay attention to any areas of tension where you're holding on to something. Wherever you might feel anything you're holding on to, be aware of the choice you have to let go. You can focus on the eyes, letting them soften, loosening your temples. Release any tension from your jaw. Loosen your shoulders. Let your hands feel soft and relaxed. Allow yourself to feel the energy and vibration inside your body."

My mind's already chattering:

My nose itches.

Am I doing this right?

Does Yasaman actually have a crush on me?

Can I really do this battle?

"If thoughts come up, don't judge yourself for having them, but see them as clouds, coming and going. Allow them to be, and then release them and come back to your breath, to the moment," she says, as if she's speaking directly to me. I try to do as she says, focusing on my breath as much as I can.

Is this what she means?

I don't judge. I allow it to be. I let go.

Louie's still dead. No matter what I do he will always be dead.

Another cloud. Just allow. Let go.

This continues on and on and on. My attention travels from Ms. Murillo's soothing voice, to how uncomfortable my ass feels, to my thought clouds, to my breath, back to my thought clouds, to the part of me willing to let go, to the part of me judging myself and thinking I'm doing a horrible job at this, to the part of me so ready to get the fuck out of this room, and then back to breath. I'm obviously a horrible meditator, but instead of opening my eyes and seeing what everyone else is doing or checking out and falling asleep, I let myself sit in this internal space and just let everything flow.

I'm tense, then relaxed, then annoyed, and then calm, thinking about time, love, the future, the past, how much longer we have, and then letting go. Every time I let go, it feels like I'm peeling a layer off, getting a tiny inch closer to my core, to the quiet, calm center that feels so foreign to me. Is this what Louie was after? Soon I hear the sound of three bells.

"Let's close the session by focusing our practice on a meditative thought. In Buddhism there's something called the second arrow. The first arrow is the event or trauma or whatever's happened to you, and the second arrow is all the judgment and shame and fear that comes after it. We might not have control over the first arrow, but the second arrow is always in our own hands, so the choice is yours. Are you going to keep stabbing yourself with it, or are you going to release it and finally be free?" she says, as if she is so in tune with my heart right now that she knows these are the exact words I need to hear.

"When you're ready, feel your feet flat on the floor, wiggle your fingers, and come back to your body. Open your eyes when you feel ready," Ms. Murillo says. I wiggle my fingers and open my eyes, and although I don't feel enlightened or anything, I definitely feel more relaxed and in my body. I stay sitting for a while trying to process everything that's just happened.

Buddha Boy comes over and, without saying a word, hugs me. He's skin and bones, but so warm and loving.

"Yo, just keep at it, okay? The silence and the words, nothing is your enemy," he says, and I nod yes like I've been hypnotized by him.

Before I leave, Ms. Murillo checks in with me.

"How did that feel for you?" she asks.

"It was actually better than I thought it would be. I mean, nothing has really changed, but there's more space in my mind, and everything isn't so jumbled up."

"It definitely takes practice. It's important to be alone and quiet with yourself sometimes, Rana. It'll help you be your own safety net," she says. She starts rearranging the desks, and I help her.

Even though she just told me to find the quiet within myself, I open up. "It's gonna be one year soon. Of Louie being gone, I mean." Ms. Murillo stops moving the chairs and looks at me in this way that is both pitying and understanding. I suddenly feel on the spot and continue moving the desks back where they were. She follows my lead. "One year feels hard, Ms. Murillo. Like it's a circle that's closing, and I'm not ready for it."

"I felt the same way with my husband. Like one year meant it was real, it was over, and I had to be over it too. But fuck that," she says, "you do things on your own timeline. This is your journey, and no one can tell you how to do it right."

Kids are starting to come in for her next class, but her eyes stay on mine, and she reaches over and hugs me, and I cry and cry. It's been so long since anyone has allowed me to just be my own glorious fucking mess.

16.

"Let me hear your piece," Coach says the next day. I don't have class at the end of the day, so we're meeting during seventh period. We're in his messy office, and he's bought us Subway sandwiches and is chowing down on a twelve-inch meatball sub. I'm so nervous and already ate lunch, so I save mine for later.

"Well, it's not my piece. It's Louie's piece."

"Okay, then let me hear *Louie's* piece."

I take a deep breath. It's just Coach, I keep thinking, you can do this. But I know the end goal is to do this for way more people than just Coach. I close my eyes and think of the other day at the canyon. I try to imagine Louie again, try to find his voice within mine, and release the words the way I did before.

I open my eyes and feel like the room is spinning. Coach is smiling.

"You okay?" he asks.

"Ya, I'm good," I say. "So . . . how was that?"

He takes another bite, making me wait until he's done chewing before he tells me what he thought. "That wasn't too bad"—my shoulders immediately sag with relief—"but this competition is about revealing truths. That wasn't your truth—that was Louie's. You were saying all the words, but you weren't embodying them, and the only way that's gonna happen is if the words come *from you*. I want to hear something you've written. You were always writing in your notebook before practice and games. Don't think I didn't notice," he says, and leans back in his chair, a grin on his face. He wipes his mouth with a napkin that's now completely red and drenched in oil.

"I don't have anything finished," I say.

"It doesn't matter," he says. The annoying thing about Coach Lock is also the thing I love most about him—he asks me to challenge myself and sees right through my excuses, pushing me to be a better, stronger version of myself.

So I do what I've been too scared to do up until this point: I take out my notebook and I start to read for Coach. I read my half-finished "I Am From" poem for Mrs. Mogly's class, an ode to the beautiful mess that makes me who I am. I'm reading off the page, and I don't know the poem as well as I know Louie's piece, but I can feel how different it sounds. It's like a dance between my words and me, the truth taking me on these waves that push and pull.

After I finish, Coach is nodding his head. "Damn. That's beautiful. So far it's killer, and your willingness to be that honest is dope, Rana," he says. "But if you're going to battle, you're going to need more fire. . . ."

"That's why I'm using Louie's stuff. I can't do my poem, Coach. I'm just not comfortable with it."

"Just think about it, okay?" he asks. "I think this—*that*, what you just did—was what Louie would really want." I nod yes, even though there's no way I'm reading this poem in front of anyone other than Coach Lock. Louie wanted *his* words out there, and I'm going to make sure that happens.

"Alright," Coach Lock says, standing up next to me now. "Let's see . . . more fire. First things first, when you read something silently to yourself, the energy of that piece is in your *mind*. When you release it for others to hear, the energy of the piece has to be in your *body*. It's all in your breath, your face, your arms, your legs, every inch of your body has to be present and available to the words—to the message."

He has me take a few deep breaths, shake my arms out, jump up and down, wiggle my body around, roll my head in circles.

"You have to use your breath to your advantage. It's like an ebb and flow of sound and breath, sound and breath. You have to feel the source of the sound in your belly," he says. Then he tells me to yell at the top of my lungs a few times, but to make sure the yell comes from my belly.

"Now?"

"Yes, now. No wasting time," he says.

I feel incredibly silly, and my mind is trying to control my scream—do I open my mouth first? Does the sound come from my throat? My belly? What if people can hear and think something is wrong? I yell once. A sad attempt.

"That sounded like a yawn," Coach says.

I yell again, but I know it's not enough.

"You sound like a baby cub. Let's get that mama lion roar, Rana! You're not a kid anymore. Real life is coming for you, and it wants to hear what you have to say."

I've always tried to be the peacekeeper, to keep my truths silent to not disappoint anyone around me—and it's fucking exhausting. If anything is going to change in my life, I have to try something different.

I yell one last time and am jolted by the power of my own voice. Mrs. Patel, the school secretary, comes running in. She leaves when she sees that we're laughing.

"See, that's what I mean," Coach says. "You have to channel that energy in a controlled way and grab people's attention. You have to play with the audience and take them on a journey. Now, read the first few lines with what I'm saying in mind. And take a deep breath before you begin."

I do as he says, breathe deep, feel the energy of my voice in my chest, allow it to ebb and flow with the emotions of the words, which sound so different this way—I can actually feel them vibrating inside my heart.

"See what I mean? If you feel it, we feel it."

"I feel it," I say, and I can't help but smile. We keep working on my poem this way, me repeating it until it's tattooed in my brain and I have no choice but to remember.

After school, Naz finds me and is still hung up on the whole Marcus thing. I want to tell her about what just happened with Coach Lock, but I'm still processing.

"I mean, like, have some fucking decency and at least tell me if you're hooking up with other girls. He had all of Friday to get with whoever else he wanted, why couldn't he just save Saturday for me?" I guess I must be quiet for a while because she says, "Rana? Yo!"

"Shit, sorry. You're right. He should've been more real with you. You deserve better, Naz. You're, like, the most beautiful girl in this school, and you don't have to show your tits or your ass to get attention," I say as we navigate our way through the crowded halls.

"Shit, Rana, I always know I can count on you to keep things in perspective," she says, laughing. "And I'm excited to hear you do your thing." Naz and I are having an after-school study session, preapproved by my dad, and I asked if I could share my version of Louie's piece with her, get her feedback. "How's it been going, by the way?" she asks.

"Really good," I say. My practice with Coach Lock has boosted my confidence in a way I didn't think was possible.

Before I can tell her more, though, Yasaman walks over, her face beaming with excitement. She gives Naz a hug and then gives me one too. She smells like coconut and the fleeting joy of summer just around the corner.

"You guys want to grab some Thai food? I found this hole-in-the-wall spot off White Oak. It's a Thai grandmother cooking in the back, and her grandson takes orders. I mean, it feels like you're in fucking Thailand, the food is *that* good."

"Shit, that sounds amazing. I'm starving . . . but we were going to do some work at Naz's," I say.

Naz looks at Yasaman, and then at me, and then at Yasaman again. She squints like she's inspecting a painting, and a smile blossoms on her face.

"No biggie," Naz says. "I'm not really that hungry, but if you guys wanna grab some food, Rana and I can study another time." The thing with Naz is she means what she says. I know her offer is genuine, and she won't get pissed at me for ditching her.

"You sure?" I ask.

"Don't trip, Rana. Do your thing, but you're not getting out of doing the piece for me," she says, and sends Yasaman and me off with a hug.

17.

Som Tam is the smallest restaurant I've ever been to, with only four tables. It's in a shopping center with a Ross Dress for Less and a Mattress Superstore and from the outside doesn't look like anything special, but sitting here across from Yasaman makes the air feel golden, like I'm dining inside a royal Thai palace.

"I've never had Thai food before," I tell her. The walls are covered with delicate paintings of elephants in a pond, golden temples, and monks meditating.

"That's an official crime—you know that, right? My mom and I went to Thailand a few years ago. We rode elephants and just ate our way through the country. I mean, Bangkok is madness, but if you go to Chiang Mai or the beach, it's pure heaven. You know it's the only Southeast Asian country that was never colonized by a European country?"

"I had no idea," I say, trying to get excited by her excitement. All the wisdom pouring out of her makes her glow. Her excitement about life is magnetic.

"What?" she says, sounding suddenly insecure, which doesn't seem like her style at all. "I sound like a dork, huh?"

"No, not at all. You're just passionate," I say. Then, feeling bold, I add, "I like it."

She looks up at me as she sips her water, showing me how soft a kiss would be between us if we tried.

"You know what you want?" she asks me, snapping me out of a trance.

"Ya," I say, because in my mind, I know what I want—I want *her*.

"What are you getting?"

"Oh. The food. No idea," I say.

Yasaman asks if she can just order for us, and I give her the green light.

"You okay with a little spice?" she asks me.

"Sure," I say.

"Don't worry, I didn't ask for anything too spicy," she tells me after the Thai waiter who's probably our age takes her order.

"It's okay, I trust you," I say.

"Oh my God, do your parents ever make you eat kaleh pacheh? What is that shit? Like brains and feet? My grandmother always forces me to eat it when I visit her."

"I've actually never tried it," I say. "It's your dad's mom, right? The one who lives in Iran?"

"Ya."

"You ever miss your dad?" I ask her.

"Of course I miss him."

"I'm sorry. That was a stupid question."

"No, it's cool. No one really asks me that. It's like it happened so long ago I should be over it or whatever, but you don't ever really get over it. He was this super creative soul who just wanted to spend all his time in nature. Be one with the earth and shit. I go to Iran pretty often to see my grandma, and it's cool to be in the house he grew up in. Like, he slept on this bed when he was a little boy, and this is the kitchen he ate dinner in, and these are his friends he grew up with who got to live when he didn't."

I nod and try to absorb everything she's just said as I munch on a spring roll. I watch her carefully dip hers in sauce and then take a bite too big for her mouth.

"I'm sure you think about your friend a lot," she says.

"Honestly? I think about Louie every day. It's going to be one year soon, and it just seems so final. It was such a shock, you know? It's hard to get closure when it's so sudden." My last conversation with Tony flashes through my mind. It brought up so many questions that I'll probably never get answered. "I can't help but feel like I missed something, and like I'm a shitty friend for it."

"I mean, whatever happened, it wasn't your fault—you know that, right?"

"Then why does it feel like it is?" I ask.

"Because grief can mess you up. After my dad died, I stopped talking," she says, "for a fucking year. Four and a half to five and a half I did not speak a damn word."

"Holy shit."

"I know. Of course you want to feel like you played some role in this. You want to believe you had control over something that feels so out of control. That makes total sense," she says, now pouring red chili sauce all over her spring rolls and taking a bite without even thinking twice. I decide that this is what I like most about Yasaman. Her self-assurance and her power to make you feel like there's absolutely nothing wrong with you, even if you feel like you're losing your mind.

"Lately I feel like maybe I didn't know him at all," I say. "Like there was a totally different side to him I was just blind to."

Yasaman considers that for a moment while she chews. "I mean, we all have different sides to us, don't you think? You're not the same when you're hanging with me as when you're hanging with your mom. It's hard to keep it real with everyone."

"I know, but we were so close."

"I get it. I have a family friend who turned out to be a coke addict, and I had no clue. I mean, legit snorting that shit all day, every day. I kind of felt stupid," Yasaman says, just as the waiter places a ridiculous amount of food in front of us. There are so many plates, he has to go and come back with the rest of them.

Yasaman explains each dish—papaya salad with dried shrimp, green curry with chicken and eggplant, pad thai with beef, stir-fried string beans, and panang curry. It's all out-of-control delicious. Even when my mom's not around, I can't help but feel her gaze on me as I decide what I'm going to eat, but Yasaman piles the food on her plate, and I decide to follow her lead.

"So how many different sides are there to you?" I ask her.

"A bunch, I think. It's hard for me to let people in," she says.

"Really? You seem pretty open about everything."

"I know, but on the inside, it's different," she says. She's not offering me anything and I don't want to push it, but she won't take her eyes off me. I stop eating, transfixed by her. She starts twirling one of her curls nervously. I think she's blushing, but it's hard to tell through the freckles.

"I've never actually told anyone this," she says.

"What?" I say, thrilled that she's on the verge of opening herself up to me.

"I've had a lot of issues with eating. I mean. I don't know. I guess I was pretty bulimic in middle school. I would eat everything I could get my hands on and then throw it all up. I don't know why, but it felt really fucking good. I was so out of control, but it was like I had the ultimate control. Like, have you ever just known something is so wrong, but you can't help yourself from doing it?"

I bite into something extremely spicy, and the heat spreads across my tongue, and I'm coughing and choking on my cough and gulping down all my water.

"You okay?"

"That shit is spicy," I say.

"I'm sorry. I ordered mild," she says with a quiet smile.

"It's okay. So how did you get over it?"

"My mom made me go to a treatment center, which isn't always the answer, but it definitely helped me get on the right path. I'm much better now. Like, I'm eating way too much food right now, but I don't feel bad about it," she says.

I realize that with every bite I've been taking, I've been feeling guilty without even being aware. I've been making sure I eat less of the noodles because I know they have higher carbs. What the fuck? I load a pile onto my plate.

"Here's to not giving a shit and eating whatever we want," I say, and twist the noodles onto my fork and raise it in the air. She does the same, and our forks clink together—a sound that feels so loud, I can't hear anything else in the room.

18.

The next day before third period, I run into Samantha, because her locker is right next to mine. On my better days I can pretend to be nice to Babak, but I find it impossibly hard when it comes to his girlfriend.

"Hey, Rana," Samantha says. She's wearing a crop top, and I can see her entire flat stomach. She's too skinny, and her hair is cut in this awkward bob that makes it look more like a bowl, and it doesn't surprise me at all that my brother and I have such different tastes in girls. He's been a serial dater since the fourth grade, and I've never found a single one of his girlfriends attractive. And I always end up being the one consoling my brother when they break his heart, which they always do.

"Where's the rest of your shirt?" I ask her.

"Good morning to you too, cranky-pants," she says. She checks herself in a mirror she's put up inside her locker. Her lips are small and pouty, and her eyes are a dull hazel color. "It's very fashionable to show your belly button right now. But you wouldn't know anything about that, would you?" she says just as my brother sneaks up behind her and wraps his arms around her.

She lets out a squeal. "Bobby Joon!"

"Samantha Joon," he mumbles in her ear, and it's all so disgusting, how she's using this Farsi word for "dear" like she's trying to impress him, but I'm also unable to look away, transfixed by how easy all this seems for them.

"I was just giving your sister some fashion advice," she says.

Brianna Asher comes by and gives Samantha a hug because they're good friends. They're talking about prom and how Brianna found this gold backless dress and how Samantha still needs to find one.

"Let's make an appointment to get our makeup done," Samantha says, and Brianna agrees that's a great idea.

"You going to prom, Rana?" Brianna asks me, noticing that I'm standing there. Samantha gives her a dirty look for being nice to me.

"Rana hates all that school-spirit shit," Babak says.

"I'm thinking about it," I say. Prom hasn't really crossed my mind until now with all the other shit going on, but who knows—anything is possible.

I can't really focus in my classes because I keep thinking about Thai food with Yasaman and the battle and if Coach and everyone else were right and doing my own piece makes more sense. My head is whirling, temples beating like drums.

I go to the library at lunch and find an Audre Lorde book, and reading her poems makes me feel like I can finally breathe again. I read one called "Recreation," which is extremely sensual—it's about sex, but also how we recreate ourselves, whether it's through words, art, or the way we love and allow ourselves to be loved.

Her words remind me of nights with my grandfather and Forugh Farrokhzad—the same fire, boldness, and vulnerability.

I read poem after poem after poem, trying to swallow her fire and make it my own. After a few minutes, I open my notebook and finish the rest of my poem; I don't even have to think about it.

Later, in Mrs. Mogly's class, we read an Audre Lorde essay, "Poetry Is Not a Luxury." It's about how poetry is the language of dreams, and dreams can inspire action. How as women, there's a darkness within us where all the beauty and magic of life are possible, if only we're willing to feel it. How white men are all about the mind—"I think, therefore I am"—but Black women know "I feel, therefore I can be free."

After we finish reading, Mrs. Mogly asks us what we think the title of the essay means, and everyone is silent. I can't tell if they're still processing or just uninterested now that our AP exam is done, but I feel the power of Audre Lorde's words still stirring inside me. I don't know how, but my hand shoots up into the air.

Mrs. Mogly almost falls off her stool when she sees me. "Yes, Rana?"

I think of Buddha Boy and Ms. Murillo's meditation, and how simple and easy everything feels when you're in the flow. So I take a deep breath, and instead of panicking, I turn inward, create space within me, and speak up.

"She's basically saying that as women, we have a lot of pain and darkness within us, but that darkness is really where all our creativity and power come from. I think she's directly speaking to Black women, but really, it's a message for any woman or person who's ever felt *other* or powerless. Like, all these white dudes are telling us how important it is to think, to have a brain, but she's saying that the heart is ancient and even more powerful, and that we *need* to make poetry as an expression of our hearts if we want to see our dreams come to life. So, like the title says, poetry isn't a luxury; it's a necessity."

No one says anything for what feels like a very long time. I look around, and a lot of people are nodding in agreement, some just look confused, and probably most of them couldn't care less about my moment of triumph—but Mrs. Mogly agrees with a level of enthusiasm I've never seen from her. My hands feel steady and my breath feels even, and when Mrs. Mogly asks us to pass the copies of the essay to the front, I fold mine up and quickly shove it into my backpack.

After school, I find Naz at her locker. She's talking to Marcus and has extra-red lipstick on and is covered in different black-and-white patterns so the lipstick really pops. Just as I approach, he kisses her, an intense one with tongue, and then walks away.

"That was interesting," I say with a smile. Naz was so upset about what happened that it makes me think she likes Marcus more than she lets on. I still think she can do better, but I can see this is what she wants.

"It was, wasn't it?" Naz says, slamming her locker shut. "You think I'm being stupid, don't you?"

"I think you should do whatever makes you happy," I say.

We head out the front entrance, the smell of summer—sunblock and freshly cut grass—creeping inside, teasing us.

"How was the Thai food yesterday?" Naz asks.

"Fucking amazing," I say.

Naz smiles. "This is epic, Rana."

"What is?"

"You and Yasaman! There's obviously something between you two. I've never seen you like this."

I stop in my tracks. I automatically spin out into panic mode, like a thread is coming undone and there's no way to put it back into place.

But it's Naz. Naz, who has no shame about anything and tells me things exactly as they are. Naz, who brought up the subject of me and Yasaman with not an ounce of judgment and seems happy for me. Why do I find it necessary to hide from my best friend? I wish Louie hadn't hidden himself from me, though maybe I should have paid closer attention too. Just like I wish I'd done for Louie, Naz is looking out for me—and right now, I could let her in.

"Damn, you really are the queen of vibes," I say, letting a smile creep through.

And Naz hugs me and holds on tight like she really means it, and we're both in tears. It's like I'm melting into her body, into this acceptance. I don't know what I was expecting, but this wasn't it. She looks me in the eye, really sees me, and it feels so good to not have to hide. I know it won't be this easy with everyone, but I'm grateful it is with Naz.

She kisses me on each of my cheeks. "I could never imagine a girl putting her face between my legs, but if that does it for you, then why the hell not?"

We both start cracking up, and then the tears bubble up for me again and leave me silent. I take a deep breath and try to really feel this moment of having someone I love so much know this thing about me.

"I bet you there were girls getting it on with each other when the Prophet was around," Naz says. "If men can have as many wives as they want, I don't see why two women can't be together. Religion is all man's interpretation of something super beautiful and pure anyways. God accepts everyone. It's men who fuck everything up in the end."

I'm laughing through my tears, and this feels like the core of who Naz is, *her* vibe—she's someone who loves easily and makes sure you know how she feels.

"So what's the plan with Yasaman?" she asks me.

"I have no fucking clue. I'm not really good at this."

Then Yasaman runs toward us out of nowhere, red curls bouncing, with an excitement like she might jump into my arms.

"Oh my God, oh my God. Rana, guess what? Today's the last night LACMA's showing the Frida Kahlo painting—they're staying open late and everything. We have to go. We're going to regret it for the rest of our lives if we don't," she says, huffing and puffing.

"Who's this Frida Kahlo?" Naz asks.

"She was only the most amazing, outspoken, feminist, talented, badass Mexican female artist ever. Everything she did is magic."

"Jeez, take a breath, girl," Naz says with a laugh.

"It sounds amazing, but my dad will freak if I stay out late on a school night," I tell Yasaman, "especially with finals coming up." I know I sound like a dorky freshman, but unless it's a school-related obligation or a family function, my dad will never let me go. When it's just my mom, it's a different story, but she's not the main decision maker right now.

"He's *that* strict?" Yasaman asks. I nod yes.

"Okay, let's just get a little perspective real quick, shall we?" Naz says. "Rana's dad is strict, but my dad is the I'll-hit-you-upside-the-head-with-my-slipper kind of strict. Rana's dad would never hit her. I have an idea," Naz says. We stop at the school steps, right next to a grassy patch where the hippies like to kick around hacky sacks, and we form a little circle like we're scheming something up. "You're going to owe me, like, fifty venti Frappuccinos after this, Rana, just so you know. So tonight I have my study group at the mosque. I've actually been going and learning something because I'm pretty set on using the Hadith to prove to my dad that he shouldn't send me to Afghanistan after I graduate and force me to marry my cousin. Because as it turns out, the Prophet said, 'Seek knowledge even if you have to go as far as China.' So I'm thinking education and college and all that have to be more important than marriage, and if I can use the Prophet's own words to convince—"

"Naz?"

"Okay, sorry. Enough about me. Just tell them you're coming with me. That after you hung out with my mosque friends the other night, you grew curious about what this whole Islam thing's really all about, and you want to actually study it or at least check out the study group. They'll eat that shit up, Rana. Trust me. I usually get home around nine; does that give you enough time?"

"We can definitely make that work," Yasaman says, already smiling and on board with the plan.

"Nine sounds good," I say, "but my dad will probably want to call your dad and make sure this study thing is actually happening."

"No problem. My dad's a super boring dude, so he has, like, zero friends and is desperate for attention. Sometimes I overhear him telling childhood stories to telemarketers. It's so depressing. He'd love to talk to your dad. I got you, Rana, don't worry," Naz says, which makes me feel like two thousand pounds lift right off my shoulders.

Yasaman and I have our second date tonight.

19.

Yasaman picks me up at five o'clock on the dot in front of Starbucks because I told her that would be better than picking me up from home. I was so nervous before I left home, I decided to meditate for a bit, which I'd never done alone before. I focused on my breath and tried to acknowledge and release the thought clouds as they came. At first I was itching all over, could hardly sit still from my excitement, but when I really stuck to it, I could feel my heartbeat slowing down, my chest rising and falling with more ease, the thoughts slowing down. When I opened my eyes, I was still me, but I felt more connected to the moment, to my body; the anxiety that had been clawing at my stomach had released its grip too.

When I told my parents about going to Naz's study group with her, my dad was elated.

I just think it makes sense to at least study the Prophet's words if I'm going to call myself a Muslim, I told them.

This is a very wise thing to say, my dad said. Although he's not the pray-five-times-a-day type of Muslim and doesn't take it too seriously himself, my dad associates religion with proper life choices and good-natured people, and so if one of his kids wants to hang out at the mosque, he has no problem with it.

And then, as predicted, he insisted on calling Naz's dad to see if this class was actually happening. Naz's dad somehow managed to keep my dad on the phone for almost an hour, asking him too many questions about Iran and its politics, and mid-conversation my dad just nodded his head at me, a signal that I was free to go.

Yasaman's driving an old, red BMW and has to lean over toward the passenger side to open the door for me. I came to Starbucks a little early so I could apply a thicker layer of eyeliner and mascara in the bathroom and change out of the mosque outfit I left the house in. I'm wearing an off-the-shoulder stretchy black top with little white daisies on it, black jeans, and gold hoops, which, as far as I'm concerned, turn any outfit from casual to fancy. I also kept the lipstick Naz gave me at the party, so my lips are a fresh lollipop kind of red.

Yasaman's wearing a loose black top, and I can tell she's not wearing a bra because it's easy to see the outline of her nipples. Her curls are down and not piled on top of her head, which I like, and she's wearing the green, glittery eyeliner that makes her eyes brighter.

"Everything cool with your parents?" she asks.

"I think so. Naz is a genius sometimes."

"It's totally going to be worth it," she says. "I love Frida. I'm literally dying to go to her house in Mexico City. I hear it's massive, and they just kept it exactly the way it was when she was living there. I think her bed hasn't even been touched since she died or some shit. That's where her studio was too. Have you ever been to Mexico?" Yasaman asks me. We get on the freeway, and surprisingly there's no traffic headed toward LA.

"I've never left the country. I've only been to Vegas and New York, and both before I turned ten."

"You're kidding, right? Rana, you're totally missing out. We should take a trip somewhere. You know it's less than three hours to Tijuana, right? I went last year with a bunch of friends from my old school, and it was so fun. We went down into Baja too and slept on the beach and swam with sea lions. It was amazing."

"Shit. I didn't know it was so close," I say. I take a deep breath because I'm slowly realizing what different worlds Yasaman and I come from. Even Babak, who gets special privileges because of his golden penis, would never be allowed to go on a trip to Mexico with just his friends.

I barely know this person and have convinced myself she's into me without any solid evidence other than a gut feeling and getting freaky on the dance floor. My anxiety swoops in again, and I can't close my eyes and let go of my thought clouds with Yasaman right here beside me. The thoughts come and they come, and there's no exit sign lit up for them to find their way out.

I suddenly feel so boring compared to Yasaman, and my hands are getting clammy. I roll down the window even though it's ninety degrees outside because I need some air. What am I supposed to talk about with her? I can feel her eyes on me, and she's probably sensing my nervousness and can see I'm wearing too much makeup and thinks I'm trying too hard to impress her.

"You okay?" she asks me.

"Just need some air. Sometimes I get carsick."

"I have gum if you want," she says.

"No, it's all good," I say. I don't say anything for a while, and then she turns the radio up and they're playing "California Love" by Tupac, which is the song Yasaman and I danced to at Marcus's party.

"Hey, it's our song," she says. *Our song.* I almost die on the spot.

"I love Tupac," I tell her again.

"Really? I don't listen to him much. This is the only song I really know."

"You're kidding me, right? He's a lyrical genius. I mean, this song isn't that deep or whatever. But listen to 'Keep Ya Head Up' or 'Brenda's Got a Baby,' and you'll hear it. He also has this whole superhuman vibe going because he's not caught up in being afraid to die or anything, and so he puts it all out there because he has nothing to lose," I say.

"That unibrow is pretty sexy; I can see why you're into him," she says.

"Nah, it's got nothing to do with that. Trust me, if you really listen, you'll understand what I'm talking about."

Then we just listen to the song until it's over. When the commercials come on afterward, she turns down the sound. "You ever seen him live?"

"Freshman year. That shit was epic. Louie took me," I tell her.

"That's so cool you got to experience that with him," she says.

"Ya, it is," I say. There's a long silence between us. She takes her eyes off the road and catches mine for a second. She stares at me so intensely I'm worried she's forgotten about driving altogether, and I get anxious—but with this look and all its potential, there's also something electric, something alive moving through my body.

The museum is crowded because everyone wants to see the Frida painting before it's officially gone. Good-looking twentysomethings dressed up for the occasion sip cocktails at a makeshift bar. I've never actually been to an art museum, but for obvious reasons I don't admit this to Yasaman. I kind of feel out of place, but Yasaman walks through the crowd like she owns the museum. She leads us through the bar area and then speed walks through a massive room full of art—bronze statues, a painting that just looks like a kid splattered paint all over the canvas, a portrait of an old man with hot pink pants on—clearly on a mission to show me this painting and only this painting. "It's there. I see it," she says, and soon we're standing side by side in front of *Self-Portrait with Thorn Necklace and Hummingbird*.

Frida Kahlo, like Tupac, could have been mistaken for Iranian because of her unibrow and mustache. In the portrait, thorns are wrapped around her neck, making her bleed, and a black hummingbird hangs from them like a charm. I look at the painting for a while, impressed by how bold it feels, like Frida was trying to claim her life on this canvas—but soon I'm mostly staring at Yasaman while she takes in the painting, and that image is even more beautiful to me.

"Isn't it stunning? She painted, like, fifty-five self-portraits. She wasn't a narcissist or anything like that, but she said she spent so much time alone that she was the subject she knew best. Kind of like you writing a poem about how you see yourself versus looking at something outside of you," Yasaman says. She leans into my body and whispers the words to me. I'm listening, watching her lips closely so I don't miss a word.

"Why is the hummingbird black?" I ask her.

"I mean, birds usually symbolize freedom, right? And especially a hummingbird, so colorful and full of life. But this one's black and lifeless because of all the pain Frida had to deal with. Like, she knew she was meant to be free, but she had an accident when she was eighteen that permanently disabled her and kept her in bed a lot, and she traveled whenever she could but probably felt pretty trapped at times." Yasaman whispers all this while keeping her eyes glued to the portrait. I've never had anyone break down a painting for me like this, and the more she explains it, the more I see the beauty in what Frida was trying to create.

There are also a black cat and a black monkey behind Frida. When I ask Yasaman about them, she says, "The blackness could just represent her dark parts. Maybe that darkness that lived inside her is what made her so damn good. Some people think the monkey represents her husband, though. They had a pretty fucked-up relationship, and the monkey's the one pulling on the necklace and making her bleed. People say she was actually bisexual."

"Seriously?" I ask.

"Ya," she says, and I'm impressed. Here's a woman so unafraid to show how vulnerable she is and so free with her sexuality, despite feeling stuck in her body, that she put it all on display for the whole world to see.

"How high do you think she was when she painted this?" I say, and Yasaman laughs.

"A few bong loads at least."

"But seriously, it's crazy if you think about it," I say. "One night Frida was in her house in Mexico City, smoking out of her bong, painting this exact painting. She wanted us to really see her, and here we are fifty years later on a Wednesday night in LA looking at her. That is fucking bizarre." I know I sound like the one taking bong hits, but Yasaman smiles at me, and it makes me think she's glad I'm getting something out of this.

"Art is mystical. It's not even about the painting itself; it's about the experience," she says. "I'm sure someday someone will read one of your poems and have the same thought. You still owe me a poem, by the way."

At the end of the night, I have Yasaman drop me off down the street from my house so my parents don't see her car. Before I say goodnight, I do what I've been thinking of doing the whole ride back. I take out my notebook from my bag and place it on my lap.

"I have one," I say.

"One what?"

"A poem," I say.

"Really? Okay," she says, sounding excited. She turns the car off, switches a light on so I can see, and moves her body so she's facing me.

"It's pretty rough, and I've never read it to anyone before, so . . ."

"No judgment here, Rana. I promise," she says.

My thoughts are all over the place; everything feels blurry for a second and I think I might pass out, but I take a deep breath and find the poem I wrote about my dad and the garden.

My voice trembles at first as the words leave my body, but I remember Coach Lock and this idea of the words coming from somewhere deeper, somewhere even more powerful than my voice—my gut, my instinct, the same part of me that knows I like Yasaman. The fear turns into excitement, energy, life rushing out with my breath. Here are my words connecting me to this person, hooking her into my soul in a way I've never allowed with anyone besides Louie. When I finish, my heart's beating way too fast, and it's like I've just blacked out and am coming to again. She doesn't say anything. My insecurities get the best of me, and I open my mouth to try and explain myself.

"My dad's really into gardening. He just puts all this pressure on me to make it beautiful when he's not around and—"

But she stops me with a kiss. Her tiny, strawberry-glossed lips press into mine, and instead of joy, instead of melting into it, it's a sting, a burn, like she's slapped me. I pull away; I have no fucking clue why. This is the dream. This is what I've wanted for so long, and I can't handle it. I feel like a complete idiot. Having sex with Tony feels so much easier compared to this because *this* is actually real—*this* could mean something. Here it is in front of me, and I can't fucking handle it.

"It's okay to be nervous," she says.

"I know . . . sorry." She's being so damn nice to me, which is making me feel worse about not allowing myself this moment.

"You wanted me to do that, right?"

"Ya, totally. But my brain. It won't shut up."

"I get it. Don't stress, Rana. It'll happen when the time is right," she says. But what about the one and only now? What's wrong with me that I can't ever just be in it? Why do I feel like I'm always watching myself live, and that I'm not the one actually inside my body experiencing life as it comes?

"And by the way, you're a really good poet. Like, wow. I wasn't expecting that at all," she says, and reaches over to give me a hug. I hold on to her long enough that I can feel our breaths sync up.

"I'm sorry. I've never. I just . . . ," I say, but she keeps saying it's okay.

"Don't worry. Stop apologizing, Rana. It's really okay," she says.

"Sorry. Okay. I'll see you tomorrow, I guess. Bye," I say like a blabbering idiot, the eloquence of my poem long gone by now.

20.

I'm awake by five because I can barely sleep after my night with Yasaman. I'm officially a coward, and I'm worried that now she doesn't think I'm into her and has lost all interest in me. I go outside to drink my coffee and watch the sun rise, and of course my dad, the early riser he is, is out there in his usual house getup—undershirt, boxer shorts, slippers, cigarette in one hand. A pile of weeds lies off to the side, and he squats down to yank more out.

"What did you learn last night?" he asks when he sees me—less like an interrogation and more like he's just curious.

"Last night?" I didn't think he'd actually do a follow-up. "Let's see . . . well, the Prophet thinks education is the most important thing in the world. Even if you have to go to China, you go if it means you'll get an education," I say, remembering one of the few nuggets of truth Naz has ever shared about Islam.

My dad stops what he's doing and stands up and looks at me.

"Very nice, very nice," he says. "Like I said, my friend at UCLA can give you a tour of the campus whenever you want, make sure you get all the classes you need. This is a very big deal, Rana Joon.

I'm proud of you," he says—which is really all I ever want to hear and something he rarely ever says. I don't know how to respond.

"How can we fix this?" I say, turning to the garden.

"Okay, now. The first thing we have to do is to get rid of the enemy. For this garden, the weeds are the enemy. These weeds have no value. They are like an impatient mother-in-law who sucks all the life out of you. They grow too fast and take all the nutrients the plants need," he says, squatting down low again.

"I don't get it. Some of them are so beautiful," I say. Most of the ones he pulls feel dried out and thorny, but he's also taking out green ones with stunning pink flowers growing on them.

"Yes, but sometimes beauty is just a trick. The mother-in-law can wear a nice dress, always get her hair done, smile at you when you walk by, but in reality, she just wants to destroy you," he says. I'm not sure where this mother-in-law analogy is coming from, especially since from all of my grandfather's stories, my grandmother seemed like one of the kindest women to ever walk this planet. "These weeds, they don't know their limits. They become greedy, and so nothing else will be able to grow. Come help me," he says.

I put my coffee down on a nearby table and squat down with him and start yanking the weeds out by their roots. Mother-in-law or no mother-in-law, the whole process feels gratifying, like biting my nails or pushing down on a bruise—I know I'm causing some real damage, but man, does it feel good.

It's a Thursday, but instead of flat ironing my hair after pulling up weeds, I spend the rest of my time before school working on my "I Am From" poem. I read Audre Lorde's "Recreation" again for inspiration because the last few lines have wrapped themselves around my entire body and just won't let go:

my body
writes into your flesh
the poem
you make of me.

This is what Yasaman is asking of me, and I don't know if I have it in me to give it to her.

I try to find Yasaman between passing periods. She's not at her locker or by her art class or in the girls' bathroom. I head to my locker and see she's standing with Naz, waiting for me, which makes me almost get down on my knees and praise Allah. *She doesn't hate me,* I want to yell. *She doesn't think I'm a coward!* Turns out I didn't totally fuck things up last night. I give them hugs and open up my locker.

"How was last night, you guys?" Naz asks. I hesitate and look at Yasaman.

"It was dope as hell. Naz, has Rana ever read you one of her poems? She's legit good."

Naz smacks me on my arm.

"You little bitch. You read her a poem? I've been begging you to read me one for over a year now," she says.

"I'm sorry. It just happened," I say. My face is hot with embarrassment. I look into my locker for my Spanish book, and peeking out is the pink flyer Jordan gave me. I pull it out and stare at the page, Jordan's voice clear in my head—

Don't get stuck in the mud, Rana. You ain't no mud type of girl.

"I'm actually entering this," I say, handing the flyer to Yasaman. "I'm doing one of Louie's pieces, though. He wanted to do it and he can't, so I'm doing it for him. Coach Lock's helping me not look like a total idiot." If I'm going to do this thing, I want to do it right, and I need people who aren't strangers in the audience rooting for me—as many as I can get.

"Holy shit, this is amazing. But why wouldn't you do your own piece? You really are amazing," Yasaman says.

I shake my head. "I can't."

"Why the fuck not?" Naz chimes in. "I mean, go big or go home, right?"

"Louie would one hundred percent want you to do a Rana original. Speak your own damn truth for once," Yasaman says, with a smile that creeps up on her face. The way she's looking at me, I know she also believes that the mud is no place for someone like me and that she wouldn't mind it if I made a poem out of her, wrote it onto her flesh.

During seventh, Coach Lock and I meet in his office. I prepare myself to do Louie's piece for him, but instead he tells me to sit down.

"I got something for you," he says, and closes the door.

He takes a deep breath and, like a superhero, suddenly transforms into a different version of himself:

> *Your love speaks revolution under my skin.*
> *Molecules like madmen, magnetic to this sin,*
> *I'm drowning in you.*
> *I don't know if you can see through*
> *Me and the way I wish I could just be a part of you.*
> *Do you even see me?*
> *Do I even see me?*
> *These broken mirrors a blur, am I even bleeding?*

Glass breaks through skin, through heart and blood.
Is this the real deal or did I just make it up?

I'm mesmerized. The words are powerful, but it's how they shoot out of his mouth, how they immediately wrap themselves around me, making me a part of his world in an instant, that's so electrifying.

"You see, a poem is meant to be read in the silence of someone's mind. But what we're trying to do here is much different, Rana. It's an experience. You're taking everyone on a journey. Make sense?"

I nod yes and ask him to do it again.

21.

I watch my parents from the back seat. My dad is driving in that hectic way he drives, like it's Iran and there are no laws to the way people navigate themselves on streets. He curses at the cars, and every time he does, my mom's whole body jumps. My mom's back to her usual awkward-wife self, doing what she does, which is fill up the air with words. She talks about her cousin Ladan's son, who just got engaged, and everything Ladan's told her about the proposal, how he asked her while on a trip to Paris, under the Eiffel Tower. Isn't that so romantic?

Of course my parents are dragging me to this engagement party while Babak gets out of it so he can go to a friend's birthday at CityWalk; just another example of penis privilege. Ladan's son just graduated from med school at thirty-five and has landed himself a twenty-one-year-old fiancée. In three and a half years I'll be twenty-one, and I haven't ever been in a real relationship. How the hell does a twenty-one-year-old think she knows who she should spend the rest of her life with?

Iranians, especially Iranians who live in LA, love throwing

parties. To have fun and gather the people they love together in one place and suck the marrow out of life, sure, but it's also a great opportunity to show off.

Imagine this: You were living a lavish life in a country that proclaimed itself the "Paris of the Middle East." You owned property, you had your own business or were a prominent doctor. You stayed away from politics because it was too messy, and you liked your king because he made your country look good, even though he was torturing anyone who spoke up against him. And then everything got turned the fuck around, the religious assholes took over, and you had to get the hell out or you knew your life would never be the same. I'm not saying everyone's story was like this, but many of them were. I know all this because of my grandfather. He made sure I knew that those who got out—no matter their religion—hadn't betrayed their homeland but were survivors who knew when it was time to let go.

A lot of people came before the revolution and could sell their properties or get their money out of the bank, but a lot of people, like Ladan's family, waited too long and came here with only the bills they could sew into the inseams of their coats. And so hiring valet parking and inviting three hundred guests to her son's engagement party is just another way of saying:

WE FUCKING MADE IT. I FUCKING MADE IT. I AM REALLY GOOD AT TURNING VERY LITTLE MONEY INTO A LOT OF MONEY. EAT YOUR SPICY TUNA ROLL AND AS MANY CREAM PUFFS AS YOU WANT AND TAKE THESE ORCHID CENTERPIECES HOME SO YOU CAN REMEMBER THIS FACT FOREVER AND EVER.

It's kind of obnoxious, but also understandable, and even though I'd rather be hanging with Naz or Yasaman, I can get down with all the free food. There's a sushi bar, a guy carving a big roast, and a huge table just devoted to desserts set out, even before dinner.

We enter through a side gate into the backyard, where the party is, and all say hi to Ladan. Her house is big on its own, but the backyard looks like a hotel garden—tennis courts on one side, a pool, fountains, an enormous gazebo that's been transformed into a dance floor tonight. Her gold-sequined dress pokes my skin, and I can feel her damp armpits when she hugs me. She sticks her dark red lips to my face and then squeezes my cheek like I'm a five-year-old.

"Rana Joon, how pretty you look," she says. I'm definitely underdressed in the same black lace dress I wore to Louie's funeral; short, open-toed heels my mom forced me to get from Nordstrom for the occasion; and my go-to hoops. Most girls are wearing poufy dresses or something shiny that's probably way too expensive. I did, however, do a phenomenal job flat ironing my hair, and I'm wearing more mascara than usual and, again, lipstick, which made my mom extremely happy—I actually think I saw her in tears when she watched me applying it before we drove over—so maybe Ladan is noticing that.

"Inshallah, God willing, you'll be next," she says right as the DJ starts blaring "Livin' La Vida Loca" by Ricky Martin way too loud.

"Inshallah, I won't," I say.

"Her time will come, Ladan Joon," my mom says, trying to politely take the pressure off me, but it doesn't feel like enough.

"Khob hala, soon, soon, finish your school like Negin and then we find you a nice boy while you're still ripe. Wait too long and you'll become like rotten fruit," Ladan says, and then someone calls her over and she frantically scurries away.

"That woman has lost her damn mind," I tell my mom.

"She's just happy. Her son is getting married. It's a big deal," my mom says, nervously scanning the crowd. When my dad's around, she becomes incredibly awkward at family functions, like she has to prove something to everyone. I know she's nervous about seeing her sisters because she hasn't really been talking to them since my grandfather got sick and they all totally disappeared.

When they serve dinner—over twenty-five different dishes, from stews to salads to bedazzled rice—my mom finds me and shows me to the table where she's sitting with my dad, my two aunts, and their husbands. Of course none of my cousins are here on a Friday night, because they're all in college and are all boys with golden penis privileges and are probably out at some Hollywood club opening.

I see skinny-ass Bod and his parents and his uncle sitting at a nearby table because everybody knows everybody, so of course they're here too. "Why can't we sit with Bod and them?" I ask my mom. Even though Bod is annoying, I definitely prefer him over my aunts.

"This is our family," she tells me.

"They sure don't act like it. They treat you like shit, Mom," I say, but she shushes me quickly and says now isn't the time.

We sit down with my aunts. Khaleh Mojgan is the chubbier one who always wears black to make herself look slimmer. She likes to start the gossip about so-and-so's divorce and about how Ladan's dress is a little too much. Khaleh Nahid looks more like my mom, but while my mom's makeup is impeccable, Nahid's lipstick always goes beyond the lines of her lips. She usually is the one asking nosy questions.

My mom tries to insert herself into the conversation and comments on the food—how salty the stew is.

"It tastes good to me," Khaleh Mojgan says. "Not everyone is an expert chef like you. How are your cooking classes going, by the way?"

My dad squirms in his seat, and my mom hurries to find an answer.

"Oh, I'm taking a break. You have no idea how busy we get," she says. "We haven't had a moment to just sit and do nothing." She squeezes my dad's arm while he chows down, and he nods his head like he's trying his best to uphold this sham, but also he's hungry as hell and just wants to shut my mom up.

Khaleh Nahid asks me about college. My mom blurts out, "She had a hard time deciding between her many acceptances, but in the end she chose UCLA so she can live at home." What she really should be saying is that I'm only allowed to go to UCLA because they want me living at home.

"Eh, very good," Khaleh Nahid says. "Ali can show you around. He has many nice-looking single friends too. It's time to think about these things, Rana Joon."

"Can't wait," I say, giving her a thumbs-up, and take a large spoonful of rice and shove it in my mouth.

My mom puts her hand on mine and tells me under her breath, "Movazeb bash." *Be careful.* As in *Watch it.* As in *Every spoon of rice you eat, it becomes less and less likely that we'll ever have a night like this for you.*

"Baba Joon would be very proud of you. He didn't really make time for our kids, but with you and Babak he always had a special connection," Khaleh Mojgan chimes in.

"Ya, that's because my mom actually spent time with him and

wanted us to get to know him. She didn't just disappear when he was dying," I snap at Khaleh Mojgan, but really at both of my aunts, because it's the truth my mom would never dare speak. All this pretending is starting to make me feel nauseous, and it's starting to click for me that words have way more power when people can actually hear them.

Everyone's eyes are bulging out of their sockets, but my dad looks like he's having a stroke.

"You're embarrassing yourself," my dad barks at me. "Apologize. Now!"

His harshness immediately makes me feel like a little girl, and it's possible I might start crying. "I'm sorry," I mumble.

"Louder," he says.

He couldn't care less about my aunts. He couldn't care less about how many times I've had to be there for my mom since my grandfather died because my aunts and him weren't. He can tell me he's proud of me, but who really cares when he's so oblivious he can't respect my truth? All he really cares about is our reputation as a family, and above all else, his own reputation as a father.

"I'm sorry," I say again, this time louder.

"Please excuse her. Kids these days just don't know their boundaries," my dad says, and everyone nods in agreement.

I look at my mom, who's looking down at the table. She's quiet, even after everyone moves on, and my dad's talking to his brothers-in-law about how shitty the economy in Iran has been since the war, and my mom's sisters are talking about where they think Ladan will be throwing the wedding. I can't say for sure, but from where I'm sitting, it looks like my mom might be smiling.

When dessert is put on display again, everyone else avoids the table for fear of looking like a fat ass, but I dash straight toward the éclairs, grab one, and stand by the dance floor so I can eat it in the semidark without my mom saying anything. The next thing I know, Bod's standing next to me. He's also grabbed an éclair.

"Hey," he says.

"Hey."

"You look nice," he says.

"I didn't get the memo about this being some sort of beauty pageant," I say.

"I'm serious, though. You look nice."

I smile at him even though he's a complete dork. He's wearing a shirt that's buttoned up too high and slacks that come to his ankles.

"How are things with your dad being here?" he asks me.

"It's fine."

"Is it weird?"

"Why would it be weird?"

"I don't know, you haven't seen him in, like, a year. A lot can happen in a year."

"So?"

"So? That's kind of weird."

"It depends what your definition of weird is."

"Okay, now *you're* being weird," he says.

Bod has these perfect parents who always go out together, actually hold hands, dress nice for each other, compliment each other—he wouldn't understand even if I tried to explain my family to him. But there's no one else to talk to here.

"I guess it's a little weird," I say. "My mom just becomes way more neurotic when my dad is here, like everything has to be wrapped up in a perfect fucking bow. There's no room to breathe."

I look up and see Bod's parents dancing with each other under the gazebo, Faranak's head on her husband's shoulder. "Do you think your parents still have sex?" I ask him.

"What? Ew. That's disgusting."

"They just always seem like they're so in love. You ever hear them doing it? I bet you they're super noisy."

"I'm not talking about this with you right now," Bod says, and walks away from me, which is fine because I have to pee anyway. It's so crowded outside I can't find access to get inside, so I end up walking along the side of the house, hoping I can swing around the front and find my way to the bathroom. Halfway down I find a side door and am about to use it when I see that the gate we entered through is open, giving me a view of the driveway—where my mom is smoking a cigarette with Bod's uncle.

The image is bizarre because (a) my mom doesn't smoke, and (b) she looks at least ten years younger. I realize her black dress makes her boobs look huge, and her high heels make her butt look extra round, and she looks so alive standing there next to Bod's wannabe-Hollywood-star uncle. She looks like a stranger, smoking her cigarette like an expert, and I guess he looks handsome in a black suit and white button-down shirt. He's probably five years younger than my mom but has salt-and-pepper hair, so he looks mature.

I'm pretty sure she's flirting because she puts her hand on her chest and laughs in this exaggerated way, but I know that's as far as she'll ever take this. It has to be. My mom would never put her needs first. She's hung on to this charade with my dad for so long, all because she doesn't want people talking behind her back. She wouldn't dare ever start something with Bod's uncle, and especially not while my dad's around. Right?

My mom sees me, puts out her cigarette, and casually walks toward me.

"What are you doing?" I ask.

"Smoking a cigarette. It's not a crime," she says. She takes out a little compact mirror, applies a fresh layer of lipstick under the dim outdoor light, and then offers me some, which I refuse.

"Come, let's dance, Rana Joon. It's been so long since we've danced together," she says—and somehow I let her drag me to the dance floor, where we spend the rest of the night together.

22.

It's Saturday night, and Naz and I are hanging out in
my room. She's lying on my bed and I'm sitting down, trying to get
her to give me the scoop on Marcus, but she wags a finger at me.

"Nope. You're not getting out of this. I wanna hear your
piece."

"Now? Can't we just chill? I'll let you do my makeup," I say,
because that's Naz's unfulfilled dream.

"Damn. If you can't do it in front of me, I don't know how
you're going to do it in front of a room full of people. I mean, if
they throw eggs at you, I'm not cleaning that shit up," she says.
She turns away from me like she's pissed, but I know she's just jok-
ing and is trying to push me.

"Fine," I say.

I stand at the foot of the bed, and she perks up and adjusts
herself.

I focus on my breath just like Ms. Murillo told us to do while
meditating. I allow the thought clouds to come and go but don't
hold on to anything for too long, and I see Louie's words in the

darkness of my mind before I let them go with my voice, my breath, my body—his words that get a chance to live again. When I refocus on Naz, she's stunned into silence.

"Who the fuck are you? I feel like you were just abducted by an alien or something. Holy shit," she says, clapping eagerly. I can't help but laugh and allow myself this little slice of joy. I might not win, but fuck, it feels good to hear my own voice sounding like this.

"I wanna hear *you* though. Like, that was cool and everything, but I want a Rana original," she says, getting serious again.

"I'm not ready," I tell her, sitting back down.

"You don't have to perform or whatever. You can just read it to me," she says, sitting on the edge of the bed now so we're facing each other.

I look into her eyes and can see how much she cares. There's so much I didn't know about Louie and so much I don't know about the ones I love, but Naz is asking me again to let her in, to help her see me fully, and it feels impossible to say no to that.

I grab my notebook and read her my "I Am From" poem off the page, my hands shaking, and I don't look up at her until the end. When I do, I can see that her tears have reached her chin. She doesn't say anything, but wraps herself around me, and together we become a big messy ball of tears.

It's not just the poem. It's life, all of it—the loss and the joy, the rawness of it, and everything that goes unspoken like an electric impulse moving through the room.

"Fuck, Rana. Don't hide that shit from people. That's your magic," she says. She goes to the mirror and fixes her makeup quick. "We have to celebrate this triumph! Like, now. High school is almost over, Rana. We need to have some fun. Let's go out—you can invite Yasaman," she says, because she knows it will work.

"What the hell do I say to my dad? He's still pissed at me for telling my aunts to go fuck themselves last night," I tell Naz. Even though I'd apologized at the party, he'd been trying to punish me through silence and disappointed looks ever since.

"Honestly, the amazing thing about the mosque is that the study group is always going on and I've actually been pretty into it. A lot of people show up so it's hard to keep track of who comes and goes. So—you get ready now, and I'll go pop in at the study group, show my face and offer my profound wisdom, and then come back here and pick you up. That way, if my parents ask around, people will remember my brilliant insights and will definitely confirm I was present. Just tell your dad you're coming with me again, that Allah is calling your name and you can't ignore it."

I agree to Naz's plan, and when I'm done getting ready, I head to the garden, where my dad's working. I'm surprised he hasn't even yelled at me to come outside so he can show me what to do with all these new plants he's bought. He must still be really mad. I don't think I was in the wrong last night, but if I want to go out tonight, I have to make the first move.

There's nothing left in the cardboard boxes that were filled with plants he bought from the nursery. He's sweaty and has dirt all over his legs because he's on his knees planting tomatoes, herbs like mint and rosemary, succulents, and purple flowers that are only buds. Everything seems so small and unimpressive at this point.

"It looks like it has a lot of potential," I tell him. He stays quiet and keeps patting down the dirt around the last few plants. "Are you going to show me how to take care of them?"

He looks at me, the disappointment making his eyes beam with even more darkness.

"You embarrassed me last night," he says. "Not only me, but your mother."

I want to tell him that she seemed fine, that she seemed so okay with everything she was sneaking off smoking cigarettes. I want to ask him: *What's more important, embarrassment or actually facing the truth? You don't know me anymore. You don't even know Mom.*

But instead I say, "I know, I'm sorry. Can you show me what to do so I take better care of the garden this time? Please?" I ask him in the most innocent voice possible, keeping the focus on what matters to him most. This seems to loosen him up a bit.

"Well, it's all new for them and it's very hot these days, so we need to water every day."

"But the soil looks so dry. It's like clay," I say.

"Don't worry. I put some fertilizer; it will be good."

I stand there and make a mental note of how much water he's giving the plants and how long he stays on each section of the garden.

"You have to water them with love. Really pay attention when you do it. If it's still wet the next day, you know you've given them too much, and you can start doing it every other day. It is like having a conversation with them. They know how to communicate with us; we just have to know how to listen," he says. It's amazing how he can look at these inanimate objects so lovingly but can't show his wife even a little bit of affection.

"Naz invited me to her study group tonight."

"Again?" he asks.

He stops watering the plants and examines my face closely, as if waiting for me to break down and reveal to him my real plan of making out with Yasaman, but this time doing it right—not turning away from it but writing a poem onto her lips.

"I like this Naz," he says after a moment. "She is a good influence. Have fun." I'm so excited he's said yes that I give my dad a hug. It's stiff and uncomfortable for both of us; it's been too long and we're both unsure how to manage each other's bodies. But it's something. I leave him alone in his own private paradise.

23.

Naz and Yasaman and I go to the Top of Topanga to get high. This is my go-to spot whenever I need to get away and want a killer view of the Valley. It's up Topanga Canyon, not too far from Ventura Boulevard, but far enough that you feel like you've entered another world. This is the same road Louie was on when he crashed. We dropped Naz's car off at Yasaman's, so Yasaman is driving. She's playing Tupac's "Changes," and our windows are down, and the almost-summer air is warm but fresh, and anything feels possible. I think of saying something about the significance of this road, but I don't want to be a downer, so I just sing along to the song.

It's after eight and there are only a few cars when we get to the parking lot, probably all with people hotboxing or making out in them. There's a sign that says the viewpoint closes at sunset, but there are no chains or anything to keep us out. The entire Valley is down below, and it sparkles and makes me feel tiny and insignificant and like my soul has a greater purpose and might just burst all at once.

"I've never been up here. It's so beautiful," Yasaman says.

"It's the perfect spot to get faded," Naz says. She takes out her dinky wooden pipe shaped like an owl and packs a bowl. The three of us pass it around while sitting in Yasaman's car, and by round two, the bag of Doritos is already open.

"Don't you guys find it weird that we'll never ever know what happens after you die, until we actually die?" Yasaman says. "I know there are all those people who have near-death experiences and say they saw the light and came back or whatever, but . . . there's no way of actually knowing what it's going to be like. And, if you think about it, no one's mentioned going to the other side and seeing fire or hell or whatever. It always sounds so peaceful. Maybe it's not so bad."

Naz and I start cracking up.

"What the fuck, Yasaman?" Naz says, licking the Cool Ranch off her fingers.

"I'm being serious. You know in ancient Egypt, pharaohs' brains were removed through their noses before they were mummified? Can you imagine that?"

"That's fucking gross," I say.

"They actually removed all the organs. The only thing they'd leave was the heart because they thought it was the essence of the person," Yasaman says quite seriously, like she's some sort of museum docent.

"How the fuck do you know that?" Naz asks her.

"What? I read a lot," she says.

"The brain through the nose? That's one big-ass booger," Naz says, like she's a five-year-old, and we all start laughing—the giddy, out-of-control laughter that has no beginning and no end.

"Pony" by Ginuwine starts playing on Yasaman's car radio.

"Hey, turn it up!" Naz says, and Yasaman does. "We have to get out and dance. All of us. Get the fuck out. Now."

We leave all the doors open and get out to dance. We're each in our own world—Naz is grinding the air, Yasaman is letting the beat roll through her body, and I'm sticking my ass out and waving it around like no one's watching. We're out of breath, laughing too hard, singing the lyrics loud.

At some point we all look like cowboys riding horses, and I can't keep my eyes off Yasaman. Naz goes inside the car to smoke more weed and finish the Doritos off, and Yasaman and I sit on these big boulders to catch our breath with our backs to the car and a stunning view of the Valley in front of us and only trees and bushes surrounding us.

"This is my favorite thing to do when I'm high," Yasaman says, and she grabs my arm and starts tickling my forearm up and down, like her fingers are a harmless, delicate spider. I close my eyes and let her touch become a part of my body. *I want this,* I keep saying to myself, *just let go. Let go.*

"That feels so good," I say. She takes my hand and starts drawing circles on the middle of my palm.

"Your parents ever do that? I think you have to say 'Gili gili hosak' or some shit," she says, like she's singing a song. "It's like a nursery rhyme or something. I don't know what it means, but it's one of the few things I remember my dad doing with me."

"I think so," I say. Her fingers travel in between mine, and soon we're holding hands.

"This okay?" she asks.

"Ya. It's good. I'm chill, don't worry," I say. My heart's beating so fast, I think I might throw up. Her touch makes me feel lightheaded, so I close my eyes and breathe. She wiggles her hand out from mine, and I think she might be getting up, but when I open my eyes, she's inching her face closer to mine. Even in the dark I can see the electricity in her green eyes. She watches my lips, then my eyes, and then my lips again, and I let myself melt into the moment as our tongues touch, and this time it doesn't feel like a slap. There's no sting, just tongues twirling, wet with spit and the complete joy of this moment. She's touching my face as we kiss, running her fingers through my hair as if trying to make sure I'm real, leading us through the push and pull, push and pull of our bodies. Tony's kisses are always so dry, so bland, lifeless—but this, this is a merging, a oneness I've never experienced before. Everything I ever thought to be true about myself feels like a firework now exploding in my belly. I'm lost in the black hole of Yasaman's mouth, and I don't ever want to be found. I almost get up so I can straddle her, so I can feel her throbbing with me, but then she comes up for air and we take a break.

"Holy shit," I say.

"What?"

"Nothing. That was just . . . amazing. Different."

"It was," she says with a surprisingly shy smile. We stare at the view for a while, the city lights, cars zooming by, the stars our only witnesses. I take deep breaths and try to calm down a little.

"Hey, I was thinking. We should go to prom together," she says.

"Like as a group?"

"No, like you and me," she says.

"Like, you would be my date?" I ask, surprised by her proposition. I'm still reeling from our kiss.

"We don't have to make an official announcement or anything. You don't have to buy me a corsage or rent us a limo. But I like you. I think it could be fun if we went to prom together." She grabs my hand again. The words *I like you* vibrate in my ear. My heartbeat spreads to my throat, my head. With each bang of my pulse, the bold me, the me who just kissed Yasaman and actually let herself go, starts to shrink.

Instead of saying *fuck yes* to her invitation, I'm silent and scared shitless. She seems so comfortable with the idea, like she wouldn't mind people seeing us together, holding hands, slow dancing, kissing even. I want to say, *Yes, of course, I thought you'd never ask*, but the thought of letting the whole school in on this makes me nervous. The whole school includes my brother and other Persian kids who'd definitely talk and spread gossip to their parents, who'd eventually spread it to mine. And under no circumstances can my parents find out about this.

I pull my hand away from Yasaman.

"You don't get it," I say, staring out.

"It's not easy, but you gotta start somewhere."

I shake my head. "It's not the same for me. You don't have your dad breathing down your neck. I mean, you don't have to explain yourself to someone who will never in a million years understand. Or even *want* to understand. If I go to prom with another girl, somehow my dad will find out and my life will be over. You're lucky you can be so free."

When I finally work up the courage to look at Yasaman, there are tears in her eyes.

"You think I'm lucky my dad's dead?"

"No! No. Fuck, that was so stupid of me," I say, reaching for her hand again. To my surprise, she lets me hold it. "I'm so, so, so sorry, that's not what I meant at all. It's just really complicated for me."

182

"It's complicated for everyone, Rana. Your dad's strict. He comes from a country that thinks being gay is a crime. But he's only here one month out of the year—are you really going to live your life for him?"

It's a question that has made a home inside me, but to hear someone else say it feels so different and makes the answer so clear. I put my hand on her thigh and she turns toward me and this time, I lean in for a kiss, trying to savor this moment, this sweet thing that feels like it will surely make all my monsters disappear.

Then I hear footsteps approaching.

"What the fuck?" A voice slashes through our kiss, and I look up to see Ramptin zipping up his pants. He's obviously just taken a piss in one of the nearby bushes.

I want to die.

"Hey, Ramptin. What's up?" I say, trying to sound casual.

"Rana the Frog sucking face with a girl?" He's laughing, and I have no clue what to say. Ramptin finding out means he will one hundred percent blab to his mom, and his mom knows my mom and will do the dutiful thing and call my mom immediately and make sure she knows the ugly truth about her daughter.

"Ramptin, please. You can't tell anyone," I say, perfectly clear on how pathetic I sound.

"Who the fuck is this?" Yasaman says, looking at me.

"Yasaman, this is Ramptin. Ramptin, this is Yasaman. Ramptin's family is friends with mine," I say, staring at the ground.

Yasaman responds with a heavy "Oh." She knows what this means. My stomach churns, and I might throw up.

"It all makes sense now, I guess," Ramptin says.

"What the fuck are you talking about?" I ask, building up the courage to look him in the eyes.

"Why you wouldn't give me a blow job in middle school," he says, cracking up.

"What did you say to her?" Yasaman says, standing up like she's getting ready to pounce on him. I pull her back.

"You better keep your fucking mouth shut about this," I tell him.

"You fuck with her, you have to deal with me," Yasaman says.

"Oooooh, I'm pissing my pants over here. So you're her knight in shining armor then?"

"At least I'm something to her. You're an irrelevant speck of shit."

Ramptin's eyes widen, and he has nothing to say in response.

I can't believe this is happening. "Ramptin," I say. "Seriously. I know you're pissed at me because I didn't suck your dick a thousand years ago, but I need you to swear on Biggie's life you won't say shit."

"Whatever. Peace out, lesbos." Ramptin makes his way to a huge SUV parked close to our car and drives off, while I'm frozen to the spot.

"Fuck, I'm so screwed. He's going to tell his mom, and she's going to tell mine, and my dad is going to force me to go back to Iran with him or—"

"He won't do that, Rana. He's a dick, but he wouldn't go that far."

"You don't know him," I say. I'm trying to take deep breaths, but my mellow high has turned into aggressive paranoia. Yasaman tries to take my hand again, but I pull away. "Let's just get out of here."

"Doritos are finito. I need some real food. Jack in the crack or In-N-Out?" Naz asks us as we get in the car. Neither of us says anything.

"What the fuck? Did you guys get attacked by coyotes out there or something?" Naz asks.

"We're good," Yasaman says.

"Rana?" Naz leans forward from the back seat and looks at my face. "Are you okay?" she whispers.

"I'm fine," I snap.

The drive down is mostly silence, and then Naz cuts through it. "I think we should all go to prom together. Fuck having a date."

It's clear at this point that Naz is some sort of vibe wizard. Yasaman looks at me for a second; I can see her out of the corner of my eye.

"You guys down?" Naz says.

"Sure, sounds good," Yasaman says. "But I'm pretty tired right now. Mind if we skip the food and just head back?"

"We can't finish the night without a Double-Double!" Naz says.

"Naz, drop it," I snap at her.

"Jeez, fine."

Yasaman drives us down the canyon. The silence between Yasaman and me is so thick, I can't seem to find my way through it.

I can't fall asleep. I sit up, close my eyes, and try to meditate, but my thoughts are crashing into one another, intense waves that make my whole body feel tense.

Ramptin knows my secret. Ramptin, who hates me. Ramptin, who takes pleasure in seeing me suffer, has this power over me now. This is a fucking nightmare.

Yasaman didn't say a word to me the whole ride back. She was trying to defend me, to protect me, to help me speak my truth, and I'd wanted nothing but to run away.

This level of disappointment from another person is unbearable, and I don't know what to do with it.

My parents insist on turning the AC off when we sleep at night, so I'm in bed with a T-shirt on and the sheets rolled off me. The high from earlier in the night is gone, and all I'm left with is an empty, lonely feeling that I think might last forever.

I've been dreaming about girls since the third grade, when Brianna Asher wore her leggings with the lace trim at the ankles and her brand-new white Keds and got the new hairdo with the bangs and wore five slap bracelets on each of her wrists. Every girl wanted to be her, but I wanted to be next to her, to look her in the eyes, to slam the tetherball she'd touched, to give her some of my tater tots.

I stare at my hand, the dips between each finger where Yasaman slid her own to show me she was serious, that she was ready to link herself to me and didn't care who would see. My whole life is an unfulfilled urge, my whole fucking body a magnet wanting to be touched and be loved, but connecting in this way doesn't feel simple at all. I roll over in bed, and then turn back to the other side, and smack my sweaty pillow around, but no matter what I do, I can't get comfortable.

I get up and open the window and sit on a chair and look out at the dark night and the millions of stars that are only visible this far away from the city. People who live in the city just can't see shit like this.

I shoo a few mosquitos away, and instead of coming up with a plan to make sure Ramptin doesn't blab my secret to the whole world, I picture Yasaman's face. No matter what I say to myself, she's inhabited my sacred internal space, and I can't stop thinking about her and how easy all this seems for her.

I close my eyes again, focus on my breath, and sit with whatever comes up. And then I cry in a way I haven't cried since the day of Louie's funeral, in his room with Tony holding me. I cry like it's the beginning of my grief. Like my tears and the howl of my voice are the only things that are making me feel alive right now. And then I get my notebook and write.

This speckled, starry night
Cracks me wide open,
The possibility of my whole life crumbling,
And all I can think about is kissing you again.

I lie back in bed, take off my shirt, and stare at my body, painted with moonlight. My dollar-coin nipples. The trail of hair on my belly. The handful of fat on either side of my hips. Would Yasaman really want all this? All of me, just as I am? I close my eyes, and all I see is red. I touch myself until my body feels like the stars outside lit up by the moon, so far away and yet so close, I can touch them.

24.

I wake up to my mom yelling at me to pick up the phone. I turn over in bed and grab the cordless in my room.

"What the fuck happened last night?"

"Jesus, Naz, at least let me wake up first."

"Sorry, dude, just wanted to make sure you were okay."

"I'm not. Ramptin saw us making out last night, Naz. He was taking a piss in the bushes. I'm fucked," I say, lying back down and putting the cover over my head.

"You guys made out?! It was good? You liked it?" she asks.

"Ya, I liked it, but that's not the point. Ramptin is going to fuck this up, and I know it," I tell her.

"Guys like him talk a lot of talk, Rana. He doesn't have it in him. He might throw it in your face or something, but he's not going to tell anyone. Trust me. Do you want me to talk to him? Or I can tell Marcus. . . ."

"Nope, I'm good. I'll handle it somehow."

"Please don't stress about this shit. Soon it'll all be over, and you won't have to think about these people ever again—

well, except Yasaman and me, of course."

"Of course," I say, and we say goodbye and hang up.

I get up and go downstairs for breakfast. My family is already gathered, and Babak tells my parents that he's going to ask Samantha to prom. (He's a junior, but she's a senior like me, so he gets to go with her.) Of course my parents have no problem with this.

"I'm going to buy a whole pizza and then arrange the pepperoni slices so they spell out '*Prom?*'" he tells my dad, who looks confused while he cracks the top of a runny egg, peels the shell, and dips his bread into it.

"Pepperoni? What is this? Buy her a plant. She can keep it and help it grow, and when she looks at it, she will always think of you," my dad says, giving him his best version of dad advice.

"I think I'm going to go with the pizza thing. More original," Babak says.

"Nothing is more romantic than processed meat," I say.

"What about you, Rana Joon?" my mom asks.

"I don't know," I say, pouring a cup of coffee. *My life might be destroyed by prom* is what I want to say. I might as well tell them, right? It's better for them to hear it from me than through a random phone call. In my mind, I imagine telling them I'm going with Yasaman—a half-Iranian, half-white girl with red hair, freckles, and a zest for life and art and love that's contagious. We kissed last night, and it was magic. Very soon after this revelation, I can see my dad having a heart attack, hand reaching for his heart, my mom and Babak running to his aid and staring back at me like, *Look what you've done to him.*

"I'll probably go with Naz or just stay home or something," I say instead.

"Well, in case you decide to go, I can take you shopping for a dress," my mom says.

"It's okay, I have the one I wore to Ladan's house."

"Rana, it's prom. People will be taking pictures. You can do better. You should go all out," Babak says, as if he's the expert on fashion suddenly.

"We can go after school tomorrow," my mom says, sounding way too excited about it. I've never attended any school function before, and unlike my dad, who I'm sure would rather I go in an XL jogging suit to avoid any male attention, I know my mom sincerely wants me to look my best.

"Okay," I say.

"You should get her roses. You know that if you bury a banana peel in the soil when you plant roses, they grow so much faster?" my dad says, still stuck on romantic suggestions for Babak. He's really letting the bread soak, and when he pops it into his mouth, the egg yolk runs down his chin like spit.

At school the next day, everyone is popping the question in their own unique, dorky ways. Dudes dress up like bears and hand deliver flowers; Douglas, the skateboarder from my English class, graffitis the question on a girl's locker. Boys recite poems, sing songs, do backflips, bring cupcakes.

I show up early to Señor Mariani's class, tell him I'm not feeling well, and ask to go see the nurse, because at this point, my strategy is to avoid Ramptin at all costs.

"We're reviewing for the final," he says. "Your life will be a lot harder if you leave."

How do I tell him my life is already exceptionally hard and staying will only make it worse?

I take a seat, and Ramptin walks in two seconds later with a smirk already on his face. I stare down at my notebook, doodling different shapes. I can't focus on anything Señor Mariani is saying and am just quietly praying that Ramptin doesn't say a word to me.

"That was really hot the other night," he whispers into my neck.

I inch my desk forward, but there's nowhere to go.

"Who do you think would be more disappointed? Your mom or your dad?" he whispers again, louder this time.

I'm melting in my seat, my whole body on fire with every word that leaves his cruel mouth. I'm stuck to this seat, but also, if I stay here another moment, I will explode. I get up, grab my things and the bathroom pass, and run straight to Ms. Murillo's classroom, despite Señor Mariani yelling at me to come back.

She has her prep this period, so when I walk in, she's grading papers and playing Spanish flamenco music. I'm out of breath when I get there, and after she looks in my eyes, she doesn't say a word, just turns off her music and quickly comes over to me.

"I can't . . . I feel like . . . it feels like I can't breathe," I tell her, gasping for air.

She walks me to her corner of Zen, where she puts some colorful pillows down and has me lie on them.

"Here," she says, opening up a vial and putting oil on my temples and under my nose. "Just close your eyes and breathe."

I shut my eyes and am flooded with the scent of lavender. I take a deep breath, the first one I've taken in a while.

"Whatever is happening isn't forever," Ms. Murillo says, sitting above me on the couch. "No feeling is forever, Rana. The hard part, though, is that you have to feel it. If you don't, it just gets stuck inside you. There's nowhere for it to go."

"It's too hard," I say, the heat of my body now felt in the tears rolling down my face.

"I know it's hard, but it's the only way."

"It's too much," I say through the tears.

"The more you resist it, the harder it is."

In the darkness, I follow her voice like a beam of light. I focus on my breath and feel my heartbeat slowing down. She guides me to follow my thoughts—to not get stuck in regrets from the past or concerns about the future, but to stay in the moment.

"Listen to the sounds around you. Let them be a part of this experience too. There's nothing wrong with you, Rana. This is just what it means to be human," she says, and her voice and the air-conditioning and the footsteps in the hallway and the creaking of the window are all a part of me now, just like all the beauty and pain of life. It's like I'm floating, like I'm so fully in my body, I don't even have one. The clenching of my heart is gone, and I just feel open, open, open.

After a while the bell rings, which means Ms. Murillo's next class is going to start filing in.

"Are you feeling better now? I can walk you to the nurse if you need," Ms. Murillo offers.

I shake my head. "I think I'm okay now. I just . . ."

"No need to explain yourself, Rana. I'm here if you need me."

And I know she means it.

It's still passing period, so I wait for Yasaman by her locker because I feel pretty shitty about the other night and we haven't talked since. After what just went down in Ms. Murillo's room, I'm in the right headspace to see her again. Yasaman's walking over with Rain from my World Religions class, and they're midconversation and don't really stop talking when they see me.

"Oh my God, I can't believe you've actually seen *Guernica* in person. What was that like?" Rain asks Yasaman.

"Unreal. I mean, it's huge. I sat there for an hour just taking it in. You'd think because it's black and white it's not going to really stand out, but the size of it just takes your breath away," Yasaman responds.

They both say hi to me but continue their conversation.

"What are you guys talking about?" I ask.

"Just our art class final. We have to research a painting together and then create something in the artist's own style," Rain says.

"Cool," I say. I stare at Rain so maybe she'll get the hint that I want to talk to Yasaman alone, but she doesn't budge, and Yasaman's switching her books out and isn't paying too much attention to me.

"Can you give us a sec?" I finally ask Rain, and she nods and gives us some space.

"Hey, I'm really sorry about the other night," I say to Yasaman.

"Which part?" she says, her eyes still on her books.

"All of it. I shouldn't have brought up your dad like that. I could've been real with you and just told you that coming out in general scares the crap out of me. And then the whole Ramptin thing sent me into a total panic. You were trying to protect me, I know, but he's been torturing me for years, and now he knows this huge secret of mine—"

"I get it, Rana. It's not easy. My mom is a freaking hippie, and it even took her a minute to process, but like I said the other night, at some point you're going to have to start living for yourself. Whatever Ramptin does or doesn't do, you always have a choice."

"It just feels like I want it so bad, but I don't actually deserve it."

"What don't you deserve?"

My voice is small, but I find the courage to say it out loud. "Love."

Yasaman drops her bag and reaches for me. We hug, and the thought of letting go makes me want to cry again, but I push the tears back.

"Rain's waiting. We have to work on our final," she says.

"Right, of course. We're cool, though?"

"We're cool," she says.

"If you're still down to go, would you want to go to prom with Naz and me? I know she can be a little intense, but she means well. It'll be fun," I say, knowing how stupid I sound inviting Naz as our third wheel, but she feels like a buffer I still need.

Yasaman hesitates for a second and then smiles. "Sure."

"I think Naz said she can drive, so we'll just—" But before I can finish, she's talking to Rain again. I watch as they walk off, arms linked, headed to the library.

25.

"I don't want anything too tight," I say as I browse the dresses at Nordstrom with my mom after school. I can't believe I've actually agreed to do this. Everything she picks out is either too shiny or fluffy, exactly what you'd expect someone to wear to prom.

"Eh, Rana, it's like you're just saying no because I'm picking it," she says.

I clearly have to lay down some restrictions, so I say, "I want something black, and no poufy skirts."

"It's prom, Rana Joon. It's okay to dress up."

A saleswoman with blond curls and exotic-looking rings on each of her fingers approaches us. She's wearing a loose skirt and doesn't look fancy enough to be working in this section.

"Can I help you ladies?" she asks.

"Yes, we need a very elegant, sophisticated dress for my daughter's prom."

"Not too elegant. Something black, but different," I say.

"Maybe something sparkly? Sparkles can be different," my mother chimes in.

"No sparkles," I say to the saleswoman.

"No sparkles. Got it," the saleswoman repeats as she guides us through racks and racks of dresses and picks out as many black ones as she can.

My mom insists on sitting in the fitting room while I try them on.

"I need some privacy," I tell her.

"Don't be silly, Rana, the mirror is in there. I can't keep coming in and out," she says.

All the dresses are pretty much the same in the end. One has no back, which I can't wear because there's no way in hell I can get away with not wearing a bra; one has a slit on the side that comes all the way up to my crotch; one has lace sleeves. But at the end of the day, none are flattering or really *me* at all. The only one my mom kind of approves of is a black one that has gems all over the neckline, but I hate how bedazzled it looks.

"Maybe something that flows, so everything is not showing," my mom says as I try on the next dress. I can feel her eyes examining my naked body, probably wondering what happened to the pretty bra she bought me or how my thighs got so big.

"It must be nice," I say as I unzip the next dress and find my way into it. I wasn't thrilled with all the beading, but my mom insisted.

"What?"

"Everything looks so good on you. You don't have to deal with this shit," I say.

"That's not true," she says. "I've always been a few pounds too heavy." That's laughable, and I actually do laugh.

"Ya, but you've never had these," I say, grabbing ahold of my love handles.

"Eh, een karoh nakon, don't do that. You know if you wear a girdle, it will really help with that." She says this so gently, totally convinced she's being supportive, but it just makes me feel like shit.

"You know what? I think I just want to be me. No girdle or push-up bra or stupid cayenne pepper cleanse to fit in an ugly dress for one night. Can't I just be myself? Is that a fucking crime?" I snap at her, and then catch her eyes in the mirror before I pull the dress all the way up. It looks like she might cry, but she holds herself back, smiles, and just nods in understanding—which is shocking because I assumed she'd get defensive or tell me that she was doing everything out of love, couldn't I see that?

"Sure," she says. "I'm sorry."

"Can you help me zip this up, please?" I ask her, feeling guilty now.

We both stare at the finished product in the mirror—me wearing something I would never in a million years think to put on my body, but somehow it actually looks good on me. My curves look amazing, and though the beading is black, it shimmers purple in the light. I actually look sexy and mysterious, and I'm totally comfortable with my legs, which are my greatest asset, showing.

"I love it," I say. My mom doesn't say anything for a minute, and I'm thinking she probably hates it and here we go with her criticisms—but all of a sudden she's crying.

"You look beautiful. I'm sorry I don't say that enough, Rana Joon. You know I love you," she says. She stands up and pulls me in for a hug. Normally I try to stay strong in her rare moments of weakness, but this time I cry with her.

"I've ruined all my makeup," she says. She pulls out a tissue from her purse and starts wiping her mascara.

"You still look beautiful," I tell her, and she smiles.

We decide to get the dress, my mom's treat.

Afterward we're walking by the food court, and all the smells are torturing me. Crying apparently works up an appetite. I'm fucking starving.

"Are you hungry?" my mom asks.

"Kind of," I say.

"Let's eat then," my mom says. "You pick."

The fact that she's not insisting we get a salad feels even more absurd than us agreeing on the same dress. This is a side of my mom I haven't seen since I was a little girl. I walk us over to the Great Steak Company and order each of us a steak sandwich and fries to share.

"Is that okay?" I ask her, because I don't think I've ever seen her eat fries. Maybe she hates them, who knows?

"Sure," she says. She looks uncomfortable standing next to me, watching them chop up the meat they're frying, dip the fries in a basket of hot oil, but she's forcing a smile and I'm amazed by her willingness to let this happen.

"I know I've been acting strange, Rana Joon," she says as we set our trays down on the table and arrange our dipping sauces. I'm not sure which strange she's referring to—the general weirdness when my dad's around? Or her smoking with Bod's uncle like a rebellious teenager? "I appreciate you trying to protect me, but it's not your job. I have to speak up for myself."

"I just want you to be happy. I don't think that's too much to ask for in life," I say.

The way my mom eats her sandwich—mayonnaise and grease dripping on her fingers, melted cheese filling the corners of her mouth, lipstick fading, moaning sounds of bliss—is something I've rarely seen. She's focused and dedicated when she cooks with her students, with passion in her eyes as she pinches the saffron or flips the pot over to reveal a golden brown plate of crispy rice, but it's less common to see her express this type of ecstatic enjoyment from food.

"What happened to chew slower, eat less?"

"Yes. Yes, but this is very good. This is something else," she says. I nod in agreement because the combination of toasted bread, melted cheese, mayonnaise, greasy meat, and fries is everything I could ever ask for in a meal.

Maybe my mom and I aren't as different as I think we are. She's said things like *Not ever my child, not ever you,* but if she really knew the truth about me, maybe she could get past it and love me regardless. Maybe it's better she hears it from my mouth than from Ramptin's mom's collagen-loaded lips.

"You know, we didn't have prom in Iran," my mom says. "But I remember at the end of high school, I went to the Caspian Sea with my friends. I had never gone before. The water was sparkling, and the air was so fresh. It was only six, seven hours away from Tehran, but it felt like I was on a completely different planet. I felt like an idiot, waiting that long to go."

"Baba Joon let you go?"

"I lied and said it was a trip with my school." She takes a few fries and dips them in ketchup. "There was a French boy. I had a crush on him," she says, information pouring out of her as if she's drunk off carbs and doesn't feel the need to hold back any longer. "He was our age, but it felt like he was a man already. You know, very confident. He kissed me one night under the stars, and then we went swimming together." She finishes her sandwich, and I'm waiting for the rest of the story, but she's just smiling in a dreamy way, like she wishes she were right back in that sea with her French lover.

"What happened to him?"

"Oh, he was a very naughty boy. He just wanted sex, and I wasn't that kind of girl," she says—but then she adds, "Sometimes I regret it. Remember to have fun, Rana Joon. Life is so short. I wish I had enjoyed myself more, not cared so much about what other people thought."

If there was ever a right time to tell her, this feels like it. I open my mouth to tell her, making a choice that this one and only now will be about me offering this truth to her—*my truth*—but before I can say anything, she wipes her hands with a napkin and blurts, "I'm having an affair with Bod's uncle."

She doesn't look at me after that. She just gets up from the table and throws out our garbage and stacks the tray with the others.

"Um, are you going to elaborate on what you just said back there?" I ask my mom as we exit the parking lot and head home.

"Nah, khoobam, I'm okay," she says. She puts on her over-sized sunglasses, starts the car, and hits the switch to spray and wipe our windshield. "I didn't realize how dirty this car was."

"Mom, you're acting really weird," I say. I'm blinking hard and fast, suddenly blinded by the light of this truth. It feels like my whole world has imploded, and I hold on to my seat, trying to grip something for security.

All the joy I thought I'd feel at my mom finally taking a stand for herself doesn't exist. Before we were partners in our misery—and now what?

"Maybe I'm just being myself," she says. She pulls out a cigarette, lights it up, rolls down the window, and smokes it like a pro.

Maybe I don't know all the layers that make up my mom, just like I didn't know all of Louie's. And maybe I'm not the only one going through changes. Looking at my mom now, it's like she's become a different person too. Maybe this is what it feels like to grow up; everyone becomes so much more complicated than you always thought they were.

"How long has this been going on?"

"I've been smoking on and off for years. I just did a good job hiding it from you."

"No. The affair."

"Not long. Less than a year."

"Why are you acting like this is no big deal? You lied to us. To all of us."

"I thought you just want me to be happy? What happened to that? This makes me happy, Rana Joon. I want to be *wanted*. To have someone here and not there. I deserve that," she says, sucking on her cigarette with the elegance of a movie star.

I do want my mom to be happy, but is this person next to me even my mom? It's like I don't know her at all.

I roll my window down and stick my head out, and the hot air flaps my hair in all directions. Maybe I'm not even mad at her, but just jealous. She's free from her burning ball of secrets and I'm not. This was supposed to be my moment to break free, and she stole it right out of the palm of my hand.

"It's just selfish to lie like this for so long," I mutter, but at this point, I don't know who I'm talking to anymore.

26.

I spend the whole week in the library, kind of in my own world. Yasaman's been busy working with Rain on their art final, and Naz has been busy playing hot and cold with Marcus. After my fight with Tony, I can't even go to him to talk or watch TV or smoke a bowl.

Every time we practice, Coach Lock keeps drilling it in my ear that I need to do one of my own pieces, and I keep resisting. But at our last practice this week, I finally agree to read the completed version of my "I Am From" poem to him.

He's quiet for a minute after I finish, clears his throat in what feels like awkwardness, and I'm worried he might think it's too much—but then he comes over and gives me a big old hug.

"That's some real raw shit, Rana. I'm proud of you. Even if you don't use this, writing it is a triumph," he says, and I know he's right.

At home I practice in front of the mirror until my eyes are watering and my throat feels like a cat is trying to scratch its way out. I do

Louie's piece at first, but halfway through, I switch to my own. For some reason I can't really explain, I decide to undress and stand in front of the mirror, wearing only a bra and underwear, and in that state, I release the words from my body—the truth of who I am. The words I wanted to say to my mom are no longer suction-cupping my heart into a tightness that makes it hard to breathe, and instead, my spit unleashes them like a flock of butterflies destined for one thing—flight. The more I repeat my words, the lighter my body gets, and soon I'm floating.

I stare at myself in the mirror, not a half-assed gaze or a look that pinpoints only my flaws. I take all of me in and get closer and closer to the glass, until I can see my breath on it.

I'm alive. I'm alive. I'm alive, I quietly tell myself. *Stop acting like a dead person. Stop acting like you have no choice. Like you have no voice. You ain't no mud type of girl.* If my mom can be honest, why can't I?

But she wasn't announcing her affair over the Persian radio. I'm probably the only person who knows. This feels different. Sharing my words at the Way of the Wu would be cracking my heart open, sharing my soul with an entire room of sweaty, hyped-up strangers.

I lie down in bed, close my eyes, and fantasize about Yasaman on prom night. What will she wear? Will she want to dance with me? Could we find a hidden corner to make out in? Or maybe just say fuck it, and do it under the flashing laser lights of the crowded dance floor? Life is for the living after all, and it doesn't really feel like I've been living since Louie died. Maybe it's finally time.

The night of prom, I don't dry my hair after my shower and start my usual ritual of flat ironing it. Instead I use some shit the white-haired saleswoman at Ralphs said was great for frizz control, and I let it dry on its own.

I'm thrilled with what I see in the mirror because it's new and unfamiliar, and there's something so disorderly and free about the curls—the same chaos as Yasaman's, only dark brown instead of red. A part of me feels like this is what I'm meant to look like. I put on my dress and my wedge heels, plus a black choker around my neck, a heavy load of mascara and eyeliner, and red lipstick.

My door swings open, no knock or anything, and Babak is standing there with spiky hair and a tight-fitting black suit.

"Whoa, Rana. What the fuck happened to your hair? You look like Sideshow Bob. Not a good look."

"What the hell is wrong with you? Like I don't already get enough criticism from Mom about how I look," I say, turning to face him.

"I'm just being honest. You're going to be taking a lot of pictures tonight."

"I don't care about the stupid pictures. It's none of your business how I do my hair or what I eat or how much I exercise. Jesus, your head is so far up your ass, you don't even know . . ." I almost tell him but stop myself quick. My mom's truth isn't mine to tell.

"What? What don't I know?"

I don't know why it's taken me this long to be real with him, to put up boundaries, but then again, our family is very skilled at pretending like everything is A-OK. I've been pissed at my mom since she told me about the affair, enraged even, but maybe I can learn something from her.

"You just don't get it. You'll never get it. You get to stay in a hotel tonight, and I have to be home by eleven. You do whatever you want with whoever you want, and I have to tiptoe and manipulate my way into having just a little bit of fun. And the most fucked-up part is that you're blind to your own freedom. It's your ignorance that makes you an asshole."

Even with his thinly waxed eyebrows, I can see the shock on his face.

Instead of feeling overwhelmed or anxious about what to say next, I'm empowered in a way I've never experienced before.

"Dude," Babak says. The words that should come next are *I'm sorry*, but they don't. He just says, "Dude," again and again like a scratched-up CD.

"I don't have time for this. I'm gonna be late." I push him out of the doorway and make my way down the stairs.

When I come downstairs, I expect my mom to be excited by the heels and the makeup, but instead she says, "Eh, what happened to your hair?"

"I needed a change. It's not a big deal," I say, pulling on my curls. My mom and I haven't talked beyond the car ride home from the mall, and there's distance from her that makes my chest tighten.

"This dress is too sexy-mexy. Do you have a shawl to cover up or something?" my dad says.

"Baba, stop. It's a hundred degrees outside," I say.

"Ebi Joon, she looks beautiful," my mom says, finally realizing that I need her on my side. Somehow this shuts him up, but then he goes on a whole rant about not drinking and being home by eleven p.m. sharp.

"Okay, I get it," I say. My mom's taking tons of pictures of me while my dad awkwardly watches from afar. I hear Naz honking and say bye.

"Oh, Rana. This girl called for you before," my dad says.

"What girl?"

"Yasaman. What is her last name? Do you know her last name?" he asks, because knowing someone's last name means he can figure out if he knows the family or knows someone who knows the family and can do his background check on the people I choose to spend my time with.

"What did she say, Baba?"

"She said she will meet you at the dance. She went early to help, so you don't need to pick her up."

My heart sinks a little, but at least she'd called to tell me, which meant she wasn't intentionally trying to ditch me.

"You couldn't have told me sooner?"

"I'm sorry, it's hard for me to remember these things," he says, and reminds me one more time to be home by eleven.

27.

Naz is wearing a tight black-and-white checkered jumpsuit, red fabric wrapped around her hair, and lipstick to match. She did her makeup in the car, and her eyeliner is super thick, but that just makes her eyes look even more gorgeous.

"Fuck," Naz says, "we clean up good. Your hair looks dope."

"At least one person thinks so."

"Why don't you ever leave it like this?"

"It feels weird," I admit, "but I think I like it."

"And why the hell don't you ever let these babies out, Rana? It's a fucking crime. I bet you Yasaman will dig them," Naz says, patting down my boobs.

I flick her hand away and tell her Yasaman is meeting us there. Naz turns up the music, and we're off.

Prom is at some fancy hotel by Universal Studios. Inside, everything is Paris themed; there's a huge cardboard cutout of a Parisian café strung with lights, croissants and little sandwiches on display, a chocolate fountain, a photo booth with an Eiffel

Tower background. The dance floor is already packed. I look around for Yasaman.

"Do you see her?" Naz asks.

"No, but . . . I'm sure she's looking for us too. I'll go find her," I say, even though my heart already feels defeated, wondering if Yasaman has forgotten about us—forgotten about *me*. I look everywhere for her—in the bathroom; at the tea-and-coffee station, where the croissants and sandwiches are; in the hotel restaurant—anxious the whole time that her phone call was just a courtesy and she doesn't actually give a shit if I even show up. But I want to find her and tell her that I'm ready now, that I'm done questioning everything so much.

I go through the back door of the hotel and see a girl with red hair. This girl's hair is long and stick-straight, falling midway down her back, and it can't possibly be Yasaman, but she turns around at the sound of the door opening, and I see it *is* her.

She's wearing a dress as red as fire, orange lipstick, drinking out of a silver flask with Brianna Asher, whose gold dress looks like it was sewn onto her body. They're laughing at who-the-fuck-knows-what and passing the flask back and forth.

Yasaman runs over to me.

"Holy shit, your curls," she says, giving me a hug. "You look amazing."

I wasn't expecting this level of excitement from Yasaman, but by the smell of vodka on her breath, she's obviously a little drunk.

"Hey, Rana," Brianna says.

"Hey," I say, and then to Yasaman, "I thought we were picking you up?"

"Shit. Ya, I called your dad. Didn't he tell you? I ran into Brianna at the mall, and she asked me if I could help set things up."

"But the plan was to go together," I say.

"I mean, it was a group thing, so I didn't think it was that big a deal," she says, and takes another drink from the flask.

My whole body is vibrating in anger. Seeing her out here with Brianna, acting like this night isn't a big deal to me, has set me on fire.

"What's that?" Brianna asks, because I forgot that I bought Yasaman a corsage and it's in my hand. Shit.

"Oh. Um. It's for me," I say.

"You bought yourself a corsage?" Yasaman asks.

"Ya. I thought that's what you do at prom," I say like an idiot, and slip it onto my own wrist.

I want to give it to Yasaman, but she feels so far away suddenly with Brianna by her side. I want to tell her to stay the fuck away from Brianna Asher because this is supposed to be *our* night.

Brianna hiccups, and then spits a laugh out. "I'm sorry, I'm not laughing at you. I've had the hiccups for, like, the last forty-five minutes. They keep coming and going. It's insane."

"Let's try again," Yasaman says, and then stands directly in front of Brianna, so close they could kiss, holding her shoulders and looking in her eyes. "Just hold your breath," she says. "Ready?"

I stand there and watch Yasaman count. I should walk away, but I don't. Brianna breathes again, and the hiccups are gone.

"I can't believe I start summer session in a few weeks. Cal is so intense," Brianna says.

"Holy shit. That was my top choice. I got on the waitlist, so we'll see," Yasaman says.

"I didn't know you wanted to go there," I say to her, and she doesn't say anything. One of them passes me the flask; for some reason I take it instead of leaving, and it goes round and round.

"You're going to UCLA, right?" Brianna asks me, and I nod yes. "I can't believe you quit, Rana. You could have totally gotten a full ride playing ball."

"Wait, you were on the basketball team? I didn't know," Yasaman says, and I can't tell if she's impressed or slightly hurt that she didn't know this one important thing about me.

"She wasn't *just* on the team. She was really fucking good. My only real competition. I don't think I'll ever understand why you did that to yourself," Brianna says, taking another swig from the flask. Her compliment is a blaring alarm in the pit of my stomach, another reminder of how I've fucked up. "Cal has this amazing program where you go to Paris your sophomore year and learn French and go to like a French university or something. We should totally do it together if you get in, Yas," Brianna says.

"That sounds amazing," Yasaman says. "I'm all about traveling. Like, why would anyone ever want to stay in one place? My mom and I are actually going to Mexico City the day after graduation to see Frida Kahlo's house—"

I crack up, cutting Yasaman off. "Yas?" I say to Brianna. "Who the fuck is Yas? Her name is Ya-sa-man," I say, feeling tipsy now and overdoing my Persian accent.

"Rana, it's cool," Yasaman says, side-eyeing me.

"But it's not cool," I say, the vodka burn giving me a courage I'm not used to. "You're all about keeping it a hundred percent real and being honest about who you are, right? If she can't even say your name right, then does she really even know you? You can't expect everyone else to be honest about who they are if you're walking around letting some stupid white girl call you *Yas*."

"I think I'm gonna go inside, Yas," Brianna says.

"No, it's cool. I'll go, *Yas*," I say.

I quickly walk inside and hope to God that Yasaman will follow me—but she doesn't. Everything feels like it's spiraling out of control suddenly. This was supposed to be our night to shine, and now I just feel like a five-year-old who wants nothing more than to sit in the corner and eat croissants.

I go back into the banquet room and stand by the tiny sandwiches and put a bunch of them in my mouth. I follow them with a couple croissants. The only way I won't have a complete breakdown is if I keep eating. Just stay away from Yasaman and keep eating. If I move from this spot, if I try to be a normal person and dance or take a picture with the Eiffel Tower, I'll end up screaming or strangling someone.

Everything I imagined happening at the beginning of the night—Yasaman and I walking into prom together, my corsage on her wrist, dancing, holding hands, kissing freely—feels like a stupid fantasy with no foundation in reality at all.

My brother and Samantha grab some food next to me, and then Samantha in her ugly silver puffy skirt and sequined top says, "Come dance with us." She actually sounds like she means it too.

"Ya, come," Babak says, shoving a sandwich in his mouth.

"Don't be so depressing," Samantha says.

"My stomach just hurts," I say.

"You okay? Want some ginger ale or something?" Babak asks, sounding genuinely concerned.

"I'm okay," I say, and they're over it quickly and head to the dance floor without me.

Naz suddenly appears. She's out of breath from dancing so hard and is holding a water bottle.

"What are you doing over here like a grandma? It's fucking prom! You gotta get down or go home!" she says, obviously drunk. "Here." She hands me her water.

"I'm not thirsty," I say.

"It's vodka, bitch," she whispers in my ear. "No one ever suspects the Muslim girl." She starts laughing like an out-of-control hyena. "I don't know what's going on with you, but you can either stay in your shitty ass mood or get fucked up with me and have a good time. Marcus came solo too, so it's about to go down! And he can totally drive us home. I just told him he'll have to make a run for it as soon as we get to my house so my dad won't murder him, and he said one of his boys can pick him up down the street."

I drink from the water bottle and let the sting of vodka soothe my heartache, and soon Naz and I are on the dance floor releasing all our pent-up hormonal high school energy, like the world is about to burn to the ground tonight and we can only put out the fire with our sweat.

I'm pretty drunk at this point, grinding with Naz and jumping up and down like my wedges are sneakers, as if Yasaman doesn't even exist at all. Suddenly someone's hand is on my ass, and at first I think it's just Naz, but I turn around and see Ramptin. His hair is slicked back, five o'clock shadow like a thirty-year-old man, a white button-down shirt with too many buttons open. Most girls are probably dying to dance with him, but to me, he just looks like he's trying too hard.

"What the fuck are you doing? It's me, Rana," I say, because maybe he doesn't recognize me with the curls.

"No shit. You look hot," he says. I can smell the weed on him like cologne.

"You're high as fuck," I say, and turn around to get back to Naz, but I've lost her in the crowd.

Ramptin stays close and gets even closer. "I like your hair like this!" he shouts over the music. I have no clue why he's complimenting me. I nod at him and roll my eyes, too dizzy and drunk to go looking for Naz, and suddenly "California Love" comes on and Ramptin pulls me in closer, his hand on my ass as he presses me into his crotch, and I can feel how hard he is. I'm too drunk to be grossed out, and it feels good to be wanted like this, to this song especially. "You're so fucking hot, Rana," he tells me in my ear. "You're the sexiest girl in our school, and you don't even have to try. One night with me and you'll never want to be with any girl ever again," he says.

I can feel his breath on my neck and then his lips, and it feels like it's too late to undo this. Maybe life can be this simple, as simple as my own mom thinks it is. Maybe I can be the type of girl who welcomes and embraces a world that's this black and white.

I pull his face toward mine and kiss him. I forget where and who we are and how much I hate this human being and lose myself in touch and spit.

"What the fuck?" I hear someone say, and it snaps me out of my drunken make-out trance. I see a hand smack Ramptin away from me. I turn around to find that the hand belongs to Yasaman.

"It's not what it looks like," I say, even though it's exactly what it looks like. I'm kissing the guy who's been bullying me and trying to make my life miserable for years now, the same guy who Yasaman tried to protect me from. I'm making out with Ramptin when I should be making out with Yasaman.

"What? You're jealous or something? I could get down with the both of you if that makes you feel any better," Ramptin says.

Yasaman looks at me like she's expecting something to happen—like she's waiting for me to do what I was planning to do all along, to grab her hand and make this night about us—but my confidence is totally gone. I look down.

"See? She was having a good time with me, and you ruined it," Ramptin says.

Yasaman looks so pissed off, I think she might punch him in the face, but instead her fierceness crumbles into sadness. There are tears in her eyes, and she runs through the crowd trying to get away from this whole scene as fast as humanly possible. I should run after her, but I don't. I'm feeling too sick.

"I think I'm going to throw up," I say.

"Shit. You know where the bathroom is. Good luck with that," Ramptin says, and darts off.

I look for Naz everywhere, trying to hold my vomit in. I find her sweaty and stuck to Marcus.

"Naz, I'm going to puke," I say, grabbing her arm. "Come to the bathroom with me?" She looks at Marcus, and then at me, and then at Marcus again.

"Don't you dare move from this fucking spot," she tells Marcus, then takes my hand and rushes me over to the girls' bathroom. We squeeze into a stall, and she pulls my curls back as I throw up. I should be done, but there's definitely more. I put my finger down my throat, like I'm trying to touch my own heart and make sure it's still there. I can feel the slime inside me, and everything buried below it, full, ready to be flushed out. I gag, my ears and head aching from the pressure, and then after a couple dry heaves, I vomit again.

"I fucked it up," I keep saying over and over again as I try to catch my breath. "Yasaman hates me, and I'm a fucking voiceless loser—" I manage before I puke again. "Louie's dead, Naz. He's still fucking dead. There's so much he should've done, and now he can't do any of it," I say, and I'm a ball of tears as she wraps me up in her arms. I don't hear what Naz is saying, but her touch and her voice are the only things that are keeping me from losing my damn mind.

28.

Marcus drives Naz's car since Naz is wasted too, and they drop me off a little after ten.

"Want me to come inside and tuck you in?" Naz asks as we pull up in front of my house. She's lying down across the back seat. I pass Marcus a worried look.

"Don't worry," he says. "I'll take her to In-N-Out and sober her up a bit before I drop her off. My buddy will pick me up from her place."

"You know her parents will kill her if they see you."

"I'll make sure they don't," he says with a reassuring smile.

"I love you, Rana," Naz says. "I love you so much it hurts. Everything is going to be okay. Okay? Are we ordering yet? I'll get a 3x3 Animal Style with peppers, Animal Style fries, and a strawberry milkshake, extra shake, please."

I squeeze Naz's hand from where I'm sitting. "Good night, you guys," I say, and head inside. I'm sure my parents will be up, waiting to interrogate me, checking if there's alcohol on my breath, but when I walk in the house, it's dark and quiet. I turn on the lights, thinking they might just be tricking me and are sitting in the dark waiting to surprise me, but there's no sign of them. Except my dad's pants, hanging from the chair by the front door. His stupid fucking pants that he thinks he can just take off whenever he wants and lay out for everyone to see, and no one is allowed to disagree with him. The men in our family don't have to hide shit—it's the women who have to bear the burden of secrecy. It's fucking exhausting.

I go outside to the miniature, pathetic garden I helped my dad recreate and throw his pants into the bushes. I take a look at the plants and flowers, the tomatoes that have started to grow on their silver cone, the jasmine with its undeniable scent, the purple flowers that look healthy and alive, everything lit up by the bright circle of moon above. Slowly, everything's beginning to grow, and soon it will all be left for me to take care of.

I could water and nurture them, care for these living things despite how careless I've been with the ones I love. This could be the one thing I don't fuck up. Everything else good I've tried to do has ended up a complete disaster. Maybe this is how my dad feels too—that loving these plants and watching them grow is the one thing he can't completely screw up. He ruined his marriage, he's been a half-assed dad, but this garden is something he can care for with all his heart, leaving us with something alive and beautiful to remember him by.

But who am I kidding? Who is he kidding? Life just doesn't work like that, and I know myself; it will all come to a ruin once he leaves us again. The garden isn't a gift but a burden.

Right now I hate this fucking garden. I hate the wet stink of the soil and how delicate and fragile and green everything looks. And I hate that I'm unable to speak my truth when it matters most and that I didn't have the courage to run after Yasaman when that was clearly what she wanted. I get down on my knees and start crawling around the garden, pulling everything out by the roots. I find pleasure in the tearing sound—in my power to destroy something so easily. I yank the flowers out. I dig hard with my nails and pull the tomatoes out from deep down. I'm clawing at the leaves, the soil, the rosemary, the mint, anything I can get my hands on. There's dirt on my legs, on my neck, in my hair. I pound on the ground again and again, as if waiting for the earth to fight back.

I tear up the thick vines, stomp on the tiny tomatoes with my heels, rip up the little basil seedlings, like I'm finally fighting back. My whole dress is covered in dirt, and I'm throwing everything around like I've completely lost my shit, but I don't care anymore because life is a fucking mess, and our family is a fucking mess, and I don't want my dad thinking he can leave this place without that being known. I ruin his garden—*our* garden, *our* paradise—because it's the only thing left that I can get my hands on.

I'm a dirty mess when I walk inside. I'm grabbing a glass of water in the kitchen when I hear the door open, and the lights turn on suddenly. I walk toward the door and see Babak standing there, a bag of greasy Jack in the Box in his hands.

"Hey," he says.

"Hey," I say. I know it's coming—him telling me I look crazy, disheveled, a fucking mess.

"You want some?" he asks, extending his bag out toward me with one hand.

I nod yes and immediately start crying. Babak walks me to the couch, puts his arm around me, and lets me cry into his shoulder.

"Dude, it's going to be okay," he says, munching on some curly fries while he comforts me. I grab one from him, and he hands me the container of ranch because he knows that's my go-to dipping sauce.

"Why are you being so nice to me? Why aren't you at the stupid hotel with Samantha?" I say through my tears.

"I was kind of over it. Sam was up Brianna's ass the whole night, and she kept bugging me to find a dude for Brianna to hook up with. It just got annoying. Having a girlfriend kind of sucks sometimes," he says. I burst into more tears and stuff my face with more fries.

"You're gonna be fine, Rana. Just chill out. Breathe," he says.

"You don't even know why I'm crying."

"I know—but you're about to graduate, and you got into your dream school. Your life is about to begin, Rana. Fuck all this high school bullshit. Whoever talked shit about you or whatever Naz did to piss you off, it doesn't matter because—"

"I'm a lesbian," I blurt.

He laughs a little, but when I don't say anything else, he turns to face me. I keep eating, letting my curly fries drown in the ranch before I pop them in my mouth.

"You're serious?" he asks. I nod yes but still don't look at him. The look on his face will tell me so many things, things I don't think I can handle right now, things that might mean he'll never look at me the same way or that he'll somehow use this against me. "Dude, why didn't you say something?" he says. His tone isn't accusatory. It's inviting an answer in.

I look up and see the boy who used to play ball with me, the boy who I'd wrap my arms around when our parents were fighting and we'd eavesdrop on them through the wall in my room. I see a boy who misses having a real father too and who also lost a grandfather—a boy who, like me, never learned how to say, *This fucking sucks and I don't know what to do with all the suckiness.*

"I guess I was embarrassed. They think you're so perfect. You could never do wrong in their eyes, and I'm going to be the child who ruined their lives forever."

Babak just shakes his head at me.

I look through the rest of his bag. I open a box of tacos, take one for myself, and hand him one. "But I'm still me."

"I can't believe I didn't know or, like, I couldn't tell or whatever. I thought you were into Louie's brother. You're always sneaking off to get high with him."

"I mean, we've hooked up, but it never felt right," I say, opening a packet of hot sauce with my teeth. It feels so good to say all this out loud. I load some hot sauce onto my taco and hand the rest to Babak, and for once indulge without feeling guilty or like Babak's going to make some stupid comment.

"Wow," he says.

"If you tell Mom or Dad, I will fucking murder you."

"I won't say anything, I swear. But . . . you have to tell them, Rana," he says as he pulls out more things from the grease bag—a chicken sandwich, regular fries, onion rings, a burger.

"I don't know how," I say, and he doesn't have an answer for me because we're in uncharted territory. There's no road map for this, no one to tell me how to do it. "Did you order everything off the menu?" I ask him.

"I knew you'd be home and want to eat all my food. Just wanted to make sure we'd have enough," he says.

I laugh a little. It's like Babak has been possessed by douche bag demons the past few years, and tonight he's finally turning into a human again—a human who seems to be surprisingly accepting of my truth.

"What the hell happened, by the way? What's up with the dirt?"

"Oh, I just destroyed Baba's garden with my bare hands," I say, and we both laugh so hard, there are tears in our eyes. I forgot what it was like to have a brother, someone on your side, someone to laugh with, someone who wants to make sure you always have enough.

29.

I pull the covers off to find myself still in my dirty
dress. So it wasn't all just a bad dream. I contemplate staying in
bed forever but get up and take a shower instead.

Downstairs my mom is making breakfast and my dad's sitting
at the table, drinking tea and staring down at the table in silence.
Babak is quietly munching on cereal. I pour myself a bowl, and
my mom doesn't say anything, but just gives me this worried look.
The four of us sit around the table in silence, and I'm not really
sure what to say to my dad. It's obvious he's seen the garden, but
he probably thinks it was a raccoon or coyote or something. I
could go along with that—but I decide to be honest, at least, about
this one thing.

"It was me. I did it."

Babak raises his eyebrows, clearly impressed. My mom passes
me a look of surprise, and the veins in my dad's forehead suddenly
emerge.

"Chi dari migi? Why did you do this to me?"

It's clear I've hit a real nerve; I've never heard him sound so confused, lost. He's not even yelling, which I can tell surprises Babak.

I don't know what to say. It's too late in our lives for me to tell him I needed him to stay because I can't do this all on my own. And I don't know how to say my heart feels broken or that I love girls in a way he'll ever understand.

"I don't know. I guess I wanted to hurt you, and destroying the garden felt like the easiest way," I say.

"Saket! Silence!" my dad snaps, and my whole body jolts at the sound of this thunder—now that's more like it.

Babak surprises me by speaking up and saying, "It's not the end of the world. It's just a stupid garden. You should be proud of her, not always yelling at her like a fucking dictator."

"The garden is not—"

"Oh my God. Fuck the garden!" I say, so loud I surprise even myself. "My best friend died last year. If you were actually here and an actual part of my life, you would know that. I loved him, and he's not here anymore, and it still fucking hurts! And last night was really shitty for too many reasons to list. So ya, I couldn't care less about your garden right now," I yell in a roar that comes from deep down.

"Rana Joon, calm down," my mom says, and puts one hand on mine, but I pull away.

I'm tempted to bring her drama into this, to put her actions under the microscope to take the attention off me, but I stop myself. I turn my focus back to my dad, who looks ill-equipped to handle my outburst. I've never talked to him like this. But there's no going back now. I've already dug myself a hole I can't possibly get out of, so why shouldn't I keep going?

"You can't just come here once a year and expect us to love

you and respect you like you're our full-time dad. It's not good enough for us, and it's not good enough for *her*. And if you weren't such an asshole, maybe you'd know all this and I wouldn't have to explain it to you."

"You two have become selfish American teenagers!" He slams his fist onto the table like he's trying to reclaim his own sense of power, and the force feels almost worse than a slap. "You and your brother have no value for anything anymore. This summer, you are both not to leave this house. You will stay home and help your mom around the house and do exactly what she says. That's it. You take your finals, you go to your graduation, but no parties, no friends, no nothing. That's it," my dad says.

"Okay, great. That solves everything, then," Babak says.

"Rana Joon, your father deserves your respect. He has done so much for you," my mom says, back to being the ever-dutiful Persian wife. It's like the woman smoking a cigarette and casually talking about having an affair never existed. I don't know her anymore—and I realize that scares me more than my dad's anger.

"I have a life and my own problems, and I can't just sit here and pretend like I can be whoever you want me to be. I'm a fucking human being. I'm not your puppet," I say.

"Eh, respect your mother," my dad says, suddenly protective of her. At this point, there's nothing left to say, so I storm off to my room. My dad yells at me to come back, that I need to fix this or else, but I yell at him to leave me alone and slam my door and pray to God they don't come knocking.

But of course, my mom knocks on my door every hour to tell me I should eat something, and that it's okay if I come out of my room.

I still have no appetite, but I do enjoy listening to my mom beg me to eat.

I don't respond at first, but after a few rounds of knocking and begging, I call to her, "I'm fine." And I'm actually being truthful. Even though things are messy as fuck, saying those things to my dad made me feel so alive.

My mom opens the door a crack and watches me as I edit my "I Am From" poem for Mrs. Mogly's class. "What are you writing?" she asks.

"Nothing," I say.

"Don't be like this, Rana Joon. Your father leaves soon. I know he was harsh with you, but he loves you."

"I can't believe you're still defending him. You're having a fucking affair, and you're still on his side?"

"I made French fries for you. I'll leave them here," she says, putting them on my desk with tears in her eyes and closing the door behind her.

The French fries taste better than they smell, and they smell really good. They're cut thick from fresh potatoes and fried in a huge pan of oil, just like how my mom's been making them since we were kids. It's wild how food has this power to transport you to another place, another time, when things were less complicated, and you knew you could rely on your mom making her fries the same way each time, and everything felt stable and permanent. And I think maybe this is my problem with food—I'm always trying to return to the past, to go back to that other place where I didn't feel so lost, where I wasn't yet aware of how complicated it was to be different.

The French fries are never for me anymore. But this time they're all mine.

I decide that these French fries aren't the transporting kind, but the forgetting kind that will help me erase all memory—and it's true that while I eat them, I can imagine I didn't ruin my dad's garden, and I didn't miss my chance with Yasaman, or lose my best friend and my grandfather, or disappoint my parents, or keep lying to the whole world about who I want to love. The French fries make all of that disappear.

I sit in my room and watch myself watching the French fries. I watch myself eating the French fries. I watch myself examining each one as if it's a new lover I've yet to know. I watch myself almost kiss a fry. I watch myself pour a small circle of ketchup on each one and then take careful bites because it's common knowledge that a lady eats French fries civilly. I watch myself eat half the plate and almost stop because I can't take anymore, and then I watch myself pour more ketchup and continue the ritual, and it's so obvious no one has ever loved fries as much as I do in this moment. No one has wanted to forget something so much as I do in this moment.

It doesn't matter what my mom will say when she walks in and sees they're all gone. I'll tell her the truth—that I was hungry and I fucking love French fries—but not that other truth, never the truth beneath the truth, never that I'm gay, because I know it would break her.

My mom knocks again, and I tell her to come in. She doesn't say anything, but I see her eyeing the plate.

"Yes, I ate them all. You think I'm disgusting, don't you?" I ask her. "Just say it. You want me to be skinny like you so I can find a decent boyfriend and you can marry me off—but what if I don't want those things? What if those things won't make me happy?" I say.

She sits next to me and wraps her arms around me. My mom's arms feel safe right now, like we're suddenly back in a place where her main concern is to protect me and she's not so worried about the outside world. She looks me in the eyes and says, "It's not my place to tell you what to eat all the time. It's not fair to you. I've been trying to control you because my own life is falling apart, and that's not right."

At this, I open my mouth to tell her the truth, the whole truth, but the words are stuck like a sharp blade in my throat.

"I don't like seeing you like this. You're not happy," she says.

"Neither are you. You can't keep lying," I say—to her but also to myself.

"You're right. We can't just change who we are when your dad is here," she says, and she squeezes me tight, the truth emerging like one of those ridiculously beautiful weeds in the garden, so sharp that if you touch one, it'll make you bleed.

When my mom leaves, I try to get back to editing my poem, but it feels impossible. So I decide to try meditating again. I close my eyes and sit in uncomfortable quiet, immersed in the messiness of my own thoughts. I try to watch them move through me like clouds, not getting attached to any of them; to breathe deep, tune in, stop fucking running for once. I still don't know if I'm meditating right, but I get lost in the nothingness.

I'm not sure how much time passes. When I open my eyes, I immediately reach for Louie's notebook and open it up—for some inspiration, for comfort, for advice? I'm not really sure why.

I see another page with a folded-down corner and flip to it. The piece on it is all about listening to and following your inner voice.

Intuition is God speaking to you.
Ignore the noise, the chaos too.
Follow your heart before it's broken in two.
Life isn't waiting to let you through—
Whatever it is can't wait for tomorrow.
You can't loan your love;
It ain't something to borrow.

When I flip past that piece, toward the end of the notebook, I see a good chunk of tattered paper stuck in the spirals, like several pages have been removed, and it's impossible to know if it was Louie who ripped them out or somebody else.

30.

Tony opens the door when I ring the bell. He's sweaty, like he's been working out.

"You look like shit," he says, because I'm in my pj's and still pretty out of it, and my hair is a big pouf ball after showering in the morning and skipping on products or the flat iron.

"I feel worse than I look," I say.

"So prom sucked, I take it?" he says.

"That's one way of putting it," I say. I follow him into the house and sit down on the white leather couch in the living room. I'm glad he let me in, at least, because I need to talk to him, but it feels weird being here again after the fight we had a couple weeks ago—and after everything that's been going on with Yasaman that Tony has no idea about.

"You wanna smoke?" he asks me.

"I'm good," I say.

He sits down next to me, lights up, and starts smoking right in the living room because he couldn't give a shit if his mom smells it when she walks in later. Then I pull Louie's notebook out from my bag and place it on his lap.

"What the fuck? Where did you get that from?" he asks.

"I took it from his room. I'm sorry."

"You've lost your damn mind."

"Please don't be pissed. I just missed his voice," I say. "I wanted to feel him again, maybe even understand him in a way I couldn't when he was alive."

"And what did you find, Sherlock?" he asks. He seems pretty calm, so I decide to go ahead and ask him the question I came here with.

"Why did you rip the back pages out?" I ask him.

Tony starts coughing on the weed as if he were an amateur. He reaches down and chugs from his water bottle that's sitting on the floor. Then he says, "I've never touched that thing. If you remember, I wasn't that into what Louie had to say. He probably got insecure or something and ripped those pages out himself."

"Louie was an edit-as-he-went, perfect, crisp-black-ink-over-Wite-Out type of guy," I say. "He wouldn't just rip out pages if he didn't like what he wrote."

"You know, it's possible that he wasn't as perfect as you remember him to be," Tony says, but his voice goes up, and he suddenly looks wide-eyed and paranoid.

"What are you protecting?" I ask. "You guys weren't exactly best friends. Either he devoted the last ten pages of his notebook to bashing you and you couldn't handle it, or there was something on those pages you didn't want anyone to see."

"Are you serious?" he says. "Why are you so obsessed with this? Just drop it, Rana. Get a fucking life already."

"You know denial is the first stage of grief," I say.

"What? You a therapist now or something?"

"No, but I think you're stuck there. I think you've been stuck in denial from day one, and you think you're safe there because you don't have to actually feel anything. Fuck, he was your brother, Tony. How come you just want to forget him?"

There's a moment where it's like I'm getting through to him, like he might soften and open up his rock-hard heart and tell me something real, but the moment passes in a split second. He throws Louie's notebook so hard at the wall, he hits a framed photograph of him and Louie and their mom. It falls to the ground and the glass shatters, but it feels like something deeper has come undone.

In my room, I play *All Eyez on Me* on repeat. I'm too angry to cry. If Louie was hiding things from me, and my mom's been secretly having an affair, and I've been keeping my truth from most everyone, then what the fuck are we all even doing? I want nothing more than to call Yasaman, but what the hell would I even say? I call Naz instead.

"Dude, I'm so hungover," Naz says. "And this fucking onion breath won't go away. Did we eat In-N-Out? I'm pretty sure you threw up, right? And what the fuck happened with Yasaman?"

"I don't want to talk about it," I say through sudden tears.

"Shit, Rana. I'm sorry. I was so caught up with Marcus."

"It's not your fault. I'm the dumbass."

"You're not a dumbass. You're amazing in every possible way. You're my Persian queen."

"H-How are you always so confident?" I ask her, stammering as my snot drips. I turn on my side and curl into fetal position.

"I guess I spent all of middle school feeling like a tiny speck, like the weird girl who wears this thing over her hair, like, totally and completely unseen, and once high school hit, I decided I wasn't going to let anyone else dictate how my life was going to flow. That shit has to come from within, Rana. *You* have to create it."

"Are you hiding anything from me? If you have secrets, I need to know them, Naz. All the people I love have just ended up feeling like strangers. But I won't let it happen with you."

"Let me see. Nope, nothing really. I tell you pretty much everything about me, except, maybe, how often I take a shit," she says.

We say bye through our laughter and hang up, but before we do, she says, "You create your life, Rana. Don't ever forget that."

I grab my notebook from the foot of my bed and open it up. I reread my "I Am From" poem a few times—this is me and everything I know to be true. This is what Louie was pushing me toward: this release, this opening up, this revelation. It's not even about a promise anymore or what Coach Lock thinks will win; it's about true and deliberate freedom. It's about being the creator of my life and not a fucking bystander.

I close the notebook, press it against my chest, and the tears start flowing. I decide that there is nothing left but to do my own poem for the battle.

31.

On Monday morning, I'm dreading going to school— not only because it's finals week and I've barely studied, but also because I don't want to see Yasaman or Ramptin and be reminded of the mess that prom turned out to be.

I pray to God that Ramptin doesn't show up to Spanish, but when I walk in, he's already in his seat right behind me. I expect him to yell something stupid about us making out or how I have a lesbo girlfriend and make a big scene, but then I remember he's way more subtle and manipulative than that.

While Señor Mariani passes out the Scantrons for our final exam, Ramptin whispers in my ear, "You still dreaming about our make-out session or what?"

His hot breath is on my neck, and I want to fucking scream. I ignore him and try to fill in the lines with my name, the date, and the period.

"I didn't know Rana the Frog would go for a redhead. Just doesn't feel like your style," Ramptin says, a little more loudly. I shush him aggressively, hoping to get the teacher's attention, but

Señor Mariani just passes me a look like I'm the one who needs to be quiet.

I'm not even on question two when this asshole pipes up again.

"Is she all red down there too? I bet you she is. Why don't the three of us get together after school, and you can show me how you like to get down?"

My mind flashes back to that moment on the dance floor at prom, that split second when I had a chance to say or do something and I didn't—that instant when speaking up mattered, and I chose to stay silent.

In just one moment, everything can change. You can lose your best friend, you can quit the team, you can choose to be a coward instead of standing up for the person you care about. But in that same split second, things can change for the better, too. You can meet a girl who's infatuated with life and art and won't stop hiccupping, or one of the most loving people you will ever know could invite you to a Tupac concert, or you can finish a pint of ice cream with your grandfather as his mouth unravels a poem, or the first line of the greatest poem you will ever write can pop into your head.

I turn around, lift my body up out of my seat a little, and lean toward Ramptin like I'm going to kiss him again—but instead I say, "Ya, I'm a lesbian. So what?"

I try to whisper, but it comes out pretty aggressively, and I watch Ramptin jump in his chair like I've punched him. He looks around to see if anyone else has heard. I think we both expect more people to care, but most are too focused on the test or just shushing us for being annoying. The kid next to us passes us a dirty look but doesn't say anything. I watch Ramptin's face as he tries to process my truth—as he moves from anger to humiliation to wanting to laugh at me. Meanwhile, I'm getting the same rush I felt when I read Yasaman my poem—the power of my voice to be a vessel for truth, and not just something hibernating deep inside my body.

Ramptin does end up laughing, sounding a little hysterical, and then he gets up and walks toward the front of the room, and I'm thinking, holy shit, he's going to stand up there and announce it for the whole class to hear. It's okay though because I'm ready for it. Let him tell everyone. I refuse to be silent this time. But instead he just goes to the sharpener attached to the wall and spins it around and around and around, making a loud, obnoxious noise. Everyone is telling him to stop, to be quiet, and he just keeps going and going like he's hypnotized, until Señor Mariani has to yell at him, and only then does he finally stop.

My whole body is still shaking as I head down the halls, looking for Yasaman. Telling Naz or Babak was one thing, but I feel completely different after Ramptin. Fear has no place in my body. There's a buzzing throughout, an aliveness I've never felt before. I need to find Yasaman now. I need to apologize to her, tell her what just happened, tell her about deciding to do my own piece for the battle. She's not at her locker or in the bathroom or in her art class or in the cafeteria. The warning bell rings, and I walk outside to see if maybe she's coming back from going off campus for lunch—and there she is with Rain, with a Starbucks cup in hand.

I run up to her. "Hey, can I talk to you?" I ask, interrupting their conversation.

Rain seems more annoyed with me than Yasaman, who nods, gives Rain a hug, and says she'll catch up with her later. She sips on her drink and waits.

I take a deep breath and then let it all out in a rush. "I just want to apologize for everything that went down. I've always had a huge crush on Brianna—she's really the only girl I ever liked before you, and she stopped being friends with me after I tried to kiss her, and we never even talked about it—so seeing you with her just did something to me. You didn't deserve any of that. I was too afraid, and you were just trying to push me to be better and more honest with myself, and I couldn't bring myself to do it. But I'm ready now. You won't believe the shit that went down with Ramptin in Spanish class. I told him, 'Ya, I'm a lesbian, and so what?' It was fucking amazing."

Instead of the joy and congratulations I expected, Yasaman just shakes her head slightly and says, "I'm really happy for you, Rana, but that kid is the definition of a douche bag. I don't get why you care so much what he thinks."

"It wasn't just him. I told Babak and Naz too. I told you, I'm ready." I reach out for her hand, but her arm stays down at her side.

"I'm happy for you. Anyway, we're cool or whatever. I shouldn't have expected you to come out to the whole school right after we kissed. You were nervous from the beginning, and I was pushing it. My bad. I should've given you more space," she says.

Space? No. I don't want space. I want the opposite of space.

She chucks her drink in the garbage behind me. In the movie version, this is where we passionately embrace and kiss each other, but at least on her end, the spark feels totally gone.

"That's it?"

"I don't know what else you want from me," Yasaman says. "I just can't get the image of you making out with that douche bag out of my head." The final bell rings, and security starts chasing people down to send them to the office for being tardy. "I think I need some time."

She walks away from me and doesn't look back.

32.

On my walk home, it's so hot, my jeans are stuck to
me, and I feel totally out of it. The excitement of putting Ramptin
in his place has faded into a numbness that feels worse than anger.
I hear someone calling my name and see Tony standing outside of
his house, wearing nothing but Adidas shorts and his tattoos. It's
as if he's been waiting for me to walk by.

Tony keeps calling me, and I keep walking. I'm not in the
mood for him right now.

I hear him running behind me to catch up. "Hey, hey, hold up."

"What?" I snap, turning around.

"Listen, I'm not trying to get in your way. I just wanted to
give this to you," he says, and hands me a stack of lined paper—
the missing pages from Louie's notebook. I can tell right away
by the ripped edges. I snatch the pages from his hands, hungry
to hold a new piece of Louie, especially after what went down
with Yasaman. But as I look through them, I don't recognize
the handwriting—it's messy, unclear, like scribbles or notes in

anticipation of a final draft. It looks nothing like the rest of the notebook.

"I don't understand," I say.

"Just read it," Tony says, and I do my best. What follows aren't rhymes. The writing on this page is more like a manic stream of consciousness, with no cohesion or purpose to the words other than to get thought onto paper:

> *Up north the trees look different. Dad owes me.*
> *Dad left us for love, so he must know a thing or*
> *two about it. How many different kinds of love*
> *are there? Mom taught me how to hate him.*
>
> *Tony says I'm an idiot for going. He's a*
> *hoarder of life. He sits on his ass all day, does*
> *nothing. Tony, Tony, Tony equals nothing,*
> *nothing, nothing. He will never love you. He*
> *will never help you. Help you help me. Who's*
> *even listening anymore? Anyone out there?*
> *Fuckkkkkkk no.*
>
> *Dad didn't know I was coming. Wanted it*
> *to be a surprise. Wanted him to be proud of me.*
> *Wanted Mom to be wrong. He's not the asshole.*
> *He said I was acting crazy. But the trees are so*
> *different here. They're so beautiful, and the air*
> *is so different. I can breathe here. I already have*
> *enough responsibility, he said. Two other kids.*
> *Two new kids. A new life, a new wife, a new car.*
> *Who knew so many new things could be so nice?*
> *This will swallow me whole. I don't know*

*you anymore. Who are you? Where did you come
from? Who made you, you? What's the point to
all of this when we are all spirit anyway? Maybe
our bodies are just holding us down.*

"This doesn't sound like him at all," I say.

"I know."

"This can't be right. Maybe . . . maybe he was trying out a new voice, a character or something. This isn't him, this isn't—"

"Shit, Rana, this *is him*. The truth is he went to see my pops. And when he was gone, I found his meds in the trash. Not a good combo. And as I predicted, the bastard slammed the door in his face. That type of rejection stings. Especially for a sensitive type like Louie—*especially* when he was off his meds. We got in a huge fight when he got back. I told him he couldn't just stop taking them, that he needed them, and that really pissed him off. I told him it was a dumbass move going to see our dad; I rubbed that shit in his face. That day he tried to knock me out. The first time in our whole lives, he hit me. And later that day, he crashed," Tony says.

The black eye Tony had at Louie's funeral. Louie put it there.

"This whole year I've been thinking, 'What if I'd done more to stop him from going? What if I'd told my mom about the meds first? What if I just listened instead of putting him down?'" Tony says.

His voice is so soft, insecure, that it doesn't fit his tough exterior at all. I hear something slam and look up the street and can see my dad standing there in the distance, hovering over our garbage cans. He'd never approve of me associating with a guy like Tony—tatted, buff, and half-Black—and I expect him to yell for me to come home now, that my mom needs me and there's no time to waste. He just stands there, though, and doesn't move.

"Is that your dad?" Tony asks.

"Ya, I don't know what he's doing."

"This shit is tripping me out. He's just staring at us. Say something to him," Tony insists. So I wave, and after a moment, my dad just goes inside.

"Listen, I totally get why you'd feel responsible, but you can't blame yourself," I say. "If he was off his meds . . ." I don't even know how to finish that thought, so I move on. "Why keep all this a secret for so long? Why rip out those pages?"

"I just didn't want things getting messy, you feel me? Something was up with him for sure, and I didn't want my mom to think he'd done anything intentionally. Maybe I wanted to protect his ass for once. Protect him from himself."

And I finally say what I never wanted to question out loud. "Do you think he wanted to die?"

Tony sighs. "I have no idea, Rana. Maybe?"

I nod at this, and the tears come. Tony comes close to hug me—not the kind of hug that will lead to anything more than us being friends, but the kind that feels safe and constant.

As it turns out, there are multiple layers to any human being, and just because you're unaware of a few of those layers doesn't mean you can't truly know a person. Louie was my best friend, but he was also many other things to many other people, and just because he hid things from me didn't mean he loved me any less. If anyone can understand this, it's me. Maybe Louie just needed me to see his Zen'd out, mystical side—the layer that was trying to feel centered and at peace with life, the layer he believed would inspire me to feel the same, the layer that would save him from himself.

"You guys weren't all that different from each other, you know?" I say to Tony. "I mean, your tats and life philosophies were different, and your taste in girls, probably, but deep down I think you both have the same heart."

"I can't believe it's going to be a year next week," he says.

"Me neither." I hadn't forgotten. The anniversary was always there, sitting in the back of my mind. It had been front and center for so long, but with everything happening, it had slowly started to drift away. I guess that's the thing—as much as I didn't want the circle of this year to end, life was always happening and moving me forward. Louie wasn't here anymore, but he would never be forgotten. And I was going to make sure of that.

"Did Louie ever mention the Way of the Wu to you?" I ask Tony.

"Ya, he talked about that shit all the time, but he never had the balls to actually do it."

"Well, I have the balls," I say, and Tony looks me up and down like he's seeing me for the first time.

"No shit," he says.

"I'm going to do it for Louie, and your ass is going to be there to witness it," I say, because for this moment I want to be sure the room will be filled with important people—familiar faces, people who matter to me and can learn this layer of me and maybe even understand it. Sometimes it feels safe to keep a secret until it starts rotting inside you, like a tooth that no longer belongs, until the only choice you have is to pull that motherfucker out.

"Louie was lucky to know you. Like, you really fucking care, Rana. That shit is rare. I'm sure you're gonna do him proud. And soon you'll be all sophisticated and in college and shit and forget all about us little people," he says. We both start cracking up.

"I've actually been dreading this year being over. Like, it would mean time is up on missing him or something."

"Naw, we're going to miss that kid forever," Tony says.

"Forever and ever," I say. We hug again.

"I should probably go. I think my dad's pretty pissed at me," I say.

"Ya, I actually have to get back too—I'm working on a letter to Principal Denado about starting up again next year. I know Louie would never get over me not graduating."

Now it's my turn to look impressed. Tony just smiles and walks back toward his house, and for a moment, I just watch him. It feels like I'm watching Louie—kind, sweet, hopeful, loving, wise Louie. Not the complete him, because he'd never walk around without a shirt on, but a pretty big chunk of who he was.

33.

When I get home, it sounds like no one's here, and I'm thinking maybe my dad didn't feel like dealing with me and just went upstairs to nap. I peek outside from the kitchen and see him standing in the middle of the garden (obviously, pants off). He's assessing the damage and gathering up everything I've ruined, and even though I know he's kind of an asshole, I can't help but feel bad for him. Not necessarily because my mom's been cheating on him, but because he's so guarded and lonely and his tongue has no way of speaking about what's really going on inside.

I spend the rest of the day eating a bag of Cheetos I snuck into my room and replaying my conversation with Tony in my mind. Louie had been secretly suffering, and I hadn't seen it. But that wasn't my fault. I hadn't been a shitty friend, and Tony wasn't a half-assed brother. This is just a fucked-up situation with no saviors or martyrs. We both just have to deal with the fact that someone we really, really love is gone.

I grab the picture of my grandfather when he was a young man in Paris. I remember what he said when I asked him once if he missed my grandmother. She had died before I was born, and he had never really been with anyone since. His words come alive suddenly, like my ears are popping from too much pressure and I'm finally able to hear him again. *Yes, of course I miss her every single day, but I can't just sit here and feel sorry for myself. I have to live—for her and for me. That's what she would want, for me to be more alive.*

I lick the orange powder off my fingers and practice my poem, the one I wrote with my own sweaty hand, over and over again until each line becomes a limb, an eyelash, a curl on my head.

I have no idea how much time has passed when my mom walks in and tells me dinner is almost ready.

"I have a lot to do. Can I just eat later?" I say. She looks surprised, I think, because I've never passed on food, and I can smell the lamb shank she's been roasting the past few hours. But I need to keep practicing, and nothing can get in my way.

"Your dad is leaving soon, Rana Joon. He expects—" she starts to say, but then catches herself. "Okay. That's fine. I'll just tell him you're studying for your finals." She's about to leave but sits down on my bed instead.

"What are you writing? It is a big secret or something?"

"Just poems," I say.

"Read me one," she says. The last thing I want to do right now is read my mom a poem, but she seems so genuinely interested. "Your grandfather, may his spirit be happy, was such a good poet. He would read me his poems when I was a little girl. You must get your gift from him," she says.

"You don't even know if they're any good," I say. She smiles, and some of her lipstick has smudged on her teeth. It's a small flaw and one that could easily be fixed, but it makes her feel more human to me. I flip away from the "I Am From" poem and pick another one out of my notebook to read to her, about my grandfather and our midnight poetry sessions:

It's midnight on a Tuesday and I'm thirteen.
We're eating Rocky Road ice cream and
You spit out the nuts
And ask me what marshmallows actually are,
Tell me poetry is in my blood,
And I don't believe you quite yet.
You say sometimes life is beautiful
And sometimes life is hard.
We don't get to choose what happens when,
But the real secret is that all of it is magic,
And I don't believe you quite yet.
You tell me love is the most beautiful feeling,
That the heart is the master,
That there is no other way,
And I don't believe you quite yet.
We've finished the whole pint
And you pour us each a glass of water—
To erase our sins, you say—
and then wish me the sweetest of dreams.

I expect her to tell me it's good, that she had no idea I could actually write, and then maybe question me about whether it's true—did I sneak ice cream with my grandfather in the middle of the night? But instead she's crying and can't get any words out.

"Mom? What is it? I'm sorry if I upset you—"

"No, no. It's just so good, Rana Joon. I had no idea you would do this with him," she says through her sobs. I give her a hug. "I really miss him. It hurts too much to think about it," she says, and I let her cry and snot all over me, giving her the space to finally come undone.

The next morning, I walk into Coach's office unannounced. All coaches have to help admin with graduation prep since they're not teaching actual classes, so he has a pile of papers on his desk and looks stressed when I walk in, but he smiles when he sees me.

"Well, if it isn't my favorite poet. I thought we were practicing after school?"

"We are. But I couldn't wait, Coach. I've decided to do my own piece," I say, and I still feel good about it even though my palms start sweating when I say it.

Coach drops his pen and smiles. "You're my hero. Honestly. I know that shit is hard for you, and you're going for it. Let me hear it!"

"Now? You're busy. I'll just . . ."

"I'm good. Graduation can wait," he says, and he leans back in his chair and looks at me expectantly.

I take a few breaths and open up the center of me, let the words rush out, my story come alive. I'm transported above place and time and exist only on the tip of each word. I've never felt so alive—and by the look in Coach's eyes when I'm done, and the tears that have started to flow, I know he felt it too.

That night, I wait for everyone to fall asleep so I can practice my poem in front of the mirror in my room. I let the energy move from my chest into my throat, and I sense the meaning of each word inside my body. I let myself pause where it feels natural, slow down to build momentum, and speed up when the emotion feels rawer and urgent, I let the repetition create a rhythm that expands way beyond the space of my room—beyond my house, my street, my city, as far out into the universe as it can go. I let my body dance and move with the poem and make sure to take my time at the end, to look into my own eyes as if I'm the audience I'm so desperate to connect with.

I stay up pretty late doing this, barely get any sleep, and am up with the sun. I take a shower and slick my hair back in a ponytail.

I take my cup of coffee outside, expecting to be alone, but my dad's sitting in a white plastic chair, steaming chai in one hand. I almost think he's an intruder for a second because he's fully dressed—pants on and everything—but no, it's him. I haven't really seen my destruction of the garden in daylight until now, and the guilt rises quickly as I sit down in the empty chair next to him. It's six thirty a.m. and the air is wet and cool, but the sun's out and the potential for intense heat is already brewing. My dad doesn't look at me and takes long, loud sips of his tea. Unsurprisingly, he's been avoiding me since I destroyed his garden and basically told him to go fuck himself. I'm waiting for him to call me irresponsible, to lecture me on how I need to be more focused in life, to tell me I shouldn't hang out with that Black kid down the street, and I'm ready to get defensive or scream or cry.

He says, "A garden is like paradise on earth. Every memory I have of my father before he died is in our garden. Us Iranians, we take our gardens very seriously. Your whole life can be a complete disaster, you can be poor and lost, but if your garden is beautiful and growing nicely, you can feel like a king. A garden is full of hope, you understand?" My dad has never sounded this poetic before, and he also never talks about his parents.

"You know, when I was a little boy, after my parents died in the fire, any insect I could get my hands on, I killed it. Flies, spiders, moths, grasshoppers. Even the butterflies, or what are those red ones with the dots?"

"Ladybugs?"

"Yes, even those. I was very happy to kill them. It felt good to be in control. But the older I got, the more I realized that killing these things would not bring my parents back. There's more power in helping things grow than destroying them."

His vulnerability, so unexpected, pierces something inside me. The man sitting across from me isn't just the father who left, isn't just the man who's been a shitty husband, but is also someone with scars that never healed, just like me. "I'm sorry I did this to the garden. I promise to fix it up over the summer," I say.

"I still think about them every single day, you know. The ones who die, they never leave us," he says, which is his way of saying, *I'm sorry about your friend.*

"I know," I say.

He takes out a string of amber beads from his pocket and moves the beads down the string one by one with his thumb. It's my grandfather's tasbih. Using it was his way of meditating—each bead, each movement of the finger a way to stay present. I haven't seen the tasbih since he died, and there are tears in my eyes because I didn't know my dad had the beads or used them or appreciated them in the same way my grandfather did.

"So, you chose English as your major, huh?"

"How do you know that?"

"Your mother says you're writing all the time. I'm assuming this is something you really love."

"Sorry to disappoint you."

"Just don't forget that us Persians are the greatest poets who ever lived," he says, and chuckles in a way I haven't seen since I was a little girl—his whole upper body shaking, like the joy can't be contained in his body.

We both sip from our drinks and stare out at the ruins of what's left—the chaos of what was starting to take root and blossom—and are silent for a moment, because it's hard to say what comes next.

"Why don't you ever ask Babak to help you with the garden?"

"Eh, that boy only thinks about himself. I know this is something he could never do," he says, and then adds after a moment, "You know that if I were always here, your mother wouldn't be very happy. You think she needs me, but she's much better without me. She's a very strong woman, like you. You will take good care of her when I'm not here." He says it not like a question, but a fact, an expectation, a promise.

34.

A week later, it's the last day of high school. I wake up, take a look at my watch: it's six ten a.m. *Louie was still alive one year ago today* is all I can think. By six p.m. he was gone, but one year ago, right now, this early in the morning, he was still breathing, still dreaming, still had a whole life ahead of him.

I get up, and before I even get dressed, I'm practicing my piece in front of the mirror, feeling the ebb and flow of breath and body. I look into my own eyes, deeper and deeper until I lose myself and then find myself again.

Ms. Murillo's final should be easy because I've done all the work, showed up for all her classes, and can write extensively on any topic she'll throw our way.

When I sit down, I see the topic for our five-paragraph final essay on the board: analyze one of the religions we learned about this semester using articles, readings, and documentaries as evidence, and also do a personal reflection at the end on how understanding this religion on a deeper level has impacted us. Done and done. I'll pick Buddhism and use the article she had us read about a monk who burned himself in protest and some Alan Watts excerpts as my evidence.

Before we start, Ms. Murillo explains the prompt and gives us a minispeech that has everyone, including her, in tears.

"I'm so proud of you guys. Life is the most beautiful, meaningful, scary ride of all, and I can't wait to see what amazing things you do. Just know that I see you and all that you're capable of, all that potential that lives inside you. I really, really see it. And no one can take that away from you." Then she hands out blank paper for us to start.

I write the date down and stare at it for a while. Ms. Murillo comes over with her flowy sundress, looking like some sort of Greek goddess, and lowers herself so we're eye to eye.

"It's okay if today sucks," she says, because unlike most everyone else in this school, Ms. Murillo remembers. "Whatever comes up, just embrace it. Try not to be too hard on yourself, Rana."

I nod in agreement, take a deep breath, and start writing.

At the start of seventh period, I run over to the library to make copies of the battle flyer, fold each one up and write a little personalized note for everyone I want to be there, and slip the notes in their lockers. Last, I drop one off in Ms. Murillo's box in the main office, and then I run to Coach Lock's office so we can practice together one last time.

"Okay, give it to me," he says. "I've got to do the graduation run-through with the rest of the coaches in half an hour." He stands up and walks around the desk so he's facing me. I know I have it down, but still, somehow when I'm face-to-face with another human preparing to spill my soul, my body tightens up, my breath held hostage, sweat rising everywhere.

"You look like you're about to have a heart attack. Shake your arms out. Take three deep breaths," he says, and we breathe in and out together. My heart settles, and I keep telling myself to use the nerves as energy. "Go for it," he says. And I do.

I let the poem explode out from inside me. I see Coach Lock, but I don't see him. I don't think about the words or what lines come next; I let them flow through me. My mouth is just an instrument with a story carved deep inside—my story, but the story of my mom and my dad and my brother and my grandfather too. It's the story of Tony and Louie, and Naz, and Ms. Murillo, and Yasaman, and really everyone who's ever felt like there was more than one side to them, like they were being pulled in so many different directions, it became easy to lose themselves.

I know right now my grandfather is listening, that he's been listening this whole time and that he's helping me create this moment, and I know Louie is too.

Coach Lock is quiet for a minute after I'm done, and he rubs his face like he's either in pain or disbelief.

"Holy shit, Rana," he says, "this is something. You've really found your voice. This is coming from somewhere way deep. You could actually win this shit," he says.

I'm so high off my own words and Coach Lock's excitement that I can't stop doing it again and again. We go over the poem a dozen more times. And every time, Coach Lock gives me feedback—tells me when to be louder, softer; when to pause completely; when to use my arms; when to scan the room.

"Remember—just own it," he says. "God blessed you with a gift, and it's up to you to let other people in on that. And respect the mic." And with that, the bell rings, and high school is over, and Coach Lock releases me out into the world with the sound of my own voice, my own power, ringing in my ears.

When I walk outside, I expect fireworks, a parade of elephants, confetti flying everywhere, but people are just high-fiving, yelling, ripping up their notebooks, and letting the pages fly free. I want this moment to be important, but I can't seem to find anyone I know amidst all the excited bodies. I go to my and Naz's usual spot at the back of the school and sit down by myself while people run around yelling, *Fuck high school!*

Two forty p.m. He was still alive. This time last year, Louie was off his meds, struggling in secret, but he was still alive. There was still a chance for him to find peace. I want to savor these final moments before the circle comes to full completion, before I have to go searching further and further in the past to find Louie.

"Aren't you supposed to be streaking through the school or something?" I look up and see Naz standing above me. She's wearing all white, and if it weren't for her almost-black lipstick, she'd look like an angel with the sunlight surrounding her. She sits down next to me.

"Probably. I feel like I should do *something*."

She holds up the flyer I left in her locker. "This feels like something," she says.

"I've been practicing like crazy, Naz. Coach Lock's been helping me."

"Well, I have no doubt you're going to kill it."

"I can't believe this shit is over. I think I'm going to actually miss it. Not all these morons but the feeling of it. You know what I mean?" I say.

"I'm just glad we had each other through all the insanity. I know you were always closer to Louie, but we got something good going on here too."

I can't help but smile. "We do. I think we're pretty dope," I tell her. And then I continue, "You know it's one year today?"

"Shit, really?"

"I miss his ass," I say.

"Well, if you didn't miss him, I'd be concerned, you know? Like, maybe you missing him so much is just equal to the love you had for him. I don't know, I'm not an expert on death or anything, but it makes sense to me. Plus, if you want to get all spiritual about it, the Prophet did say, 'People are asleep and when they die, they awake,' so maybe we're still living inside a dream, and Louie gets to experience reality. And who knows, what comes next could be way cooler than this. Like venti Frappuccinos and getting your nipples sucked all day long," she says through her laugh.

We're quiet for a moment, and I realize with all my shit, I don't even know how Naz has been doing. I missed so much with Louie—and I don't want to do the same with her. "So how are things with your dad? You still gonna be around next year, or should I start looking at flights to Afghanistan?"

Naz laughs. "Looks like I'm not getting shipped off quite yet. I've been drilling it into my dad's head, this whole idea about the Prophet and education. I even told the imam at our mosque about my situation, and he's actually pretty forward-thinking and has been talking to my dad a lot, so I'm in the clear for the next four years at least."

"That's awesome, Naz. We get to start our next chapter together. I wasn't ready to be a bridesmaid yet, so it works out pretty well for me," I say. She smacks my arm, and we both laugh.

"Did you invite Yasaman to the battle on Friday?" she asks.

"Not yet. Things are kind of weird between us." I still have her invite in my bag.

"You can't get shy now. You gotta go out with a bang," she says, and claps her hands together hard to show me exactly what she means.

35.

At graduation a couple days later, a bubble of excitement surrounds us. Everyone's screaming or pumping their fists in the air or tossing beach balls around. It's easy to get caught up in it, but I find myself searching for Yasaman. I don't see her anywhere.

Before we walk out in our assigned lines, I go to the bathroom. I stare at my reflection in the mirror. My red lips remind me of my mom's. My thick eyebrows, although nicely tweezed to give them shape, definitely come from my grandfather. My nose is average, which comes straight from my dad, but my eyes—my eyes are big and black and entirely my own. They remind me of no one I know. In the mirror, I see Brianna Asher come out of the other stall and go to the sink to wash her hands.

"Hey," I say.

She looks at me and smiles. "Hey, Rana," she says.

This should be the moment where I tell her how fucked up it was that she stopped being my friend, and how she pretty much came between me and Yasaman, and lay it all on her, but it seems like she's so oblivious to everything, and maybe I've just been really good at blowing things way out of proportion. Maybe this is the moment to finally forgive. She checks her hair in the mirror, adjusts her cap, and takes a few deep breaths like she's trying to avoid having a panic attack.

"You okay?" I ask.

"Ya. Just this stupid speech. I'm so nervous," she says. I totally forgot that she was selected to give a speech at graduation.

"You'll be fine. Just respect the mic and own it," I say.

"What?" she says. She seems more annoyed than inspired by my advice.

"Nothing. Good luck at Cal," I say.

"Ya, good luck to you too," she says, takes one last breath, and then leaves.

As she walks away from me, I realize that when it comes to Brianna Asher, and probably a lot of other people in my life, I've been seeing what I want to see—this version of her that validates the story I've been carrying around. She's been the one who fucked me over. An unreachable being. But she's just a girl my age who gets nervous before giving a speech and doesn't have everything figured out.

We have to sit in alphabetical order, so I'm not even sitting with Naz or anyone I've ever had an actual conversation with throughout the past four years. I keep trying to spot Yasaman in the crowd of almost a thousand students, but her bright red head is nowhere to be found. I'm not sure exactly what I'll say to her if I find her, but I want her there at the Way of the Wu tonight.

Brianna gets up and gives her speech. It's as boring and

generic as high school graduation speeches get. You know, stuff about being ready for the real world, whatever that means. The crowd still goes wild for it.

My row has to walk up, and I hear my name and walk onstage, and someone hands me a fake diploma, and there's a flash because they're taking staged photos of us. As my row's walking back to sit down, I hear Yasaman's name, and I turn around to see her, but there's a line of people behind me, and they yell at me to just keep going.

It's another full forty-five minutes of hearing names that I've never heard before recited, and then the ceremony is over. My parents have bought every bouquet of flowers available at Ralphs, and they hand them all over to me in one big heap, and even my dad kisses me over and over. My life is about to begin in a way theirs never got a chance to. Babak hugs me and tells me he's proud of me. My mom asks a random woman to take too many pictures of us, and I can't focus at all.

"Look at me," the woman with her obnoxiously big sun hat says. "Over here. Smile!" she says.

I look at her and force a smile. My eyes go back to the crowd. Bod and his parents find us and give me more flowers. My dad insists everyone come over to our place.

"We can order pizza. I haven't had a good slice of pizza in years," my dad says.

"That's a great idea," Bod's dad says. "I will eat anything with melted cheese on it."

"This husband of mine always thinks with his stomach," Bod's mom says, and gives him a kiss like she means it, and Bod looks grossed out.

It's so crowded I can't find Naz, which is fine because I know I'll see her later tonight at the battle. But I never got Yasaman her invite, and I'll never be able to find her in this chaos.

We're walking to our car, and I look like one of the people trying to sell flowers on the corner before the ceremony. In the parking lot, I spot Yasaman putting her own flowers in her trunk while her mom gets into the car. I run toward her without saying a word to my parents.

"Hey," I say, out of breath. She has orange lips and is wearing a yellow sundress and huge silver hoops, her curls draped around her.

"Hey," she says, slamming the trunk shut. She looks a bit startled, and she takes a few steps back from me. I drop all the flowers onto the ground and pull out a folded-up flyer for her I'd stuck inside my bra.

"Look, I know you said you need time, but I miss hanging out with you. The thing is, I don't actually know how to talk about my feelings or how to be straight about what's going on with me. I think it's genetic, but I'm working on it, and it would really mean a lot to me if you'd come tonight."

She opens the flyer.

"You actually doing it?"

"Ya. And I think you're going to think my piece is dope. You've taught me a lot about myself in so little time. Please come. You have to come," I say.

I can hear my mom yelling at me from the other side of the parking lot to hurry up, that everyone's waiting for me.

"I'm leaving for Mexico City tomorrow morning with my mom. We're going to see La Casa Azul. I haven't even packed yet, so I don't know . . . ," she says.

"Of course. That makes sense," I say, working really hard to hold back tears. "I just wanted to make sure you knew it was going down and that I wanted you to be there."

She looks into my eyes like it's the last time she's ever going to see me. I think she might kiss me again, she's gotten that close. "Maybe I'll come for a bit. I'll see how much I get done," she says with a smile.

I watch her walk away from me—a beautiful red force against the now-setting sun.

After dinner, my parents and Bod's parents drink tea and play Rami at the dining room table; they're telling jokes and laughing.

Meanwhile, Bod and Babak are dorking out with their comics in the TV room. I go in there, grab the comics from them, and demand their attention.

"Hey, what the hell?" Bod asks.

"You guys, I need a favor," I say. "There's a poetry competition tonight—well, it's more like a rap battle or whatever; it doesn't matter what it is, but I'm performing in it. It's kind of a big deal, and I need you guys backing me up so they'll let us go. They'll never let me go solo, but the two of you with your magical, golden penises can pretty much do no wrong in their eyes, so I need you." Getting permission from my parents to actually *go* to the competition was something I'd been putting off for way too long, and this was the best solution I could come up with.

"Sounds weird," Bod says.

"You're sitting around reading stories about wolverines and shit. You gotta live a little. Think of it as a graduation present to me," I say.

"Dude, Rana. We're on it," Babak says. I smile; Babak's on my side. It feels fucking amazing.

The three of us awkwardly interrupt our parents' card game.

"Is it okay if we go out? One of my friends is having a graduation party. Babak and Bod want to come too," I say.

"Who is this friend?" my dad interrogates.

"Ebi Joon," my mom interrupts, and in her voice it's clear that she's asking him to lay off for just one night, and his scrunched-up face turns soft, which means he's finally learning how to listen to her.

"Okay, okay. It is a special night. But no alcohol, no boys, and be back by ten," my dad says.

"Eleven is okay," my mom says. My dad gives her a dirty look, but she laughs. "Chi? What? She's not in high school anymore," she says. At that, my dad starts laughing too, though a little uncomfortably.

We kiss everyone goodbye, take pizza for the road, and hop in Bod's car. I hold my notebook to my chest while I sit in the back seat, my heart thumping against all the words living inside, waiting to be set free.

36.

The venue is small, so about seventy-five people packed inside makes it feel claustrophobic. I've watched a few local bands play here before, but I've never seen it this crowded. Predictably, the place is filled with dudes, mostly Black and Latino. There are some girlfriends who've shown up for moral support. There's no official bar or anything since it's an all-ages venue, but it's easy to spot people drinking out of flasks, and the whole place reeks of weed. I try to spot anyone we know, anyone I invited, and more specifically, Yasaman. We all look out of place, especially Bod, who looks like a Persian Steve Urkel with his cardigan and glasses on, but I don't care because I need to find Jordan so I can sign up and make sure I get to actually do this.

"I need to put my name on the list."

"Rana, are you sure about this?" Babak asks, scoping out the crowd. Bod looks scared, like he's allergic to a crowded room.

"Yes, I'm sure," I say. I leave the two of them and find Jordan setting up backstage.

"Hey."

"Wassup, Rana?" he says. He has a clipboard and a walkie-talkie and is setting up the mics and looks very official.

"Where do I put my name down?"

He hands me the clipboard, and I sign myself up for the eighth slot. "This shit goes by fast, so just stay back here until it's your turn. Cool?"

"I'm not leaving," I say. He lights up a joint and asks me if I want some, and I say I'm good because I want to have a clear head.

"Good luck. I knew you weren't no mud type of girl. You're a real lotus now," he says.

I hover by the side of the stage for a while, and my stomach turns in anxiety. My heart beats so fast, I can barely say hi when people pass me by and say what's up. I doubt any of them think I'm about to go onstage. None of them seem nervous—probably weed and alcohol helping, but also these dudes are the real deal. I might vomit. I wish I were going first and not eighth so I could get this shit over with, but I hear Coach Lock's voice in my head—*having the mic is a privilege*—and this is a privilege Louie never got to experience. Waiting isn't that big of a deal.

I'm still watching from the sides as Jordan walks onstage to get things going, and suddenly everything starts to feel real. Jordan gets the crowd amped up and explains the rules: each rapper has two minutes, and if you go over, you're automatically eliminated. He introduces the three judges, all musicians or artists, and thankfully, one of them is a girl—a poet named Tessa who runs an open mic in Sherman Oaks on Fridays. He explains the philosophy behind the Way of the Wu, a version of what we talked about that night at the party.

"Our external conditions don't define us, but it's how we evolve internally that shapes our paths. You can let the mud swallow you up, or you can rise above it. The Way of the Wu is about being responsible for yourself and your journey on this planet—fulfilling your own destiny, no matter what. Now make some motherfucking noise if you hear me!" Jordan shouts into the mic.

The crowd is into this, and I see most everyone's hands go up to form *W*'s in the air. I close my eyes and take a deep breath and try to shake the nerves out. Every guy who goes up before me looks and feels like he's at least ten years older than me. No stumbling, no insecurities; they work the crowd, left to right, move across the stage, project their voice. I'm too frazzled to try and hear what they're actually saying, and it's making me nervous watching them, so I step back and take more deep breaths.

This is for Louie, I repeat in my head. *This is for Louie. This is for Louie. This is for me. This is for me.* This becomes my mantra, something to focus on, tune in to, keep me from running out of this room and saying fuck it. And the next thing I know, I hear my name being called. The crowd cheers, and then they go silent, waiting for me to appear.

When I do walk out, I hear whispers, a few laughs. I know it's because I'm a girl, and they don't think I have it in me—also, I probably look incredibly awkward. I think I might pass out, I'm so dizzy suddenly. I'm paralyzed, and my whole body is stuck, but I hear someone aggressively whispering from the side of the stage.

"Just do you, Rana," Jordan says.

I close my eyes, take a deep breath, adjust myself so the mic is close enough, and release the words from my mouth, my throat, my chest, my heart, my soul:

I am from
A monarchy turned theocracy—
Ruby-studded crowns and lashings on bare skin
To commemorate the holiest of men.
I am from the land of poets,
From Sufis and feminists who
Used poetry as a way to love
And to let the world know they like sex and cigarettes too.
I am from the Valley heat
And protective palm trees that line streets.
I am from quiet stars who want nothing more than to listen
And a moon that lets me know I am not alone.
I am from a mother who loves me
But wishes I were different,
A once-a-year father who
Has no idea who I've become,
And a brother who
Doesn't understand what it's like to
Always be the one who can never be good enough.
I am from death and its aftermath,
From last breaths and cancer,
From burying your best friend
Even though he wanted his body burned,
Scattered in the ocean so he
Could stay in the flow.
I am Rana,
The frog,
The beautiful one.
I am from a desire
I dare not speak of,

From touching myself
But dreaming of her—
The girl with the red hair,
The girl who lit a fire up inside me—
And wanting so desperately for her to love me,
But I am too afraid of the hurt.
I am from secrets that burn holes
Like ulcers on your tongue
Until you're mute and the whole world feels like your enemy.
I am so many things to so many people
But I'm also just me,
A poet in disguise,
A shy girl more wrapped up in the fantasy
Than the reality of what it means to be alive.
Can you hear me now?
I'm alive, I'm alive!
Bless Louie's soul wherever he is,
Seventeen and gone too soon; now he's
Reading books with God
Or whirling with the dervishes—
Maybe even in this very room with us
Watching me become a better version of myself,
The only version of myself left to tell,
I am me,
Here,
I am in front of you.
I am alive.
Can you hear me now?
Can you hear me now?

About halfway through, the room faded away, and it was just me. Me and Louie. Me and my grandfather. Me and Naz and Yasaman and Tony. Me and Coach Lock. Me and my mom and Babak and my dad. All the people who got me to this moment, for better or worse, dead and alive.

When I'm done, my whole body is buzzing as I start to come to. It feels like dream and reality crashing into each other. People are clapping, hooting, and hollering. I can see *W*'s in the air, sending me the simple message—they felt it, they feel *me*. My body is fifty pounds lighter, freeing Louie through my words, through this moment he wanted so badly, but also it's me who's finally free. I get offstage, and Jordan gives me a hug.

"Damn, girl. That was a revelation. You fucking killed that," he says, and then runs onstage to introduce the person next on the list. I need air and a minute to process what just happened— how I poured my heart onto that stage, how good it felt, how I could feel Louie up there with me, how my secret is officially not a secret anymore. I head outside, and on my way, some people nod their heads in acknowledgment; fist-bumping me; high-fiving me; telling me, *Good for you*; patting me on the back with one hand while holding their blunts in the other. Some people give me the side-eye, whisper to their friends, probably talking shit, but the adrenaline rushing through my body has me so zoned in, I could care less.

I take a few deep breaths, and soon I find my people—Babak, Bod, Tony, Naz, Ms. Murillo, Coach Lock—who've all somehow found one another. Everyone seems blown away and they all give me hugs, congratulate me. I know Yasaman would've found everyone by now and would be standing here by my side with them if she'd decided to show up. My heart feels a little broken, but I still feel more alive than I have in a very long time.

Coach Lock comes in and wraps his arms around me, and then Naz is huddled in our group hug too.

I keep saying, *Thank you, thank you, thank you,* I'm not sure to who. I don't know what else to do at this point. It feels like a prayer or another poem or my soul reaching out to Louie. I don't know why he died, if he crashed on purpose or if it was a legit accident. I don't know why he stopped taking his meds, or why he only got to live for seventeen years and couldn't be here tonight to do his thing, or why I get to go to the college of my dreams and he doesn't. I'll never have those answers. But I have my words, their power, and that feels like a second chance.

Tony tells me how proud Louie would've been of me.

"I probably should've told you I was into girls, huh?"

"Don't trip, Rana. We're cool," he says, and I'm blown away by how kind—how like Louie—he really is.

Naz kisses me over and over again on my cheek.

"You're a badass, Rana. I can't believe what you just did. This is going down in the history books. I mean, you really, really didn't suck."

My brother brings his hands down in a bowing gesture. "We're not worthy. We're not worthy," he says, and then sweeps me in for a hug. I could stay here forever, wrapped up in this warmth and love.

I can hear Jordan shouting something about announcing the winner, and Naz grabs my hand, squeezing it too tightly. She seems more nervous than I am. When they announce I got third place, my group goes wild. Naz says something about speaking to the judges about getting their heads out of their asses, but I'm feeling pretty fucking spectacular. Babak and Coach push me forward, and I go up to claim my gift certificate and stand with the first- and second-place winners: tough guys twice my size, probably been doing this type of thing for years, but who acknowledge me like I'm one of them. No chance for me to open for Wu-Tang, but I got a hundred-dollar gift certificate to The Cheesecake Factory and a spot in one of Tessa's poetry workshops this summer, and I'm feeling the best I've ever felt in my whole fucking life with some of the people I love most watching from the crowd, and I'm going to hold on to that for as long as I can. Everyone's cheering for us, putting their *W*'s up, and all I see in the almost darkness are a bunch of lotus flowers, all with a story of their own, trying so hard not to let the mud keep them from blooming into something beautiful.

37.

The day after the battle, I seal a copy of my poem in an envelope and leave it in Yasaman's mailbox for her. I know she's already left, and I don't know how long she'll be in Mexico for, or if she'll actually read it when she gets back, but I figure it's worth a shot.

My dad goes back to Iran a week after the battle. I can't bring myself to tell him everything before he leaves. The battle skyrocketed my confidence, but it doesn't mean that everything has changed overnight. But he sets me up with everything I'd need to replant the garden.

"I'll do my best," I tell him, and I mean it.

"It's the only thing we can do," my dad says, and we embrace in a way that doesn't feel awkward or forced, but like two people relearning each other. I cry on the ride home after we drop him off at the airport—not because I want him to stay, necessarily, but because I wish we weren't the kind of family that needs to be apart in order to function.

My mom is a different story. After my dad leaves, I want to

tell her, but I just don't know how or when to do it. I don't want to just blurt it out, like how she threw her secret on me that day over cheesesteaks. The longer I wait, though, the more I can feel my eagerness dipping.

Summer starts off slowly, and I pass the time by shooting hoops with Tony in the afternoons. Not only does my mom not mind, but sometimes I catch her waving to him from the window.

One morning, before going out to play ball, I grab water out of the fridge, and my mom's in the kitchen listening to the radio. This Iranian man is talking to the psychologist about how he keeps proposing to his girlfriend but she always says no.

"Every year, I'm making even more money, and she still says no, Doctor," he says.

"What is it exactly that you do for work?" the psychologist asks him.

"I'm a thief," he says. The psychologist is silent for a while, and my mom and I start cracking up because the guy is for real.

"A thief?"

"Yes, Doctor, a thief. I steal from people's houses."

"What a divooneh, crazy man. Have fun, Rana Joon," she says.

She's transformed into a realer version of herself since my dad left. A couple nights before, she had asked me to read the poem about my grandfather to her again, and we sat over tea and dates and talked about death, how it gives you perspective and how the loss just becomes a part of you, like a jagged scar from a poorly stitched wound. It never really goes away, and a part of you wants it that way.

I could feel something changing between us that night, and it felt good. Maybe it was because she could finally breathe again and not just feel like she had to attend to my dad's needs, maybe it was because I'd graduated and she was finally seeing me as a real adult, or maybe it was a ripple effect from her revelation to me, her baring her truth to me and wanting me to see her head-on. We still haven't really talked about the affair, but maybe it's something I'll never fully wrap my head around.

Before I go out to play ball with Tony, my mom lowers the volume on the radio. "Wait."

I stop at the door.

"Will you come with me to see your grandfather?" She looks up at me as if she's the child and I'm the mother.

I nod yes and immediately know exactly what it is I have to do.

There's a fire burning somewhere in the distance. The sun is setting and it's a bright orange ball, and the whole sky has a tinge of orange to it too. I don't smell smoke, but it's clear something is burning.

We find my grandfather's grave.

Mustafa Mohammadi
1913–1994
Beloved Husband, Father, Grandfather

And his favorite Rumi quote:
What you are seeking is seeking you.

My mom is on her knees, weeping into the grass. She touches the stone of his grave like it's a piece of him.

"Say something," she says to me through her tears, because she can't muster up any words.

This will break her heart even more, but it's the only way. This is what my grandfather had asked me to do, after all.

"I am from / A monarchy turned theocracy— / Ruby-studded crowns and lashings on bare skin / To commemorate the holiest of men. . . ."

I can feel her looking up at me at the mention of sex and cigarettes. This isn't what she meant when she told me to say something, but I don't let it stop me.

"I am from a desire / I dare not speak of, / From touching myself / But dreaming of her— / The girl with the red hair, / The girl who lit a fire up inside me . . ."

At this point, she's standing next to me, but I just stare at the smoke-filled sky for a second, the beautiful apocalypse of this moment, and keep going until I finish.

"This poem is about you?" my mom asks me.

I nod yes.

"But I know you. This isn't you." Her mascara has spread down to her cheeks, and her lips quiver again, but she holds her crying inside.

"You don't know all of me, just like I don't know all of you."

"I don't understand," she says, and she gets back down on her knees and starts crying to my grandfather, "Nemifahmam. Nemifahmam. I don't understand. I don't understand," like he has the power to undo this. I guess I thought she'd be more accepting now that I know her secret, but that's not what's happening here at all, and my heart is breaking.

"It's a phase, Rana. You're young, you don't know what you want," she says through her tears.

I'm crying now too. "I'm young, but I live inside my body," I say. "I've been living inside it for eighteen years, and I know what makes me happy and what doesn't, and I can't keep lying to you."

"But you want to have a good life. A good family. Children," she says.

"Like that turned out so great for you? You're having a fucking affair, Mom!" I yell.

She looks up at me. Really looks at me. "This life will be hard."

"Ya, but it will be mine," I say, and she has no response to this. Her love for me has always involved some level of control, and my news is a fucking tornado through her universe.

She gets up. Wipes her mascara with the back of her hand, takes out her lipstick from her purse, and applies a fresh coat.

"Khodahafez, Baba Joon."

She says goodbye to my grandfather and walks toward our car, her heels digging deep into the wet grass.

38.

She goes on like this for weeks. Ignoring me. Talking to me through my brother. Not talking to me at all. Watching our favorite shows without me. She doesn't cook anything. She doesn't listen to the Persian radio or do her nails. She comes and goes as she pleases and doesn't tell me where she's going or when she'll be back.

Her avoidance doesn't make me angry; it just makes me sad. But I try to keep things as positive as I can. I work on pieces for Tessa's poetry workshop or go to Ms. Murillo's house for meditation sessions (something she invites a select few of her former students to do) or work on reviving the garden with Babak or go to In-N-Out with Naz. Life flows with a sense of ease and quiet joy I've never felt before. But every time I come home and see my mom sitting in the corner like she's mourning something, my heart sinks and true happiness feels incredibly far away without her acceptance.

My dad had left me all the materials to replant the garden, but still hadn't taught me what I need to know to keep it growing. I go to the plant nursery near our house and tell this older Latino man named Jesús with a white mustache and cowboy hat that I need his help.

"I don't know shit about gardening, but I want to learn," I say. He agrees to help me if I come super early in the morning before the nursery even opens; I can ask him questions while he waters all the plants. So I take a little notepad and pen with me the next morning, and I pick his brain.

"It's all in the soil," he says. "If the soil is crap, the plant is crap." He gives me soil booster to add to the soil we already have and tells me to put a lot in, and that I have to put in a weed barrier between the plants to keep weeds from sprouting up and taking over. "You treat each plant like a child, gently put it in the earth. When you come to water it, you do it with love," he says, and I'm pretty sure Jesús is just the Mexican version of my dad. "El jardín es la vida. And you can't ignore life."

I take my time with it. I dig holes and gently put each plant into the earth and surround it with fertilizer. I check on the mint and basil and sage every day, I watch the rosemary grow faster than anything else, I plant more of those bushy purple flowers and the jasmine my dad loves, and I help the tomatoes climb that silver cone. And yes, the sun might be the enemy one day and burn everything to a crisp, and the weeds might decide to find their way out, and the pincher bugs could appear and bite their way through the leaves, and all of it could eventually just die, but every day as I come back to it and care for it, I choose to believe that it's more likely that this beauty will keep on living.

I don't just do it for my dad; I do it for all of us. Even though my dad is thousands of miles away and isn't perfect—even though none of us are perfect—we deserve this private, humble paradise to call our own. It doesn't feel like a burden, but more like patience. I've learned the secret knowledge that anything beautiful in this world takes time to grow.

When I get home from the plant nursery one day, the door is unlocked, and I walk into the kitchen expecting to hear the sound of my mother's silence, but instead what I find is my mom cooking up a storm in the kitchen with Bod's uncle. There's a smile on her face I haven't seen in months. She's pretty dressed up with a navy blouse and lipstick, which isn't that bizarre for her, but there's also something light and airy about her, like she's been plucked straight out of the pages of a magazine and is trying to show Bod's uncle that she's a cool, relaxed, forward-thinking mom.

She hasn't started her classes again just yet, but she's showing him how to grind up the walnuts for fesenjoon stew. The sound of the blender suddenly overpowers the kitchen, and I'm watching him watch her, and up close I can see how hungry he is—for the food, but mostly for her. He says something to her I can't hear, and she starts laughing, a flirty laughter she never uses with my dad. The blender turns off, and I make my presence known.

"Eh, sorry, Rana Joon, we didn't see you there," she says. "I'm teaching Reza how to make fesenjoon."

"Hey, Rana," Reza says, like we're homies.

"Hey," I say.

"I invited Reza to cook with me. He's been asking me about fesenjoon," she says. I should be excited she's finally talking to me, but I can't believe she's brought him here in broad daylight. Like she's rubbing it in my face or something—*I can live however I want, but your desires make you wrong and a shame to this family.*

Reza keeps smiling at me, and I don't know how to respond.

"I heard the good news. You're officially a Bruin," Reza says.

"Ya, thanks. It's pretty cool," I say. I'm starting classes in about two weeks, but I don't really feel like talking about it right now, especially with him.

After a long, awkward pause and Reza looking at my mom, and then back at me, and then back at my mom, and then back at me, I tell them that I'm going to my room.

"Okay, Rana Joon," she says.

I turn around at the top of the stairs and duck down low like I'm a five-year-old trying to eavesdrop. I see Reza take my mom's hand and kiss it. Once. Twice. Three times. My mom lowers her head and smiles like a schoolgirl. He lifts her chin and then kisses her on the lips. I'm trying to be happy for my mom, but I'm just jealous of her.

And if this isn't bad enough, when I get to my room, I turn on the TV to find the same breaking news on every channel. I stop to listen, and before long, Tupac's face pops up. He's been shot in Vegas, and the reporter tells me, very flatly, almost like a robot, that Tupac's dead.

I'm immediately crying, not holding back like I did with Louie—but the tears are partially for Louie, too. Because grief never leaves, and Tupac was a big part of both of us, of our friendship, and now they're both gone. It's clear to me that the only way to process heartbreak like this is to really feel it, and so I allow myself to. I blast Tupac's CD, wrap myself in a blanket, and weep. I have no shame. I didn't even know this person, but he was the one who led me through my darkest times, and so I let the tears flow, I let his words surround me. My mom knocks on my door, tells me to turn the volume down. She opens the door to find me on my bed, curled up in a ball, crying my eyes out.

"What happened, Rana Joon?" she asks me, sounding worried. "Is it because Reza is here? I should've told you he was coming. I just . . ."

"No, Mom. Tupac's dead," I say, and then start sobbing uncontrollably.

My mom's never understood what I liked about his music, but she sits down next to me and wraps her arms around me. "It's okay," she says. "He's in a better place now with Baba Joon. And your friend Louie."

She rocks me how she did when I was a little girl and I couldn't fall asleep on my own—when I needed her touch to feel safe in this world—and a wave of peace washes over me.

"Since your grandfather died, I can feel him everywhere. In the kitchen, in the market, in the car, when I'm cooking food—his voice, his whole being is always with me. I am who I am because of him. We never really lose people, Rana Joon," she says, which actually calms me down a little.

"Play me one of his songs," she says, and it's a generous suggestion. I play "Dear Mama" for her, and my mom closes her eyes and nods along like she's actually enjoying it, even though I'm pretty sure she has no idea what he's saying.

"I like it," she says, and puts her hand on my face to wipe away what's left of my tears.

Naz calls a few minutes later and tries to comfort me for a while, which helps.

"You want me to come over?" she asks. "I'll be there in two-point-five seconds—just say the fucking word."

"I love you, but I think I'm just going to chill with my mom," I say, because she'd asked Reza to leave and told me she would make me whatever I wanted to eat.

After I hang up, my mom sits me down at the kitchen table and feeds me like a queen. She not only gives me heaps and heaps of the fesenjoon she'd made with Reza, but she piles it on top of crispy rice, and brings me my favorite bread with chunks of feta, walnuts, figs, mint, and three kinds of jam. She scoops me up some of Babak's stash of ice cream and puts fresh berries, crushed-up pistachios, and honey on it, and then brings me the darkest tea she could make with mint leaves floating inside. I'm a little girl again, safe in my mother's kitchen, the whole world just as it should be.

"I want to understand," she says as we dip sugar cubes in our tea and suck on them. "Not just Tupac, but what you told me that day too. If these things are a part of you, I want to understand them. You know I love you more than anything, Rana Joon," she says, and puts her hand on my hand, and I let her. I reach over and hug her, inhale her expensive perfume, snot all over her designer blouse, cry into her chest, because it's like she's seeing me for the very first time and also understands that looking away is no longer an option.

There's no ceremony I can go to, no mutual friend to share stories with, no prayer to say at Tupac's grave, so I go and sit in the only holy place I know—the garden. It's not beautiful yet, but I've put lights up now, little balls that hang above the trees like stars, and there's so much potential and life here that it's strangely comforting.

I hear the screen door open and look up, expecting to see my mom, but instead I see that wild mess of red hair I've been thinking about all summer. Yasaman walks toward me, quietly and slowly, as if she doesn't want to disturb me.

I'm too shocked to say anything and half believe I'm

hallucinating, but am brought back to earth when she says, "I can't believe he's dead," and sits down in the empty chair next to me. It feels like it's ninety degrees outside, or it might just be the rush of energy moving through my body at the sight of her. All of a sudden, I'm crying again.

"I don't know how I can be this upset over someone I've never even met. Grief is wild," I say.

"You loved him. He probably saved you when no one else could. That's what artists do," she says. We sit for a moment before she fills the silence. "The garden looks good. Lots of potential."

"I'm trying. Did you just get back?"

"Ya, yesterday."

"How was Casa Azul?"

"Amazing. Like, I can't even describe it. Frida's whole life was in that house, and it's so bold and unapologetic. God, she was such a badass. I want to be more like her."

"You're already a badass," I say, and she smiles and pulls me in with her eyes.

"I thought about you a lot. And I read your poem," she says, and takes my hand. "Rana, it was . . . wow."

"Thanks. I performed it at the battle. I got third place, but it was fucking amazing. I've never felt so alive. And I . . . I told my mom, too. I came out to her," I tell her.

She raises her eyebrows, and a smile spreads across her face. "Holy shit, you're the real deal now, huh? You're pretty amazing, you know that?" she says.

I can barely even think, so I turn toward her and lean in a little. She does the same, and I can feel the magnetic pull of our bodies. I kiss her, tongues dancing with each other, and the moment wraps itself around me. I climb on top of her and press the throbbing in between my legs into hers; I lick her neck, suck on her earlobe. I touch her breasts and she touches mine, and I'm not outside, looking in, but inside, floating, free. I realize how intense things are getting and I come up for air. We both crack up laughing, and I sit back down in my chair and try to catch my breath.

"Well, that was something," she says.

"Ya, it was."

"So, I got accepted to Cal. I'm moving up north in two weeks."

"Holy shit, that's awesome," I say.

"It's only an hour flight. Maybe you'll come visit?"

"For sure," I say. When I look at her, I see her eyes have been waiting for me. We both smile, reach for each other's hands again, and stay quiet for a little while. "Let's go to my room," I say.

"Your mom's inside."

"I know," I say.

My mom's watching *Friends* alone, and the smell of grease has filled the air because, since I've been sitting outside, she's just made me a big plate of thick French fries—even after all that food earlier—with ketchup on the side.

I introduce her to Yasaman, and it makes her happy when Yasaman says hello in Farsi. There are so many questions in her eyes, and I know that she's holding them back to not embarrass herself or me.

"Thanks, Mom," I say, and then pick the plate up with my one hand, still holding on to Yasaman with the other.

We walk upstairs, and I lock the door to my room, and we eat the whole plate, just her and me. I tell her about the battle and setting Louie free, and about the garden and what it means to me and what I've learned about soil and roots and starting fresh and that it's all about setting the right foundation and being patient, and then she tells me more about Mexico and that she wants to major in Latin American Studies. We lie on my bed for a minute, lips soaked with grease, our bodies almost touching, but in that beautiful space of not quite, in that holy place where it's possible for anything to bloom.

I turn to face her, and then she does the same. We meet in the middle for a kiss, and we keep going and going and going like stopping isn't even an option. We both take our pants off in a hurry, our underwear too.

"We just have to be quiet," I say. But I decide to live in the moment and not worry too much about whether my mom will knock on the door.

She straddles me this time, spreads me open and touches me—first slowly, but then it's clear how wet I am, so she moves faster. She asks me if I like it and I say yes. It's like a meditation; the thoughts pass by and I allow myself to live in my body. She grinds herself into me. I squeeze her breasts as we move together in a rhythm that feels so natural and right. I want to laugh and cry and let out the sounds of a wild animal all at once. We look into each other's eyes and witness the pleasure rise and then burst through us.

Afterward Yasaman asks me, "Can I show you something beautiful?" and of course I say yes.

39.

Night falls down from above, and a sharp blue sky fills the earth's remaining light. She's driven me to the ocean. The waves are full. The only sound is the crashing in front of my feet. A sour fish smell enters my nostrils. The mush of what's left of the sand melts between my toes, and I believe for a second I'm flying, but the water comes back too soon, and it's cold, and I wish I'd never even taken my shoes off.

"I've never swum in the ocean before," I tell Yasaman. We're far down PCH on a beach I've never been to.

"What?" she says, like it's a sin.

"I've put my feet in. I've gone up to my knees, but that's it," I say.

"How is that even possible? Isn't it beautiful? When I'm older, I want to buy a house by the ocean. One of those right there," she says, narrowing her eyes and pointing down along the shore where houses stand like giant gods in the sand. "I want to fall asleep to this sound and wake up to it and have sex to it and eat pancakes all day long, watching the waves move back and forth."

"I can't sleep with all this noise. I need silence."

"Silence is so overrated. When I was little, I couldn't fall asleep unless it was quiet too, but now I can't sleep unless the TV's on. It's like someone else is there, and they're awake and protecting me. I feel protected by the TV. That's ridiculous, right?" She's laughing now. We're not high, but we sound high. A wave we didn't anticipate suddenly attacks us and soaks my rolled-up jeans above the knee. I run backward, but Yasaman doesn't—she's actually running toward the foam, closer to the darkness that's creeping over the water now.

I remember the time I came to the beach with Louie right after my grandfather died. We talked about love and sex, and I told him my big secret. The memory comes flooding back to me, not just an image; the actual energy and magic of that moment are things I can feel in my body right now. My mom's right; we never really lose people, and tonight it's clear to me that the purpose of the pain is to just feel it, to not run, to let it pass through you, to honor the love you had, so you can let go just a bit and create space for even more love to come your way. Joy can exist, and so can pain. My happiness doesn't depend on my ability to not miss Louie and to not feel that ache, because the two can exist simultaneously and my heart is big enough to hold both equally.

Everything ahead of Yasaman and me is nothing, black and unknown, and beyond the waves, everything's still black and hidden, and beyond that somewhere is the sun rising for a new set of people, lighting that other world up with its flame.

"Shit!" I yell as another wave soaks me, while Yasaman's laughing. "I got my pants wet."

Yasaman unzips her shorts and takes them off and then lifts her T-shirt over her head, and I can't take my eyes off her. She's the moon, out now shamelessly, naked in her delight. She comes to me and says, "We're going in."

"Not a chance," I say.

"We're going to look back on this moment and ask ourselves why we didn't go in. If you don't do it now with me, I know you'll never do it," and in her eyes is something like genuine concern for my psychological well-being. She doesn't want me to miss out on this. She wants me to be the kind of person who takes her clothes off and goes into the ocean without any reservations. And I know now, standing here underneath all these constellations I can't name, that she wants to be the person who brings this being out from inside me. *This* is the beautiful thing she wants to show me—the person she believes I'm capable of becoming.

"Come on," she says, and she's walking backward, her eyes on me, her red mess of a head the frizziest I've ever seen it, her naked body beautiful, calling me inside the water. I unzip my jeans, but they don't come off smoothly because the bottom half is soaked. I stumble and fall over in the sand but manage to get them off anyway, and then I take my shirt off, and I look down at my body, but Yasaman's yelling my name, and I know if I'm going to live in the moment, I have to stop giving a shit about all the details, so I get completely naked too.

There's no turning back. You have to feel the waves; you have to accept them, or you'll just get pulled down. Change doesn't have to be scary; it can be exciting, thrilling even.

So I run, feet popping sea kelp with relief, my body breathing in the skin-shattering cold waves. I run and run so I can get closer and closer to her body, to that bright shining thing, the thing that will change my life forever, but it's hard to see her in the darkness. I try to follow the sound of her voice yelling my name, laughing, because her body's disappeared, and it's just my nakedness and the waves and the night and the nameless constellations and the ever-growing darkness before me. It's just me and this moment and the unknown world beyond, filling up with an endless kind of light.

Acknowledgments

So much love and hard work goes into making a book possible. A huge thank-you to my agent, Kim Perel, for believing in this story and for helping me find my way, even through all the unexpected detours. Thank you, Margaret Danko, for joining us for the ride.

Thank you to Alex Borbolla for your initial passion for this project and to Sophia Jimenez for taking over and making sure *Rana Joon* not only stayed afloat but flourished. Thank you to Jeannie Ng and Kaitlyn San Miguel for your insane attention to detail. Thank you to Salini Perera for bringing Rana to life with this gorgeous cover. Big thanks to the whole team at Atheneum for all the love and attention you have given this book and for prioritizing diversity in publishing, and to Tara Rayers for your thoughtful read.

Thank you to VONA, Breadloaf, and Squaw Valley Writers Conference and all the writers I met along the way, who helped me feel like I belonged, especially Jamey Hatley, Melissa Sipin, Nayomi Munaweera, and Ru Freeman.

Thank you to Rita Williams, my first graduate school professor, and one of the most profound. Thank you for teaching this poet how to write a scene and for helping me find my way to San Francisco State.

Thank you to Michelle Carter, Toni Mirosevich, and Peter Orner for making the MFA program at San Francisco State so special. Thanks especially to Matthew Clark Davison—I wrote the last scene of this book (my favorite!) and many others at The Lab, and I'm so grateful to have had such a space. Safiya Martinez and Sara Marinelli, I will always cherish the sacred time we shared.

A huge thank-you to Anita Amirrezvani and Jasmin Darznik for being so encouraging and giving with your time. And let's be real, if you're an up-and-coming Iranian American writer, Persis Karim is your biggest ally. Thank you, Persis, for your generous spirit and for wanting everyone to win. Thank you also to Dena Rod for your insightful feedback on an early read of this manuscript, and to Ali Alimi for your rhymes and openness to helping me out.

Thank you to the faculty and staff of Mission High School. You will always have a special place in my heart. And to the students, thank you for reminding me just how badass teenagers are.

Thank you to Miah Jeffra and *Foglifter* for publishing an early excerpt of this book.

A huge shout-out to Casey and Kate McEachern for so many things, including being the biggest cheerleaders of this book. Thank you, Casey, for being my first phone call when I knew this was finally happening.

Thank you to my SF soul sisters: Tamar Sahakian, Fakhra Shah, Eidit Choochage. I love you completely. And my LA soul sisters: Doreen Ahadian, Natalie and Yasmine Pollak, and Nikki

Jahanforouz. Thank you for a sisterhood that my soul has always longed for.

Thank you to my various teachers in this life, who have helped keep me sane and have guided me in finding my way back to myself: Tara Brach, Michael Bernard Beckwith, Pema Chödrön, Vivica Schwartz, Omid Arabian, and Azita Moallef.

The biggest of all thank-yous to my parents, who had to leave their home, their land, their lives so quickly, and were so determined to get to the other side. Thank you for always supporting me in following my dreams. Baba, these aren't short stories, but I hope I've made you proud. Lela, "thank you" isn't enough. We're different in a lot of ways, but at our core we are both fierce with our love. Thank you to my brother, Shervin Etaat, my creative twin, and the best uncle in all the land.

Thank you to Elia Chaim Lewin-Tankel, then and now, for being one of my greatest teachers in life and love. I'm certain our souls have been connected for many lives, and I'm grateful I get to witness yours in this lifetime. I miss you and I love you still.

Deepest thank-you to my son, Iman. You are a light in this world. I'm honored to be your guide and lucky to know your love. Thank you to the force that brought you to me and continues to guide me in this life.

I started this book in 2015, with no clear intention other than wanting to write about a place and time that felt familiar to me, to bury my own truths within a character who was very much not me, but also kind of like me. In 2017 my life was flipped upside down, and the thought of writing or reading fiction felt suddenly absurd to me. A year and a half later, Rana came knocking again and asked me to play; slowly I followed her lead. The story evolved as I processed my own grief.

So I guess Rumi was right, huh? What you seek is seeking you. It's our job simply to stay open and do the next right thing. And then the next. This was my next right thing.

A huge shout-out to *me* for not giving up and to *you* for picking up this book. There are so many choices out there, and the fact that you picked *Rana Joon* means the world to me.

I hope this book speaks to any person struggling to speak their truth, find their voice, live their life freely, in the moment, and in joy. To the Iranian LGBTQ+ community in Los Angeles and beyond—your stories will always matter. And to the women of Iran fighting for their freedom, you will always be my heroes.